Alley Ciz

SWEET VICTORY

BTU Alumni Series Book #3

ALLEY CIZ

Also by Alley Ciz

BTU Alumni Series

Power Play (Jake and Jordan)

Musical Mayhem (Sammy and Jamie) BTU Novella

Tap Out (Gage and Rocky)

Sweet Victory (Vince and Holly)

Puck Performance (Jase and Melody)

Writing Dirty (Maddey and Dex)

Scoring Beauty- BTU6 Preorder, Releasing September 2021

#UofJ Series

Cut Above The Rest (Prequel)- Freebie

Looking To Score

Game Changer

Playing For Keeps

Off The Bench- #UofJ4 Preorder, Releasing December 2021

The Royalty Crew (A #UofJ Spin-Off)

Savage Queen- Preorder, Releasing April 2021

Ruthless Noble- Preorder, Releasing June 2021

Holly Vanderbilt is running.

From her past, her present, her future—*everything.*
Baking is her only solace. Cookies, cakes, ingredients coming together, they make sense.
A professional fighter walking into her kitchen? Not so much.

Vince Steele is focused on his future.

The next fight.
The next win.
Nothing else matters except feeling the weight of the Light Heavyweight belt around his waist.
Until Holly.

He has what it takes to win the belt. But will Holly's past prove to be an opponent he can't beat?
He's never backed down from a fight.
He wasn't going to start now, not when winning Holly's heart could be the *sweetest* victory of all.

The Coven is back and about to recruit a new member. SWEET VICTORY is the third book in the BTU Alumni Series and can be read as a stand-alone. The book features a Christmas-loving hot mess of a baker, an alpha-dirty-talking MMA fighter, and the best group of friends ever (even if they don't know how to mind their own business). HEA guaranteed—being on Santa's Nice List...not so much.

Sweet Victory (BTU Alumni, Book 3)

Alley Ciz

Cover Designer: Julia Cabrera at Jersey Girl Designs

Editing: Jessica Snyder Edits

Proofreading: Gem's Precise Proofreads; Dawn Black

❈ Created with Vellum

For Caitie.
Vince Steele is yours, because we know you would cut a bitch if they
tried to take him from you.

Dear Reader,

Sweet Victory can be read as a stand-alone but it is interconnected in the BTU Alumni world. You do not need to read Power Play *or* Tap Out *first but they might help you keep track of the crazy cast of characters as large as The Coven and their guys. Either way I hope you enjoy Vince and Holly's story.*

Crank up the Christmas carols and jump on in.

XOXO

Alley

Text Handles

The Coven
> **Rocky:** ALPHABET SOUP
> **Jordan:** MOTHER OF DRAGONS
> **Skye:** MAKES BOYS CRY
> **Maddey:** QUEEN OF SMUT
> **Becky:** YOU KNOW YOU WANNA
> **Gemma:** PROTEIN PRINCESS
> **Beth:** THE OG PITA
> **Holly:** SANTA'S COOKIE SUPPLIER

The Boys
> **Vince:** DAUNTLESS SUPERMAN
> **Lyle:** MR. FABULOUS
> **Jase:** THE BIG HAMMER
> **Jake:** THE BRICK WALL
> **Deck:** BIG DECK
> **Ryan:** CAPTAIN AMERICA
> **Nick:** THE BOONDOCK SAINT
> **Damon:** THE GREEN MONSTER
> **Justin:** THE SEAL DEAL
> **Gage:** THE KRAKEN

Wyatt: HUGE HOSE
Griff: THE FEROCIOUS TEDDY BEAR
Ray: JUST RAY
Tuck: WANNA TUCK
Jamie: ROCKSTAR MAN
Sammy: THE SPIN DOCTOR

IG Handles

Ryan: CaptainRyanDonnelly9
Jase: EnforcedByJaseDonnelly13
Jake: BrickWallDonovan30
Gemma: GemCooksForYou

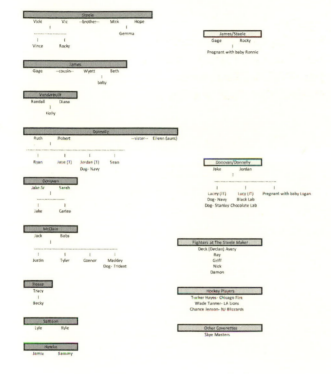

Steele

Vicki	Vic	--brother--	Mick	Hope

Vince	Rocky		Gemma

James

Gage	--cousin--	Wyatt	Beth

baby

Vanderbilt

Randall	Diana

Holly

Donnelly

Ruth	Robert			--sister--	Eileen (aunt)

Ryan	Jase (T)	Jordan (T)	Sean

Dog- Navy

Donovan

Jake Sr	Sarah

Jake	Carlee

McClain

Jack	Babs

Justin	Tyler	Connor	Maddey

Dog- Trident

Reese

Tracy

Becky

Samson

Lyle	Kyle

Hawkins

Jamie	Sammy

James/Steele

Gage	Rocky

Pregnant with baby Ronnie

Donovan/Donnelly

Jake	Jordan

Lacey (IT)	Lucy (IT)	Pregnant with baby Logan
Dog- Navy	Black Lab	
Dog- Stanley Chocolate Lab		

Fighters at The Steele Maker

Deck (Declan) Avery
Ray
Griff
Nick
Damon

Hockey Players

Tucker Hayes- Chicago Fire
Wade Tanner- LA Lions
Chance Jenson- NJ Blizzards

Other Covenettes

Skye Masters

Prologue

S *hit!*
  Shit!
  Shit!

Holly Vanderbuilt cursed herself as she scrambled to toss yet another drawer full of clothes into the suitcase open on the four-poster bed.

A plan. She really needed to have a plan.

Bras.

Why didn't I make a plan?

Underwear followed by socks went next.

How the hell did I let this go so far?

She stepped inside the walk-in closet, ignoring the fancy gowns and proper clothes hanging on the racks, instead grabbing the comfortable tunics and other "common" pieces from where they had been relegated to the back.

Seriously, Hol, you're too smart for this.

She never should have let things get this bad, she thought as she sat on top of her Tumi luggage to get the zipper to close.

A quick glance at her rose-gold Rolex made her curse. She

needed to be out of there in less than ten minutes if she was going to manage to do so without being caught.

One more cursory look around the room, double-checking she had everything of importance, and she was wheeling her two large suitcases from the room.

By the time she had her Mercedes-Benz AMG S 63 loaded she peeled out of the driveway and through the wrought-iron gates of the estate with only a minute to spare.

She prayed her call wouldn't go unanswered.

Chapter One

Vince Steele pulled open the door to Espresso
Patronum, the coffee shop across the street from
The Steele Maker gym, for the first time in weeks.
His strict diet program prohibited everything delicious the
café offered, so it was easier to not visit at all anytime he was
training. But his sister's hormones needed calming, and he
was willing to brave the temptation for her.

The scent of coffee and baked goodness filled his lungs
and his mouth watered. God, it had been a long five weeks
so far.

"Oh, be still my heart. The Man of Steel has *finally* deemed
my humble establishment worthy of his presence again." Lyle
Samson pretended to faint as Vince approached the counter.

He couldn't stop the automatic grin at his friend's
dramatic greeting. The proprietor of the coffee house was a
consummate flirt and had a personality as colorful as his
sleeve tattoos and the hot pink and neon green highlights in
his spiked hair. He also loved using Vince's fighting
nickname.

"Lyle, my man, nice to see you." He reached across the

counter to share the complicated handshake they had developed through the years.

"Where have you been hiding, handsome? Do you not love me anymore?"

"Come on, Ly, you know you'll always have a special place in my heart." He placed a hand over it. "But Gem would own my balls if I dared take one bite of food *not* from her carefully crafted meal plan. And your goodies always have me tapping out they're so good."

Unfortunately, those things proved to be too much to resist. In the midst of the most intense training camp of his career, it was best to avoid temptation altogether. It was that or face the wrath of his cousin, the gym's nutritionist.

And nope, that wasn't going to happen. The very last thing he wanted to do was piss off a member of The Coven, the group of girls who ruled the world—well, their small corner of the world of professional fighters and hockey players, but *seriously,* a person wouldn't want to get on their bad side. And since Gemma was currently in charge of every *single* calorie that went into his body to ensure he made weight in two months, anything from Espresso Patronum was a surefire way to having her rain hellfire down all over him.

God, I'm dramatic when I can't have my sugar.

"Well, if you want, I can keep your balls safe for you. I'm *really* good at handling balls," Lyle offered.

He sputtered out a laugh. "I'm sure you are. But I'm pretty sure Kyle wouldn't approve."

"What'd he do now?" Kyle asked, coming from the back of the shop and putting an arm around his flirtatious husband. "You causing trouble out here again?"

"Always, babe." Lyle placed a kiss on his cheek.

For as much as Lyle flirted for fun, everyone knew he was stupidly in love with his clean-cut husband.

Kyle's gaze bounced between them. "Let me guess, he made a reference about how he's an expert ball boy?"

This time Vince shook his head as he laughed, not at all surprised by how well Kyle knew his husband.

"Not in those *exact* words, but yeah, pretty much."

Kyle gave his groom an affectionate smile. "What can we get for ya, Vin?" He took a moment to look over the glass display case to the right of the counter but didn't see the Holy Grail of baked goods anywhere.

"Please don't tell me you're out of blueberry crumbles?"

"Ran out about an hour ago," Lyle confirmed.

"Shit." He ran a hand through his sweaty hair. "I'm not gonna be able to move tomorrow," he said to himself.

"I take it Rock's kicking your ass today?" Kyle asked.

"More like that sexy hunk of man meat she calls a husband," Lyle said. Vince didn't want to think of his sparring partner and brother-in-law as *sexy man meat*.

"Yup. She's pissed at me for something, and I was hoping to win myself a few brownie points by catering to one of her bigger pregnancy cravings."

His pregnant, hormonal—not that he would be stupid enough to say that to her face, or even within hearing distance—sister was pissed at him for something and liked to torture him during their training sessions. He'd learned a few weeks ago that EP's new blueberry crumble soothed the beast and tried to keep her full of them.

Her husband, Gage, the UFC's current heavyweight champion, could also turn her from a feral tiger to a purring house cat, but there was no way he wanted to think about what they did behind closed doors. *Gross*. That was his sister, and the less he knew about her sex life, the better.

"How do you know she's pissed at *you* though, and not just...*hormonal*?" Lyle shuddered at the last word, clearly grateful he was married to a man.

"First"—he held up a finger for emphasis—"she gave me Tweety Bird hand wraps. Do you have *any* idea how hard it is to look like a badass when that yellow bird's smiling face is staring back at you? She's ruining my street cred." He slapped his thighs in exasperation.

"Isn't Tweety a boy?" Kyle didn't even try to bite back his amusement anymore.

"*Really? That's* what you're focusing on?" He rolled his eyes. "Then she had me spar with Griff. The guy's a World Champion boxer—he can kick my ass without trying. And now I have to go back there and grapple with Gage. She's out for blood, man. *Blood,* I tell you." He smacked the counter, the sound reverberating through the shop over One Direction's "I Want".

The Samson men *did not* comprehend the severity of the situation he had found himself in. If they did, they wouldn't be bent over, leaning on each other while they guffawed at his expense.

"You know, with friends like you two, who needs enemies?" he grumbled and shoved his hands into the pockets of his BTU hoodie.

"Calm your tits, Steele," Kyle admonished.

"Tits?" He smirked. "Come on, Ky, you know I'm pure muscle."

"Prove it. Take your shirt off," Lyle suggested, earning an eye roll from his husband.

"Before my husband can sexually harass you anymore," Kyle cut in, "why don't you go back into the kitchen. I think a new batch went in earlier. They might be done by now."

Vince followed the diamond floor tiles into the stainless steel baker's dream of a kitchen.

At the island in the middle of the room, a woman was bent over rows of cookies, piping bag in hand, decorating as she belted out the words to "Please Come Home For Christmas" along with Bon Jovi. It was only the first week of November, but as a true Jersey native, he respected her song choice. And the girl had a legit set of pipes on her too.

Between the volume of the music and her own voice, she

hadn't noticed him. He took a moment to study her unde-
tected. Her face was the picture of concentration as she piped
white frosting onto what looked like unicorn cookies. He
couldn't see all of her features with her head lowered, but he
could tell she was cute.

A white bandana was tied like a headband around her
head to keep her cognac-colored hair from her face, the bow
lying lopsided on the left side. When her hand lifted to tuck
an errant piece of hair behind her ear, he noticed the tips were
dyed a deep purple.

He'd been staring at her long enough to qualify him as a
total creeper so he cleared his throat and announced his presence with a simple, "Hi."

Unfortunately, she reacted exactly like he'd hoped she
wouldn't. With a startled "*Ahh!*" white frosting shot out of the
piping bag in an arc clear across the island. Her mouth
formed a perfect O of surprise as her golden eyes shifted
between him and the path the frosting took.

Holy fuck.

She was a vision.

As a professional MMA fighter, he was trained to read a
situation in seconds, a trick that served him well in his day-
to-day life. In the time it took him to suck in a stunned breath
and release it, he cataloged the perfect berry color of those
pursed lips, the way her hair stopped about an inch before it
hit her shoulders, and how the purple tips peeking out from
the bottom brought out the warm honey tones in her whiskey
eyes.

She was at least a foot shorter than him and had an
impressive rack—what? He was a boob guy, among other
things—stretched out the cotton of her festive and highly
appropriate t-shirt that read 'Bitch better have my cookies,'
with a picture of the big man himself—Santa—pointing like
he meant business.

There was a streak of flour on her cheek and frosting on

her forearm. She was a mess and obviously Christmas obsessed, but he couldn't keep the edges of his lips from tipping up as he took her in.

"Oh, crap." The hand not holding the piping bag went to cover the spot over her heart. "Well, that was slightly porno-graphic," she said more to herself as she reached out to clean up the spray of frosting.

She may not have meant for him to hear her, but he did and couldn't help but grin at her. The answering thump from his heart had him cursing Maddey, their resident romance author, and the romance books she'd gotten him hooked on. Because as he stood there taking in the hot mess express of a baker, he was pretty sure he was already on his way to falling victim to love at first sight.

Goddamn Coven.

Chapter Two

Coming face-to-face with the Greek god of all things holy-hotness-Theo-James-looking perfection was the last thing Holly expected. Yet no matter how many times she blinked, he was still there.

Who was he? What did he want?

Piping bag still crushed in her palm after shooting a thin stream of buttercream frosting clear across the room like a world-class porn star during the money shot, she admired the faintest hint of five o'clock shadow darkening his jaw.

Unfurling her fingers, she placed the bag beside the partially finished unicorn cookies she'd been working on, wiped her hands on the outside of her yoga pants, and cursed herself for not wearing an apron when she left white streaks of frosting behind.

Jesus, I'm a mess. She felt like she was coated in flour and frosting from the hours she'd already logged baking.

Then there was the Dauntless-leader-looking Adonis. How he managed to look so flipping mouth-watering in a pair of Nike running shoes, black gym shorts, and a gray hoodie from Brighton Tynes University was beyond her. It was a classic example of why guys had it easier than girls.

Still, a part of her wanted to lick him like the mixing bowl after making brownies.

When Bon Jovi's voice faded out to be replaced by the tinkling piano keys of Bruce Springsteen's "Santa Claus is Coming to Town," she became aware she hadn't actually spoken to the purveyor of hotness in front of her.

"Can—" Her voice squeaked. She took a moment to clear her throat before trying again. "Can I help you with something?"

She didn't recognize him, and the shop wasn't laid out so customers could wander in accidentally on their way to the bathrooms.

As if her panties already hadn't felt a bit damp from the sight of him, his smile turned downright carnal, a dimple popping out in the middle of his left cheek. That damn facial imperfection was another unfair advantage to someone already so genetically blessed.

"Yes. I'm hoping you can save my ass."

Do not look at his ass, Hol. Don't do it. If you do, you're getting nothing but coal in your stocking this year. Might be worth it if the back is as good as the front. What are you even saying right now? He's facing you. You can't see his ass.

"Gotta say…even if it's a little early in my book for the Christmas music, you have one hell of a playlist." One of his hands pointed toward the speaker wailing out notes from a saxophone in the E Street Band. "Two of the greats to hail from our fair state."

"I also have a few songs by the Jonas Brothers." The playful comment slipped free without thought. Because though some of their music *might* be on her guilty pleasure playlist, they were *leagues* away from being classified with JBJ and The Boss, regardless of their hometown.

"Anyway…" She clapped quickly to get the attention off of her playlist. If they were to go down that road, he would get whiplash from her eclectic randomness. "You said you needed me to save your ass. *Not* really sure you need any help in that regard."

Shit. Did I just admit to checking him out? Oh god, I'm a mess.

The left side of his mouth pulled up again, bringing back the perfect dimple in his cheek with it.

Why the hell did it feel like he could read all of her thoughts with a look?

And why didn't she feel intimidated standing near him? He looked like he could literally break her in half if he felt so inclined, and retreat should be her first instinct. Yet all she wanted to do was lift the hem of his sweatshirt and see if he was as sculpted underneath as she suspected.

"Ahh, yes. Well, the Wonder Twins out front said they thought you were working on a new batch of the blueberry crumbles. And I'm *praying* it is true, because if it is and you can be talked into parting with a few, I might just have a chance of making it through the rest of the day in one piece."

It didn't seem right that he could manage to come across with the innocent air of a kid asking for a snack before dinnertime while his disheveled inky black hair, so dark it looked blue under the fluorescent lights of the kitchen, made her think of sex—hot, sweaty, dirty, bent-over-the-counter sex.

Whoa. Where the hell did that come from? Rein it in, Hol.

As she mentally bitch-slapped her hormones back in line, her gaze got stuck on how the gray of his eyes looked almost reflective surrounded by a thick fringe of lashes the women in her old circle couldn't manage no matter how much they paid for extensions.

"You're in luck. I put a batch on the cooling racks not too long ago." A flirty, suggestive comment was on the tip of her tongue but she bit it back. She was so far from being in the right headspace to handle anyone—let alone this example of genetic perfection—she might as well be in Narnia. Nope, best to let this go and keep her focus on her baked goods, where the only threat posed was to her waistline.

Using a sheet of waxed paper, she grabbed two blueberry crumbles from the rack and placed them inside a white paper bag before handing them over to Mr. Dauntless.

"Thank you." His fingers brushed against hers when he took the bag, a bolt of electricity shooting up her arm, while his deep voice rumbled through her own chest. "You seriously have no idea how big of a deal this is to me. With this, I might just live long enough to see my niece or nephew be born."

Lyle's voice rang out from the front of the shop, saving her from making the mistake of asking for more information. "Yo, Buns of Steel, Maddey said you might want to get your fine ass back to the gym before Rock blows a gasket."

"Thank you again," he said to her before turning and shouting, "Buns of Steel? Since when do I look like Jane Fonda?"

There was no stopping the giggle that escaped at his quick wit or the way her eyes automatically fell to said buns in all their muscular glory as he strode from the room.

She didn't get his name, but she had a feeling her carefully crafted new life was about to be knocked off its axis.

Chapter Three

Vince headed to Espresso Patronum to find out the name of the Christmas-loving beauty he'd met the day before, and if he was lucky, he might be able to wrangle a date from her as well.

It was such a rookie mistake, not locking down at least her name, but to be fair, he was more focused on not getting his ass kicked by his sister and her husband than his love life.

Once again, he found Lyle behind the counter. Skirting around the line of customers waiting to place their orders with one of the other baristas, he headed straight for him.

Lyle's eyes lit up as he approached. "Two days in a row during camp? Careful, handsome, I'm gonna think you *like* me, and I'm a happily married man."

Vince shook his head and chuckled. The girls liked to joke Kyle needed to keep him in a cage because he was not safe for public consumption, but he couldn't get enough of Lyle's outrageous comments.

"Who taught you not to pull your punches, Ly? I come in here, risking the wrath of The Coven, and you go and break my heart with a statement like that? Stone cold, man."

"Guess it's a good thing you train for the UFC and not the WWE if you can't handle it."

"Oh, you got jokes this morning, huh?"

"Always." Lyle gave him a wink. "Anyway, what can I do for you this morning? It's *way* too early for you to have pissed off Rock so…"

He was right. He hadn't even seen his sister yet.

"No. As far as I know, I'm still on her good side. Day's still young." He shrugged. Things could always change.

"Okay. So you're here because…" Lyle encouraged him to fill in the blanks.

His hands slid into the front pouch of his dark gray Blizzard's hoodie—the state's professional hockey team—a little embarrassed by having to show his hand if he wanted a chance at finding out more information on the little Christmas Elf he hadn't stopped thinking about.

"So…what's the story with your new baker?"

As suspected, Lyle's turquoise eyes lit up with interest immediately, already drawing his own conclusions. If he weren't so adept at navigating the waters of The Coven and their habit of butting into everyone's lives, Vince might have been concerned by that devilish sparkle. But, *please*, Lyle was child's play compared to the six founding members and their newest recruit.

They were damn lucky he was related to a few of them and loved them the way he did, or else there was no way he would let them get away with even *half* the shit they made him go through. Okay, *that* was a lie—they could take over the world if they wanted to, resistance was futile.

"I take it you're referring to our Holly?"

Holly. The name was perfect for his little Christmas lover. *Shit.* Did he really just think of her as his? *Don't get ahead of yourself, Steele.* The mental chastising did nothing to dissuade him from thinking of her possessively. Yet another thing The

Coven would have his ass for. Or maybe not. They seemed to have a thing for alpha males.

Dammit, Steele. Focus.

He nodded, afraid if he spoke he'd give away how jumbled his thoughts were.

"She's in the back if you wanna go see her." Lyle gestured toward the kitchen.

Not needing to be told twice, he rounded the front counter and headed down the back hallway. He grinned as he recognized yet another Christmas hit, this one *NSYNC's "Merry Christmas, Happy Holidays." And as he stepped inside the kitchen for the second time in as many days, there she was, bouncing around and singing along to the radio while decorating a set of cupcakes.

He leaned a shoulder against the doorjamb, settling in to watch the entertaining show for as long as he could before she noticed him.

This time she stood with her back to the door, letting him appreciate her heart-shaped ass as she shimmed side-to-side to the music. With each swish of her hips, the urge to grab them increased. He shoved his hands inside the pouch of his hoodie again and adjusted the semi he now sported.

It wasn't until he chuckled at her fancy celebration foot-work that she was finally alerted to his presence. She whirled around, piping bag once again in hand, with an almost iden-tical expression on her face as yesterday, eyes wide, lips in that enticing O.

Unlike the day before, no frosting went shooting across the room. When she relinquished her hold on the bag, placing it safely on the counter behind her, another smile tugged at his lips as he read the words on the pink t-shirt tied at her hip: 'Cupcakes are cheaper than therapy.'

"*You.*" The breathy tenor of her voice made him imagine all sorts of ways he could get it to hitch.

"Me." He shrugged, hands remaining in his hoodie.

"There's *no way* the blueberry crumbles are already sold out."

"That would be an accurate assumption. I think there was an entire row left when I passed the case." He forced himself to maintain his position and not stalk in her direction to claim the kiss his lips were begging for. The need to know if she tasted as sweet as the yellow frosting was primal.

"So, what brings you into my kitchen today?" Her hand fumbled to find purchase in her jeans.

"You," he stated succinctly. With his friends, he might be laid back and a jokester, but he never shied away from what he wanted. It was one of the reasons he was posed to challenge the light heavyweight title on New Year's Eve. It was about damn time he put some of that single-minded focus on his love life. Lord knew it would make his mom happy.

She slowly blinked at him.

"Did you hear me, Holly?" Her name felt good falling from his lips. He had every intention of making it a daily occurrence.

Her eyes widened to the point that he could see a clear white outline around her irises. "H-How do you know my name?" Her words were tinged with more nerves than he liked.

"Lyle." He hooked a thumb toward the front. Even though his answer had her relaxing, his internal alarms were ringing, alerting him that there was more going on than met the eye. There was a hint of fear in her eyes, but when a soft smile touched her lips, all thoughts fled his mind.

She was beautiful.

"He never was one to mind his business," she commented.

"I don't think it's in his DNA. He's almost as bad as The Coven." The last part slipped out almost subconsciously.

"The Coven?"

He waved off the question. The last thing he wanted to think about was his sister when he was with Holly.

"So…since you bake, I take it your nights are generally free?"

"Depending on the orders, yeah, most days I'm done by two."

"Perfect. Are you free Friday night?" He wanted to see her tonight but didn't want to seem like an over-eager puppy. Though puppies were cute and all, he was hoping for a hell of a lot more than a belly rub from her.

"W-What?"

He couldn't resist the temptation of her any longer. Pushing himself from the doorjamb, he strolled over, not stopping until the toes of his Nikes touched the tips of her pink Chucks. His sister once again broke into his thoughts, and he grinned—she would appreciate Holly matching her footwear to her outfit. Rocky had more sneakers than any other female on the planet.

"I wanted to know if you were free Friday night so I could take you out on a date." There was a streak of yellow frosting on her left cheek. He lifted a hand to brush it away with the pad of his thumb before bringing the finger to his mouth to lick it clean. The way her eyes darkened at the sight proved she wasn't immune to him after all.

"A date?" she choked out.

"Yeah, you know, dinner. Some good conversation, maybe a round of pool or a game of darts. Whatever floats your boat."

"What makes you think the conversation would be good?" Girl was spunky.

"Oh, Cupcake." He broke off with a chuckle, shaking his head at the ludicrous question. "You'll be with me. I'm *always* a good time."

Her eyes flashed down to his groin, causing his dick to stir again. If he were in jeans, this wouldn't be a problem, but he was once again dressed for the gym in a loose pair of basketball shorts. He needed to start thinking about something else, *anything* else except her and how she smelled up close, like one the cupcakes she was frosting earlier, or he was about to have a very obvious problem on his hands.

"I just bet you are." Her gaze finally left his semi-hard dick to meet his again.

"I wasn't talking about sex, but if I were, I can pretty much guaran-damn-tee you'd enjoy yourself." He bent so his mouth was next to her ear. "Multiple times."

She hissed in a shocked breath, and he felt the hitch of it as he trailed his nose across the soft spot behind her ear, breathing in the lingering scent of sugar on her skin. *Fuck.* He wanted to lick her all over.

"But I meant more in a big-picture sort of way."

"You're pretty sure of yourself, aren't you, Muffin," she countered.

"Muffin?"

One of her eyebrows lifted in challenge. "What? You called me Cupcake."

"As long as I'm *your* Stud Muffin, I'm okay with that." He reached to cup the side of her face.

He could see her fighting a giggle, but she eventually caved to it. "God, you're cocky."

"Oh, sweetheart, you have no idea." He trailed his thumb across her lower lip and knew before he left the room he would know what it tasted like. "But we can work toward you getting the chance of finding out starting Friday night. I'll pick you up at eight."

Her words were slow to come as she opened her lips slightly for him. "Who said I wanted to go out with you?"

"You do."

"What if you aren't my type?"

"I'm your type."

A small growl emitted from the back of her throat, and damn if it didn't turn him on and make him want to push her buttons more. "I wouldn't be so sure of that, *Muffin*," she snarked.

"This delectable mouth of yours"—his thumb stroked across it again, this time pulling her lip down slightly— "might be able to lie to me, but the rest of your body can't. Your eyes are almost black with the lust—"

"There's no *lust* here."

"Sweetheart…there's so much lust it's palpatating between us."

He brushed his other hand along her clavicle.

"The goosebumps I can see along here tell me my touch affects you as much as touching you does me. And if all that wasn't enough, the fact that your nipples look like they could cut glass would do it." His eyes dropped down to the tempting peaks. "So no. You want me. And fuck if I don't want you just as bad."

Another hitch of her breath. And when her tongue peeked out to touch her bottom lip, the last of his control snapped and his mouth was on hers.

The hand cupping her face held her in place as his tongue stroked inside her mouth to duel with hers. He hooked his free hand around her middle, pulling her body flush against his and lifting her onto her toes so he didn't have to bend as far.

Her flavor was the most hedonistic dessert on the planet, all sugar and vanilla with a lingering spice that was pure Holly. He could live off the taste of her and he'd only sampled her mouth. Lord help him when he got to experience the rest of her.

When her hands trailed up the plane of his chest, there was a momentary sense of panic that she would push him away, but it faded when she fisted the fabric of his sweatshirt.

He was at risk of hoisting her up and laying her on top of the cupcakes she'd painstakingly decorated. With a growl, he pulled back, breaking their kiss.

Though his chest heaved from the rough breaths needed to control the raging inferno of lust barreling through his body, his words were even. "I'll pick you up at eight. See you then, Cupcake." He dropped a kiss to her forehead and left the kitchen before he said screw any potential health code violations and fucked her against the counter covered in cupcakes, his now full-fledged boner cursing him the entire way.

FOUR

Coven Conversations

From the Group Message Thread of The Coven

UEEN OF SMUT (Maddey): Ummm... I thought Vin was in training camp???

QUEEN OF SMUT: *GIF of Britney Spears looking confused*

ALPHABET SOUP (Rocky): He is. We pretty much own his ass until the New Year.

YOU KNOW YOU WANNA (Becky): *GIF of Cinderella locked in her room*

MAKES BOYS CRY (Skye): Oh shit! I love when one of the boys misbehaves.

. . .

MAKES BOYS CRY: *GIF of Michael Jackson eating popcorn*

MOTHER OF DRAGONS (Jordan): Why do I feel like we're missing a piece of the puzzle here?

QUEEN OF SMUT: Well two days in a row I saw him in Espresso Patronum and I didn't think it was on his approved diet plan.

PROTEIN PRINCESS (Gemma): The fuck it is. His ass better get back here so I can check his weight. Rock if he's cheating and gains weight, you have that sexy husband of yours kick his ass across the mat today.

ALPHABET SOUP: *GIF of Michelle Tanner saying "You got it Dude"*

QUEEN OF SMUT: What I don't get though, is both times he's been here, he's disappeared into the back. So that's the only thing I can't figure out.

MOTHER OF DRAGONS: Ask Lyle what's going on.

MAKES BOYS CRY: Screw that. Jor meet in the lobby. We'll be there in 15.

· · ·

THE OG PITA (Beth): Why do I have to have a regular job? I want to come. You guys better send me some video to watch later or something.

ALPHABET SOUP: Gurrrll. You know I got you. Now go mold minds or you know whatever it is you teachers do.

YOU KNOW YOU WANNA: True. Children are the future after all.

PROTEIN PRINCESS: Madz, we'll be right there.

Chapter Five

With the birthday cupcakes finished and packaged for pickup, Holly went in search of her friends to see what needed to be replenished for the shop. She may have told her mystery guy she finished at two —most days she was there by five in the morning—but more often than not, she clocked in more than twelve hours a day baking in the back. It was the least she could do. She owed them so much more than what could be repaid monetarily. She only hoped one day she would be able to return their kindness, because without them there was a chance she would still be stuck in hell.

She tried to deny the salary they insisted on paying her but eventually caved. She would need the income if she was ever going to be able to afford her own place and stop free-loading in their guest room.

"Any special requests?" she asked Lyle when she joined him behind the front counter.

As she let him pull her in to snuggle against his side, she admired the unique brilliance of what he and his husband had created.

The Espresso Patronum was a Potterhead's dream. Scattered throughout the eclectic seating was different Harry Potter-themed upholstery. One chair had mini Hedwigs, another the Deathly Hallows symbol, one with spells scrolled across, and her personal favorite was The Marauder's Map.

Aside from the black lacquer tables, nothing in the place matched, yet it managed to come off as a sort of controlled chaos of colors, making her think of what Alice experienced when she fell down the rabbit hole into Wonderland.

How could you not love a place where the lights were upside-down coffee mugs and the bar stools at the counter were made to look like the person was an animal, or that you were looking at their ass? Seriously, they had a stool meant to make you think you were seeing a person in a thong with lips prints on one of their bare butt cheeks.

"No, Sweets. We're all good for now." Lyle looked her over from head-to-toe. "You have to be the prettiest hot mess I've ever met."

Her hand instantly went to the spot on her cheek Mr. Hottie swiped frosting from, only to have her own come away clean.

When he had touched her that first time, sweet baby Jesus, she felt her body light up like Rudolph's damn nose. She was transfixed by the guy and she didn't even know his damn name. But when he'd brought his thumb to his mouth to lick off the frosting she somehow managed to get on her face, she had never wished to be a digit so hard.

Then he had to go and call her Cupcake, and she was ready to cave like a poorly baked soufflé.

If anyone noticed that her nipples were doing their best impression of googly eyes, she would blame the cold air that followed each customer pushing through the doors. No one needed to know it was caused by a guy who managed to consume every one of her thoughts—both asleep and awake. Because if her friends got the barest whiff of the pheromones her body released around him, they would go into full-blown matchmaker mode.

A cocky man too sexy for his own good was not on her New Life list at the moment. Nope. First up was finding her own place to live, one where if she had roommates they weren't a married couple. Romance was so far down her list it wasn't even in the same notebook, let alone on the same page.

When he mentioned the date, she was so firmly planted in Denialville that she was the flipping mayor and couldn't think of a way to decline on the spot. Now she had two days to figure out how to get out of it.

Lost in her thoughts, she missed Lyle's next comment, only jolting back to the present when he lifted her left hand to show her a long streak of frosting on the underside of her forearm. There was also a flour handprint on the outside of her thigh, and she could feel a few sprinkles inside her bra. Her creations might be beautifully put together, but she was not.

"I love how even growing up in that stuck-up family you still manage to be so uniquely you. How you didn't let them browbeat you into becoming another Stepford carbon copy I'll never know."

"Almost." She frowned, thinking of how long she played the dutiful daughter, letting her parents control her life, barely bucking the system for twenty-three years. She shuddered at what it took for her to take her life back in her hands.

"Hey." Lyle booped her nose, bringing her back to the present. "You got out. That's all that matters. Now the fun really begins."

She loved this man so much. There was no better guy she could have picked for her childhood friend to marry. Lyle was four years older than them and the complete antithesis of the highbrow, old money, Daughters of the American Revolution, debutante world she and Kyle hailed from.

She'd never forget the day her friend told her about the

guy he met at a hockey game of all places. First her friend bucked the system, choosing to attend Princeton instead of Yale like the rest of the Huntingtons, then he started dating a man. Oh, the horror.

For years, she had known Kyle was gay, but with parents who were the definition of upper-crust elitist and liked to brag they could trace their lineage back to the Mayflower, anyone who didn't conform to their cookie-cutter way of life was ousted.

And her friend? He ticked off every box on the way to being disowned.

Not follow in family footsteps in choosing a college?

Check.

Marry someone not of appropriate breeding and bloodlines?

Check.

Come out of the closet and declare your love for a member of the same sex?

Double check.

She was there the day Kyle brought Lyle home and announced he was in love—with a man. The entire thing went down in flames like the Hindenburg.

She grew up in a world of custom-tailored suits worth thousands of dollars each, yet none of them looked as good as her mystery man managed to make a hoodie and gym shorts. It was like he *oozed* sex appeal out of his pores.

Alpha had never been her type. And the guy was pure self-confidence. He was too cocky for his own good. So why did his whispered promise of getting her off—multiple times —make her instantly need a new pair of panties?

She knew she needed to resist him. But every feather-light touch and dirty word caused the fondant around her heart to crack, even as his dominant personality was enough to keep her from risking herself.

"Come on." Lyle guided her to the back counter where

they brewed the coffee. "Let's get you caffeinated so you can go back to creating whatever masterpiece is next on your list."

Lyle was the least basic person in existence and would never settle for his coffee shop's signature fall drink to be the same as everywhere else in the world. So it came as no surprise the mug he handed her was filled with his pecan pie latte, instead of the standard pumpkin spice.

A small moan escaped as she sipped the sugary goodness.

"You know," he said, quirking his pierced eyebrow as he watched her cradle the mug lovingly, "some say it's better than sex."

"I want to say that they are having sex with the wrong people, but I'm more inclined to agree." She blew across the top before taking another hearty sip. Even as she spoke, her thoughts drifted back to her no-named stud muffin. Now there was a man she'd bet could sex her up better than the latte in her hands.

The last thing—the very *last* thing—she'd expected was to hear him admit he wanted her as badly as she did him, or for his kiss to be so hot she was sure they would be permanently placed on Santa's naughty list.

Reindeer really would have to fly for her to admit how much she liked how easily he had controlled her body.

Not the time, Hol. Lyle will sniff out your lust-filled thoughts like a bloodhound if you're not careful.

Lyle's eyes narrowed as he watched her drink.

Shit, he's already got that knowing look in his eye. Abort! Abort!

She was in as much trouble as a snowman in summer.

Chapter Six

Vince used the bottle opener to pop the cap of the Sam Adams Winter Lager, wishing it was for him and not his best friend as he unscrewed the top off yet another bottle of water for himself. Water in one hand and three bottles of beer in the other—one alcoholic and two root—he made is way out of the kitchen and into the living room, passing off the Sam to Jase and the others to his two favorite nine-year-olds in existence.

"Thanks, man." Jase cheersed his beer against Vince's water, the plastic preventing a satisfying clink.

He dropped into the remaining open leather recliner, a groan escaping as he stretched his sore body out with the footrest. He was five weeks into the twelve-week—and longest—training camp of his career. It came as no surprise his father/coach opted for the longer camp since it was preceding the biggest fight of his MMA career—a chance to fight for the UFC's light heavyweight belt after Christmas.

"Camp kicking your ass?" Jase asked.

"Oh, yeah." Another groan slipped out as he adjusted in the leather chair.

"I feel ya, man. Even with preseason, nothing compares to

when the season really kicks into gear. I'm finally starting to feel like I'm settling into the grind."

Jase played defense for the New York Storm and was one of the top players in the entire NHL. Hockey was a physical game, and as an enforcer for his team, his friend wore more bruises weekly than he did.

"Well, I'm honored you chose to spend your night off with me. I love having something to taunt Rock with."

Jase choked on his beer. "Dude, you're crazy actively messing with your sister." He shook his head. "I do everything in my power not to piss JD off. *Especially* now that she's pregnant again."

It was true—things had been a little more intense now that both Coven leaders were knocked up. At least with Jordan, it was the second go-round, so they knew what to expect. Rocky was the wild card.

"You know me." He shrugged. "I like to live on the edge."

"That or you've taken one too many hits to the head."

"You're one to talk," he tossed back.

"I'll have you know…" Jase tipped his beer at him. "I rarely shed blood on the ice"—he paused in thought—"at least from a fight. Besides, Rock and Gage had a doctor's appointment. I figured I might as well hang with you since my sister chose to fly out to meet the team in Chicago while she still can." He pointed to where the pregame show for the Blizzards/Fire played on the flat-screen.

"Did she fly out with the team?"

"No. The Blizzards are on a stretch of away games. She flew out this afternoon and will stay through tomorrow to handle anything Tucker and whoever else ATS represents in Chicago needs."

"Good, that means I get a break for a few days."

"She has you doing lots of promo for the fight?"

"That's not too bad yet." He paused to drink some water.

"But she's my liaison with the women's shelter. Hell, JD is the reason I even started teaching the self-defense classes in the first place. Without her, I wouldn't be in the position I am now."

"You mean as one of the sponsors for the new shelter?"

"Yup."

Vince and the Donnellys—twins Jase and Jordan plus their older brother, Ryan—were working with another organization to build a new women's shelter. Jordan had been attacked by an abusive ex-boyfriend a few years ago, which gave all of them some firsthand experience with what some women dealt with.

Though he made plenty, thanks to Jordan's public relations company landing him lucrative endorsements, the coin needed to fund even a quarter of the shelter was something he wouldn't have until he won a title fight purse.

"How's hockey going for you two?" Vince asked Jase's younger brother, Sean, and his best friend, Carlee—Blizzards goalie Jake Donovan's younger sister—about their youth hockey league.

"It's good," Sean mumbled around the slice of pizza he was trying to shove into his mouth.

"Yup. We have the same coach as last year, so it was like picking up where we left off," Carlee added with more class than her partner in crime.

"Good. I'll be at your home game next weekend." The kids brightened at his words. There were times he forgot just how young they were. Both were mature beyond their years thanks to the time they spent with their siblings almost three times their age.

On the television, the hockey game got underway, grabbing everyone's attention as they watched their friends battle it out for the puck. At some point Ray—one of Vince's roommates and a fellow fighter at the gym—entered the room clad in a Fire t-shirt.

"So did Vin tell you about his little secret?" Ray asked Jase during a commercial break.

Jase sat up, rubbing his hands together. "Oooh, do tell."

Ray's eyes flicked his way before refocusing his attention on Jase. The guy was planning on stirring up shit. Vince couldn't blame him though—he'd do the same thing if the situation was reversed.

"Well, it seems Lyle and Kyle have hired a new baker for EP, and she is a *cutie*," Ray sing-songed the last word.

"Dude, don't use words like cutie, or you'll have to turn in your man card." Deck, Vince's other roommate and child-hood friend, said as he joined them and settled in beside Carlee.

"Oh, are you talking about Holly?" Carlee asked, excite-ment sparkling in her bright green eyes.

"How do you know about this before me?" Jase asked, sounding almost offended by being out of the loop.

"Maddey told us all about her when she picked us up from school today."

Jase's attention diverted to where his brother, Ryan, was on a fast breakaway, dekeing around their friend Tucker before sending the biscuit flying for a sweet goal in the five-hole, putting the Blizzards up 1-0 on the Fire.

"How do you know about this girl?" Jase asked Ray.

"I overheard the girls talking about her after they went on their little reconnaissance mission."

"Oh, shit, you're screwed, man, if they're involved. The Coven gathers intel better than the CIA." Jase didn't even attempt to choke back his laughter. He was pretty sure he saw a tear leaking out the corner of his friend's eye. *Asshole.*

"Don't you start with me or I'll make sure to mention to Rock that you're falling for a bunny," he threatened, and Jase's face sobered instantly.

As Jase's bestie, his sister was fiercely protective of him, having lent her support in the past chasing off some of the more persistent puck bunnies when needed. At the end of the day, all any of the ladies from The Coven wanted was to see each of their friends to be as disgustingly in love as Jordan and Jake were together, and now his sister and Gage. It was becoming an epidemic, one he'd keenly avoided at all costs until he met Holly. Now it didn't seem like such a bad thing.

That being said, he didn't need the other guys to start sniffing around her. Time to shut this down before they got any ideas.

Holly was meant to be his and no one else's.

Chapter Seven

Holly curled up in her favorite oversized chair in Lyle and Kyle's living room, full glass of wine in one hand, Kindle in the other. Today had been a rollercoaster of emotions, making it seem longer than the eighteen hours she had been awake. She *needed* the escape both the alcohol and the steamy hockey romance offered.

Once again Stud Muffin—she refused to ask the Samsons for his name—invaded her thoughts with the same confidence he'd swaggered into her kitchen with that morning.

The guy was a freaking walking, talking romance novel hero. It was like he was plucked from one of her favorite Belle Willis books and dropped into her life.

Holly had to stay focused on *herself* and *not* her love life.

She would not think about cocksure men who kissed like they taught *all* the classes in the course catalog—from Kissing 101 all the way through to the doctorate program.

Nor would she remember how gently he cupped her face while he plundered her mouth. Yeah, plundered—she was a romance junkie and she could use old school romance terms all she liked.

She certainly wasn't pondering the muscles of his well-

defined body or admitting how hot it was when he effort-
lessly maneuvered her body to align with his.

There wasn't a snowball's chance in hell of getting her to
confess to feeling up those delectable muscles.

Nope.

Not gonna happen.

And dammit, there went another pair of panties. The guy
was fucking lethal. Just the memory of him was enough to
generate copious amounts of laundry. There was ab-so-lute-ly
no way she could consider going on an actual date with him.
She wouldn't survive it.

"You know," Kyle said as he and Lyle entered the room,
"for a girl who is supposed to be lost in the world of swoony
bad boys, or whatever it is you're reading this week, you sure
look like you're thinking really hard."

"Sorry." Her cheeks heated at being caught thinking of her
Muffin. *Hehe.* Thinking of him as Muffin, without the
preceding Stud, only made her think of her vagina, which
then led her to thoughts of what he could do to it, and that
was a slippery slope she didn't need to travel.

"Want to share with the class, Sweets?" Lyle asked, a
familiar devilish twinkle shining in his turquoise eyes.

"Just working out a few new flavor combinations I want
to try tomorrow," she lied. These two were so in love, if they
had even a hint of the attraction she was feeling toward SM
they would go all supernova matchmaker on her. They would
be like if a Jewish Bubbie got together with a Greek Yaya and
had a baby, and that baby was raised by an Italian family.
They'd have her married off and pregnant faster than it took
for one of her cakes to cool enough to frost.

"Bullshit. But we'll let it slide because we have more
important things to discuss at the moment," Kyle retorted as
he pulled Lyle in to snuggle against him on the couch.

"And that would be?" she asked, her interest piqued.

"We found you a place to live," Lyle answered.

"You're kicking me *out*?" Sure, she wanted to find a place of her own when she could afford first and last months' rent —the only plans she had as far as her future was concerned, besides helping revamp EP's bakery business—but she was nowhere near ready for that.

"First off"—Kyle held up a finger for emphasis—"we would *never*. You know you are welcome to stay with us as long as you'd like. But be honest, Hol. You're itching to not be surrounded by our wedded bliss twenty-four seven."

All the tension radiating through her body drained at his reassurance. She finished her remaining wine in an attempt to rid any lingering worry.

"Even with you guys paying me *way* more than I think you should, I've only been here two weeks. I don't have enough saved up to pay the security deposit needed for a place. Even if it was a studio, I'm a few months out."

"What if you didn't have to pay a security deposit?"

"How is that possible?" She twirled the stem of her wine glass between her fingers. "I don't expect to live a lifestyle like we grew up in, but I'm not going to the ghetto." She scrunched her nose like she smelled something foul.

"Where the hell do you think we live, Sweets?" Lyle's face twisted comically. "We *don't* have a ghetto." He rolled his eyes so hard she was surprised they didn't fall out. "That's your parents' influence bleeding out."

Ouch.

"Roommates, Hol," Kyle said when it became obvious his husband wasn't going to be any help.

"Like scouring Craigslist? I'm cramping your style *so* bad you want me to risk ending up in someone's freezer when I inadvertently start living with a serial killer?"

"And you say *I'm* dramatic?" Lyle placed a hand to his chest with a flourish.

She'd lived the first twenty-three years of her life curbing her impulses, forced to be a *proper lady*. She was allowed to let her emotions flow free now—for no other reason than because she could.

"We have friends that have a room that's been sitting empty for almost a year. They would love to split the rent three ways again." Kyle continued as if neither of them spoke. "They've already said the room is yours if you want it."

"Why would they do that? They don't even know me." She wasn't used to people doing nice things without strings attached. No, her world had been filled with more strings than the cover of that one *NSYNC album.

"They know you're friends with me and that's good enough for them. All you have to do is meet and see if *you* like them. If you do, we can move you in this weekend."

She was floored. It seemed too good to be true. Instinct had her preparing for the other shoe to drop—there was always a catch. But then she remembered she wasn't trapped behind a wrought iron gate in a gilded mansion. Not everyone in the world was like the Vanderbuilts, in fact, most people were genuinely good.

"Okay." She took a deep, fortifying breath. She could do this. She could make new friends. It was time for this baby bird to leave the nest and learn to fly. "When can I meet them?"

"We already told them you'd swing by The Steele Maker tomorrow."

"The gym?" Her voice squeaked like a dog's chew toy. *Stud Muffin.* He worked out at the gym. What if she ran into him there? With her luck she would. But she wasn't sure if it would be considered good or bad.

"Yup. They both work there, so it'll be super easy for you. All you have to do is walk across the street when there's a lull in orders."

Why did she think this wasn't going to go the way her friends expected?

Chapter Eight

Cardio day dawned bright and early. Vince had a love/hate relationship with it during training camp. One of the ways to break up the monotony of having to log time on the treadmill or stationary bike was to run the five miles from his apartment in The Hightower to The Steele Maker.

He popped his Bluetooth headphones in his ears, left his gym bag by the front door for Deck to grab, and headed out.

He stretched during the elevator ride. By the time the doors opened in the building's lobby, Muse's "Uprising" was playing in his ears and he was off.

When he ran to the gym, he always left earlier than the rest of their crew in the building, but that morning he made sure to leave *extra* early so he could swing by EP and see his girl. Yes, his girl. Because whether she knew it or not, that's exactly what she was.

His normal relaxed pace of an eight- or nine-minute mile was increased closer to six by the driving need to get his eyes on Holly as soon as possible.

Brandy's "I Wanna Be Down" played through the café

speakers as he pulled open the main door. Lyle had always been a fan of the throwbacks.

With a wave to the weekday barista, he strode around the counter for the kitchen. Before he even stepped inside, he could hear Holly singing along with Ariana Grande, telling Santa to not have her fall in love if the guy wouldn't still be around the next year. She wouldn't have to worry about that if she gave in to their mutual attraction.

Her love for the big man's holiday had him convinced it would be a *very* merry Christmas indeed.

He leaned against the doorjamb, pushing his hand through his damp hair, and settled in to watch as Holly fluttered around the kitchen, taking trays of scones from the oven and placing them on the cooling racks to the left.

Unlike the previous times he'd stopped by, this time she didn't startle when she caught sight of him. The look she sent his way made him think she was expecting him to show up —again.

She was damn cute with her bandana headband and three-quarter sleeved baseball shirt reading 'Holiday Baking Team' with pictures of Santa hat-wearing gingerbread men on it. Time to step up his comical t-shirt game.

"Morning, Cupcake," he greeted her with his most charming smile.

"Stud Muffin." Her pink lips tipped up as she tossed a white kitchen towel she'd been using on the counter behind her.

"Ahh…I see you used my full name today."

"Well, when I call you just Muffin it makes me think of the phrase 'buttering your muffin' and that makes me think of vaginas, and personally I *don't* really want to be thinking about female genitalia this early in the morning."

"That's a shame," he said, crossing the distance separating them. "Because I haven't been able to stop thinking about what it would be like to butter *your* biscuit since I met you."

He bent down so his nose brushed against the soft spot behind her ear, breathing in the sweet scent of sugar lingering on her skin. She sucked in a breath as he trailed the tip of his nose along the now fluttering vein running along the side of her slender neck. Her scent was *intoxicating*.

He wanted to devour her like the peach filling in a pie-eating contest.

He trailed butterfly-soft kisses down the side of her neck that had her pushing against the hard muscles of his stomach, pressing his cool, damp shirt against his heated skin.

He let out a strained, "Shit," pulled it over his head, used it to wipe the sweat from his brow, then tossed it to the ground. He straightened and stared at her for a moment like standing half-naked in an industrial kitchen was an everyday occurrence.

His stomach muscles jumped as her fingers traced inside the deep cuts defining them, and a guttural groan escaped. He had her in his arms and lifted off her feet in a blink with a growled, "Mine."

He barely registered her shriek as he slammed his mouth on hers, the heat of the oven under his hands the last thing he was conscious of before getting lost in the kiss.

Tongues stroking.

Teeth biting.

Mouths sucking.

This wasn't a kiss. No, this was mouth-fucking at its finest. He owned her body with a single kiss.

He shifted to anchor her against the stainless steel appliance with his lower body so both hands could cup her face. His fingers tangled in her hair, the bandana knocked askew as he angled her to fit.

"Fuck, you're delicious," he rasped against her lips, sucking the bottom one into his mouth, biting down on the plump pillow then licking away the sting with his tongue.

She whimpered, clutching his sweat-soaked hair between her fingers.

"You were made to be mine."

Fuck. My. Life.

The thought played on repeat in Vince's mind as he continued to use his mouth to mark Holly as his own. He was due to be at The Steele Maker any minute, but fuck if he was able to pull himself away from this girl. Nothing, *nothing* else mattered except the sweet taste of her on his lips.

Not training.

Not his upcoming fight or his shot at the belt.

No, all he cared about at the moment was how to get *more* of her.

And fuck him sideways, if that didn't say how ass-over-head he was for this woman he barely knew—he didn't know what did.

His hips ground, the heat of her center as hot as the oven doors he braced against.

Teeth nipped.

Tongues stroked.

Hair was pulled.

He was so screwed, and not in any of the ways he had been imagining since he set eyes on her two days ago.

Two days? Had it really only been two days since he'd first seen her?

Fuck. He could give Maddey's novels a run for their money with the creativity of his thoughts lately. Most of them about how to bring Holly to a screaming orgasm.

Well, sonofabitch. I've turned into one of Maddey's best-selling books.

He would never live this down with The Coven, but hell if it wasn't already too late for him. Her flavor was birthday cake, and he wondered if the rest of her tasted as good as her mouth. He would take a lifetime of ripping from his friends if it meant he ended every night with Holly in his bed and him buried inside her.

A part of him worried he was too rough, but her fingers clenched in his hair said not to worry. So did her hips grinding against the erection trying to escape the confines of his boxer briefs and pants. And also the whimpers periodically escaping her mouth.

Each breathy sigh she released was like a physical caress to his aching dick.

"Not that I'm not enjoying the show, but I think it would be some type of health code violation if you two have sex in here." Lyle's voice popped the bubble of lust surrounding them as effectively as a needle to a balloon. "I'm not sure though. What are your thoughts on the matter, babe?"

"I think you might be right. I mean, it's bad enough our Man of Steele is half-naked, but if they actually get to the full-blown act. *Ooooh,* baby." The Samsons watched them like an HBO drama.

While the happy couple discussed them as though they weren't standing in front of them, Holly tried to hide by burying her face in the space between his neck and shoulder. Not that he would complain about her snuggling against him, but the way her warm breath blew against the lingering sweat on his skin sent tingles running down his spine and did nothing to help deflate the current situation he had going on south of the border.

"Well, my darling husband, you know *I'll* never complain about one of our boys removing clothing. Why else do you think I opened up my place across from the gym? I do love seeing all those bulging muscles on display."

"True. But maybe they should limit it to The Steele Maker and not here."

"Lyle. Kyle," Vince said once enough blood returned to his brain for him to form words.

"Vince." They returned in unison, matching knowing smirks on their faces.

"You mind giving us a minute?"

"You're not *actually* going to have sex if we do, are you?" Kyle quirked a brow.

"No. The kitchen is safe from sexual activity...for now."

Holly shuddered in his arms as he tacked on the last part. It was all the confirmation he needed that he would be laying her out and licking frosting from her delectable body.

His eyes stayed locked on the doorway until the two busy-bodies made their exit and he was once again alone with the only person he wanted.

As much as he didn't want to, he uncoiled her legs from around his waist and lowered her to the ground, making sure she didn't brush against him.

Needing a moment to beat his libido back into submission, he scooped his discarded shirt from the floor, tugging it over his head and back into place before facing Holly again.

She was retying the bandana around her head when her eyes, blown out to the thinnest rim of color from lust, found him.

"So, your name is Vince?"

"It hasn't changed from yesterday."

"Ahh." The left side of her mouth kicked up playfully. A mouth he was pleased to see was swollen from his kisses. "Well, you see, that's the thing. You never *told* me your name. We didn't *actually* do the whole introduction thing since you found out my name from Lyle. I guess it's fitting I learned yours from the same source."

Well, shit. She knocked him more off-balance than he thought if he couldn't remember to do something as simple as telling a woman his name. It was Get The Girl 101 to introduce yourself to a pretty girl you were interested in. God help him if his sister ever found out.

"Steele, if your fine ass isn't out here in ten seconds, I'm sending Madz in to get you." Lyle's voice called from the great beyond.

"Shit," he cursed under his breath and pushed a hand through his hair. "I better go before that threat turns into calling for reinforcements. But I'll stop by later, Cupcake."

He wanted to kiss her again, but if he did he was never getting out of there, and then he would have a majority of The Coven busting in on him making out like a teenager with the girl he was crushing on. Not in his top five of things he wanted happening.

He settled for a wink and walked out of the room. Before he cleared the threshold, she said, "Bye, Stud Muffin."

The goofy-ass smile those words produced stayed on his face the entire short jog to The Steele Maker.

NINE

Coven Conversations

From the Group Message Thread of The Coven

UEEN OF SMUT: Well, well, well. Looks like Vinny boy has himself a little crush.

QUEEN OF SMUT: *GIF of Bugs Bunny with heart eyes*

PROTEIN PRINCESS: I take it he was in EP again?

QUEEN OF SMUT: *GIF of Jensen Ackles pointing and quirking his mouth as if to say you are correct*

MAKES BOYS CRY: Oooo. I love Jensen Ackles.

. . .

THE OG PITA: Me too. He's my total hall pass.

YOU KNOW YOU WANNA: Oh 100% agreed. Madz you should see if you can get him for one of your covers, then we can spend all day ogling him

ALPHABET SOUP: Why is it that we always get off track and not focus on the original topic at hand?

MOTHER OF DRAGONS: Because our friends have the attention span of squirrels *squirrel emoji*

ALPHABET SOUP: For reals. And they can't even blame it on pregnancy brain like us.

MOTHER OF DRAGONS: *GIF of Khloe Kardashian saying "Hashtag, Fact"*

MOTHER OF DRAGONS: And for real, do you have any idea what these pregnancy hormones do to a girl? You can't be showing me Jensen Ackles when my hot AF husband is playing an away game.

MOTHER OF DRAGONS: *GIF of Jack Sparrow saying "That's not very nice."*

. . .

QUEEN OF SMUT: *GIF of Cher from *Clueless* saying "My Bad."
*

THE OG PITA: Dude. I only have free period for so long. Can we get to who Vince has a crush on please?

PROTEIN PRINCESS: Wait??? Is it that pretty girl we saw talking to Lyle when we were there yesterday???

QUEEN OF SMUT: Shit! Why didn't I make the connection? Hold please…

QUEEN OF SMUT: Ok, you need to spill ALL the things.

MR. FABULOUS (Lyle): OOOooo. I FLOVE when the velvet rope parts and I get invited into the "exclusive" Coven Conversations.

MR. FABULOUS: Also, is it weird I'm texting Madz when I can see her sitting 100 feet away?

YOU KNOW YOU WANNA: Nope. I'm with Rock and Gem, we do it all the time.

ALPHABET SOUP: So yeah forget about that and tell us what Vince has been up to over there 3 days in a row??

· · ·

MR. FABULOUS: Do you mean the time he came over here to beg Holly for the special treats your knocked up self was craving?

MR. FABULOUS: Or…

MR. FABULOUS: Are you referring to how Kyle and I found him with his tongue down her throat and pinned against the oven in the kitchen?

MR. FABULOUS: I'm going to need you ladies to be more specific.

ALPHABET SOUP: WHAT?!

QUEEN OF SMUT: WHAT??

PROTEIN PRINCESS: SAY WHAT?

MOTHER OF DRAGONS: COME AGAIN?

YOU KNOW YOU WANNA: VIN DID WHAT?

THE OG PITA: WHAT?

. . .

MAKES BOYS CRY: HUH?

MR. FABULOUS: Oh look, I have you all speaking in SHOUTY CAPITALS. I love when that happens.

MR. FABULOUS: Do you want to know what happened or not?

QUEEN OF SMUT: OMG you guys should see the death glare Lyle is sending me from across EP.

QUEEN OF SMUT: **Picture of Lyle shooting daggers.**

ALPHABET SOUP: Sorry, Ly. Please tell me more about the one woman who seems to have captured the attention of my darling big brother for more than 5 minutes.

MR. FABULOUS: Well she's the creator of those blueberry crumbles that baby in your belly has had you craving every day.

ALPHABET SOUP: SOLD! He needs to marry this chick.

ALPHABET SOUP: *GIF of Jensen Ackles pointing and saying "Marry that girl."*

THE OG PITA: Ooo more Jensen.

.   .   .

MR. FABULOUS: Don't try and distract me with male perfection because I haven't gotten to the best part.

PROTEIN PRINCESS: ???

PROTEIN PRINCESS: Don't ghost on us now.

YOU KNOW YOU WANNA: Maddey throw something at him.

MOTHER OF DRAGONS: OMG Lyle tell us already. My flight is boarding and I am not waiting hours to find out how this story ends.

QUEEN OF SMUT: Don't make me call in reinforcements.

MR. FABULOUS: Oh honey. Do you really think threatening to call in your fine AF brother would make me talk faster?

MR. FABULOUS: Oh shit! Tink got up from her seat. I'll talk. I'll talk.

MR. FABULOUS: You know how I asked if you'd guys would meet my friend to see if you liked her to take over Rocky's old room?

. . .

PROTEIN PRINCESS: Yeah…

MR. FABULOUS: Well…

MR. FABULOUS: It was Holly.

YOU KNOW YOU WANNA: Oh shit! Things JUST got interesting.

Chapter Ten

After being caught by her friends making out like a teenage babysitter who snuck her boyfriend over, Holly spent the remainder of her day hiding out from the world—well, Kyle and Lyle—baking up all kinds of goodies in the kitchen. She probably created more food than they would be able to sell through the day, but if she faced them, she might *actually* combust in embarrassment.

Still, being able to do what *she* wanted, even if it was working, was a refreshing change she embraced whole-heartedly.

The plus side to her mortification—she now knew her mystery man's name.

Vince.

It suited him.

She couldn't be faulted for letting things get carried away. The guy *exuded* pheromones. It was bad enough seeing him in a shirt that was like a second skin and not covered up by a baggie hoodie, then he went and stripped it off, revealing every lickable inch of his torso. Holy jingle bells, he should *never* wear a shirt. A girl could not be held responsible for her actions when faced with that much perfection inches from her face.

He *really* wasn't her type. He was so damn alpha his picture was probably next to the word in the dictionary. She'd had enough of controlling men to last her a lifetime. The *last* thing she needed was to get involved with the type of guy who told her when she could come or not.

Nope.

Not her type.

At.

All.

Fuck. Who was she kidding?

If they weren't interrupted, she was pretty sure she had been seconds away from asking if she could decorate the ridges defining his six-pack with frosting so she could clean it off him. With her tongue.

She was in serious trouble here.

She needed coffee.

Wine.

Sleep.

A lobotomy, maybe.

But for now, she had to pull on her big girl panties and walk across Main Street to the gym where Vince…she wasn't really sure *what* he did. She assumed with a body like his he did something physical, an athlete, a firefighter maybe, who knew? Regardless, there was a strong possibility he might be there when what she needed to focus on were her potential new roommates and *not* the sex-on-legs distraction.

With a damp paper towel, she cleaned the flour and other baking materials off her black leggings and headed out before losing her nerve.

She snuck behind the counter while Lyle was busy helping a customer, grabbed a to-go coffee and smiled down at its logo of a paper cup wearing the iconic round glasses, sporting the signature lightning bolt scar and brandishing a wand, all to avoid meeting Lyle's knowing gaze.

She didn't bother with her jacket, instead jogging the short distance to The Steele Maker to ward off the chill in the November air.

The building itself was a massive steel and glass structure, taking up more than half the block, and stood more than two stories tall. Like Espresso Patronum, the façade was floor-to-roof windows, but unlike the coffee house, you couldn't see through them.

As she entered the gym, she was greeted by the jaunty piano strains of Queen's "Don't Stop Me Now." A lover of a good playlist, she appreciated anyone who enjoyed the musical genius that was Freddie Mercury.

There was a large, semi-circle reception desk directly in front of the door, and she had a feeling she'd seen the pretty redhead manning it in EP a time or two.

Farther back, alongside one of the windows, she could see rows of punching bags and she was pretty sure the smaller raindrop-shaped things hanging from a shelf higher up were called speed bags. There were also a huge boxing ring and black octagon in the back.

The biggest surprise was the artistic black-and-white art hanging throughout, as well as the magnificent mural painted on an entire wall depicting the American flag and Olympic rings.

Between the displayed portraits, the amount of real estate the boxing equipment took up, and the half dozen guys scattered throughout participating in various fighting techniques, Holly figured the gym must cater to training fighters.

And in the middle of it all was Mr. Temptation himself —Vince.

Her eyes greedily took in every detail she could from her spot near the front door. He'd ditched his long-sleeved shirt and sported a gray muscle tank, the front darkened to the same stormy shade his eyes were after their panty-destroying kiss.

His hands were wrapped in black material, and she watched as he pushed a hand through his inky hair, sending it spiked out in multiple directions. Where on most people it would look sloppy, begging to have a brush run through it, on him it managed to look like it was purposely styled that way.

Unlike how most of the other fighters in the gym were paired off against each other, he was taking a fight stance against a blonde woman who had to be almost half a foot shorter than her own five-six height. *Surely, she wasn't his partner.*

Except a few seconds later, she watched as Vince wrapped his arms around the blonde's body.

Panic welled inside her chest as she watched him keep his arms locked tight as she struggled against him.

Forgetting all about the real reason she was there in the first place, self-preservation had her turning and fleeing out the door.

ONE OF THE things that made Vic and Mick Steele—Vince's father and uncle—so successful as coaches in both the MMA and boxing communities was their ability to keep those they trained from burning out, extending a fighter's career far past average. One of their tactics was incorporating some fun even during the height of training.

As much as Vince *hated* cardio day, the grueling pace of the day usually ended with some sort of ridiculousness. The only person to log more pushups with his sister on their back than him was her husband Gage. The heavyweight champ also did pull-ups with Rocky wrapped around him like a monkey—the crazy fool.

But his sister was currently gestating with his future niece or nephew, so Rocky no longer participated in the unconventional methods of training.

Since she was sidelined for another six months, he found himself at the mercy of Maddey. Yeah, *mercy*. If anyone tried to tell him a barely five foot, romance writing, Tinkerbell lookalike wasn't intimidating, they'd never had the privilege of meeting Madison McClain. As the only daughter of a retired Navy SEAL-turned-police chief, she learned early on how to keep up with her three older brothers, who had followed in their father's SEAL footsteps.

"I don't know, Vin," Maddey said as she pulled her long blonde curls into a ponytail. "I don't want to hurt you. I try *not* to get on my bestie's bad side." She hooked a thumb toward Rocky, standing off to the side and wrapped in her husband's arms.

"Oh, Tink." He waved off her concern. "I can take you with one arm tied behind my back." Not necessarily true, but he couldn't help tossing out the taunt. As expected, she narrowed her ice blue eyes at him and squared her shoulders, getting into a fighting stance.

"I hate that they told you about that nickname." She nodded at her oldest brother, Justin—former Navy SEAL and now SWAT officer—watching them from a corner.

"Love you too, sis," Justin called out, puckering his lips and making kissing noises at them. "Now come on…show this punk what I taught you last week."

Oh, shit.

"You mean how you taught me how to go all Black Widow on a person and do that fancy jump up and take down a person by wrapping my legs around their head?" There was an evil glint in her eyes as she twirled a curl around a finger, the picture of innocence.

"What? Are you training to be in the next Marvel film?" Vince smiled through the trickle of unease.

The Steele Maker had offered a women's self-defense class for a few years since learning about Jordan's psycho ex, but the McClain brothers took Maddey's training to a level far above that of mere mortals.

"Afraid, Vinny Boy?" Maddey sing-songed.

"Do your worst, Madz."

Not ten seconds later, she vaulted herself up his body, braced her hands on his shoulders and pushed herself up to wrap her legs around his head, using her body weight to take them both down to the padded floor.

Cheers rang out through the gym as their friends slow-clapped the spectacle.

"Holy shit, Madz. *You* are a certifiable badass," he said in awe.

She gave an overdramatic bow at her awesomeness.

"Okay." He clapped his hands in front of him. "Time to get serious. As kickass as your superhero-worthy moves are, I highly doubt you would *actually* use them if you were in trouble."

He went into instructor mode, switching up the way he approached or moved to attack, and each time she managed to escape. For a guy who'd made a name for himself winning fights by submission takedowns due to his wrestling background, it was mildly embarrassing how easily she slipped from his grasp. If it were *anyone* besides Maddey, he might start to question his skills, but she was a freak of nature thanks to her upbringing.

He locked his arms around her, keeping his grip firm as she struggled to find a way to break his hold.

Somewhere in the distance, he heard Becky's voice call out, "Wasn't that Holly from EP?" Everything inside him snapped to attention at her name, his arms immediately dropped from around Maddey and his head whipping up to look toward the front of the gym.

Quick like The Flash, he caught her just as she crossed the threshold onto the sidewalk outside.

"Holly," he called out, reaching out to cup a hand around her elbow.

Her body jerked as if shocked by an electrical current, and she yanked her arm from his grasp as she rounded on him.

"Shit, Hol. Did I hurt you?" He knew he didn't, but he needed to calm the raw panic swirling in her eyes.

"No." Her voice was small when she answered. "I'm fine." The hell she was. Gone was the sassy woman who blatantly told him he wasn't her type. He didn't like it.

Not. One. Bit.

Slowly—so slow he was the human equivalent of a slow motion video—he stretched a hand toward her, giving her plenty of time to move and avoid his touch if she needed to. She stood statue-still, only her eyes shifting to follow the path of his arm.

His hand snaked beneath her curtain of purple-tipped hair, cradling the back of her head while he took a few steps to close the distance between them instead of tugging her against him.

Her head tilted back to maintain eye contact. He spotted a streak of green frosting on her temple, his jaw starting to unclench at the first sign of something that was so *her* amongst the angst of whatever had just transpired.

The silence stretched between them as they stared at each other unblinking.

"Cupcake."

The nickname managed to get the barest hint of a smile, some of the color returning to her face.

"Want to tell me what had you so spooked?"

"Nothing. I'm fine."

There was that word again—fine. He'd grown up with a sister, her best friend that was *practically* a sister, and a female cousin. He knew when a woman said she was fine, she was anything but.

"Doubtful." Now wasn't the time to push the issue. "Come back inside." He nodded toward the gym behind him. "It's too cold to be out here without a coat."

It took everything inside him not to use his hold on her to get her to move, but he didn't want to do anything that could trigger her into running away again. It was seven heart-pounding seconds before she took her first step. He moved to the side, holding the door wide for her to enter.

Every eye was on them when they stepped inside the gym. Literally every single one. It was the last thing he wanted at the moment.

Cautiously, he draped an arm around her shoulders. "Guys," he called, "this is Holly. She's the baker at EP."

"Oh my god," his sister cried out. "Your food is *amazeballs*. Like, I could marry you for your blueberry crumbles. You're okay with polygamy, right, babe?" She turned to her husband.

To Gage's credit, he ignored her ridiculousness, only smiling adoringly down at her. "Whatever you want, Blue."

Man, the guy was whipped. If he was married to *anyone* other than his sister, Vince might have given him shit for it—who was he kidding, of course he gave him shit, big heaping doses of it—but he respected the guy for worshiping the ground Rocky walked on. He couldn't have asked for a better match for his sister or to be his brother-in-law.

"A baker, huh?" Gemma pushed through the crowd, her narrowed eyes cluing him to potential trouble. "So you *have* been cheating on your diet."

"No. I swear," he said vehemently. The folding of his cousin's arms told him she didn't believe him. "Really, Gem. I haven't had one thing that wasn't expressly directed by you. Not with you here whipping me into shape."

"You keep sneaking off to EP and it'll turn into a *literal* whip."

"Sorry, Gem. For as much as I love you, I think it's illegal for us to experiment with BDSM, seeing as we're related and all." His comment earned him a smack to the chest.

"*Ewww*. Don't be gross." There was no way to bite back the laugh at her disturbed expression.

"It's true." Holly came to his defense and he could have kissed her. He *wanted* to. He'd thought of little else all day. "The only time he left with food was when he came in for blueberry crumbles for who I would assume was you"—she pointed toward Rocky—"since you're the one sporting a baby bump."

"That was two days ago," Rocky stated.

"And you've been spotted leaving EP three days in a row," Becky added helpfully, holding up three fingers for emphasis. "Why else would you be going there if not to sneak in treats?"

"I bet I know why," Deck said.

"Don't be a dick, Deck," Maddey scolded.

"What?" He shrugged innocently. "It obviously worked if she's coming here to see him."

"Actually." Holly's voice brought the chatter to a halt. "I was supposed to be meeting Becky and Gemma here." She looked to where the two girls stood at the reception desk, eyebrow raised in question. Both girls nodded in confirmation.

"You were?" Vince looked down as he asked.

"Yeah."

Talk about a blow to a guy's ego. Here he thought she *was* there to see him. The memory of their scale-busting kiss was fresh on his lips. He'd hoped it was so overwhelming she finally sought him out for a change, when in reality he had nothing to do with her visit.

"I didn't realize you knew my cousin."

Her eyes lifted to meet his again. "I don't."

Now he was really confused. "Then why would you come here looking for her if you don't know her?"

"Not that it's any of *your* business…" Ahh, there was his sassy girl. "I'm supposed to be meeting them to see if we get along enough to want to live together."

"Yay." Becky clapped her hands together excitedly. "We've had a free room since that one"—she thrust an arm in Rocky's direction—"abandoned us for Octoman."

"Can you *blame* me?" Rocky retorted. "Look at him." She slid a hand up Gage's arm, squeezing his bicep in a way that probably wasn't suitable in a room with her brother, father and uncle nearby.

"*Again* with the Octoman?" Gage complained. "It makes me feel like a character in a comic book."

"Not that this isn't fascinating and all." Papa Steele commanded the attention of the room. "You're all done for the day. Get out of here. Vin." Vince turned to his dad. "You're running home today too."

Fucking cardio day.

He gave his dad an exuberant salute.

"I guess it's a good thing you are here," Holly said low enough for only him to hear. His spirits lifted at her words. "I need to talk to you." And down they crashed. Nothing good *ever* came from those particular words.

"What's up, Cupcake?" He angled his body so they were cocooned in their own private bubble.

"I can't go out with you tomorrow." His disappointment was acute.

"You have to work late?"

"No." She shook her head, the purple tips of her hair brushing against her cheeks. "I'm just not in a place where I should be going on dates right now."

The caveman inside him wanted to push the issue, the driving need to *claim* her as his own blinding in its intensity. He mentally beat that side of him back with a four-punch jab-cross-hook-uppercut combo. He could bide his time.

Because there was one thing he knew that she didn't.

They were about to become neighbors.

Chapter Eleven

Vince stripped out of the sweat-wicking Under Armor shirt while he rode the elevator up to the twelfth floor. When the doors opened with a *ding*, he wasn't surprised to see both the door to his place and the apartment where Gemma and Becky—as well as Holly soon —lived across the hall propped open so everyone could come and go as they pleased.

AC/DC was still singing in his earbuds about how they were dynamite and were going to win the fight when he stepped into his apartment to find not only those who lived in their building but all the other fighters from the gym and the remaining members of The Coven. He pulled the buds from his ears as every person in the room turned to watch him.

Seemed his friends weren't wasting any time in their interrogation. All he wanted was a hot shower to ease his sore muscles and maybe a chance to relieve some of the pressure brewing below his belt since almost taking Holly in the kitchen, followed by enjoying the extra serving of carbs cardio day afforded him. *So much for that plan.*

Ignoring the knowing looks tossed his way, he headed for the shower in his private bath.

Ten minutes later, he was showered and dressed for battle in another pair of joggers and a Blizzards t-shirt. He made his way down the hall and steeled himself for what he was about to face.

Jordan's eighteen-month-old twins spotted him first and wobbled down the hall for him, letting out a chorus of "Bin, Bin, Bin," still struggling to pronounce the V in his name properly.

Dropping to one knee, he scooped a girl in each arm and covered them both in kisses as they did the same to him.

"How are my two favorite ladies doing?" he asked as he rose.

"Nana?" Lacey or Lucy, he couldn't be sure which, held a partially crushed banana out to him. He took a tiny bite, earning him a beaming smile, and strode the rest of the way into the room.

"So?" Beth, Gage's cousin-in-law and the most recent Covenette, asked as he joined her where she sat on the floor with her own almost one-year-old.

"So," he said back, playing dumb.

"Don't even try it." She waggled a finger at him. "Dumbass is Gage's name, not yours. Spill the deets."

He looked up. *Everyone* was waiting for his explanation. Shit. Looked like there was no getting out of it. He was going to catch so much shit for this. He wasn't necessarily a playboy but he had never shown serious interest in a woman before. Lord knew his mother couldn't wait for him to settle down and start popping out some grandbabies like his sister.

"Okay, fine." He huffed out a breath. "I have a thing for Holly."

Skye let out a snort. "You have *more* than a thing from what we've heard."

"Yeah, practically having sex at EP is *definitely* more," Jordan added.

He was quick to put his hands over the ears of the twin on

his right knee. "Lay, Lu, whichever you are, don't listen to your mama."

"That would be Lucy. And please." She waved off his concern. "They're a year and a half, they don't know what sex means. And you should hear some of the stuff their father says to me. If they aren't repeating any of *that*, I think we're safe."

She had a point. Jordan and Jake were total hornballs and got it on more than most people probably expected a married couple would—especially a couple with two small children.

"How do you tell them apart?"

Lacey and Lucy were as identical as twins could get. They inherited their straight blonde hair from their mom and the bright emerald green eyes and dimples from their father. He could already feel his hair turning gray from what the future would bring.

"I'm their mom." Jordan shrugged, fingering a piece of Lacey's hair. "When you push a person out of your vagina, you kinda know these things."

He shuddered. "*So* not the visual I needed, JD."

She gave him a wink.

"Plus." She reached out to touch Lacey's yellow flower earring. "Lay's earrings are yellow and Lu's are blue." She leaned back and fixed him with a hard stare, proving yet again why she was the distinguished leader of The Coven. Girl had bigger balls than the athletes she managed public relations for. "Now stop trying to distract us. Tell us about the kitchen sex that went down this morning."

"We. Didn't. Have. Sex." He spoke each word slowly, hoping it would be enough to sink in.

"Yeah, but you *were* missing a few articles of clothing," Skye pointed out. He shouldn't be surprised they were caught up on all the details. Lyle *lived* for gossip.

"It was just a shirt. It was full of sweat from my run to the gym."

"Oh, and how chivalrous of you to shed it before you crammed your tongue down the girl's throat," Beth said.

"Did it ever occur to you to ask the girl on a date before playing tonsil hockey with her?" Rocky asked.

"I did ask her out. For tomorrow night," he said the first part with pride before his shoulders slumped.

"And where are you gonna take her?" Becky asked.

"It doesn't matter anymore. When she was at The Steele Maker earlier, she told me she couldn't date me right now."

"And that's it?" Gemma asked. "You're just going to give up?"

"Have all the romance books I've made you read through the years gone to waste?" Maddey threw her hands up in frustration. Since she became an indie romance author, their whole group had started a book club as a show of support. Now, years later, she had turned each and every member of their squad into complete romance junkies.

"Hell no, I'm not giving up." Holly was *his*. Now he just had to make her see it. "Besides…I'm about to be guaranteed to see her every day. I'll get my date."

Then he would get the girl.

Chapter Twelve

Holly was baffled by how quickly things happened after she met—and loved—her new roommates. Kyle and Lyle were waiting for her when she got back to Espresso Patronum, knowing smiles on their handsome faces. They then proceeded to tell her they already rearranged the schedule for the next day so she would be off and able to move in to her new place. She teased them about being eager to get her out of their hair, but in her heart knew it was their way of supporting her in her quest for independence.

Lyle and Kyle Samson were angels on Earth.

She used part of the morning to pack for the move, stacking the handful of bags she had by the front door, ready to go when the guys got home and could drive her over. Times like this were when she missed her car. The luxury coupe was a dream to drive, but it was the freedom having her own vehicle afforded her that she missed most.

Since the Mercedes wasn't in her name, she didn't want to risk having the cops called on her for grand theft auto, so she'd arranged for a tow truck to deliver it back to its legal owner.

She also didn't want to chance the Vehicle Finder app being used to track her whereabouts. Instead of driving directly to Kyle and Lyle's, she'd met them in Philadelphia, where she'd called for the tow truck and ditched her old phone, before riding to New Jersey with them to start her new life.

That was three weeks ago.

Now here she was, on the cusp of taking yet another step on the road to version Holly 2.0, where she called the shots and *no one* else.

The sound of the doorbell startled her, terror flooding her system. *They found me.* The thought played on repeat as she tiptoed to the window to the right of the door. Inching up slowly, she peered out one of the decorative panes to see who was at the door.

She blinked, then blinked again. No way. The sight before her did not compute. Because if she *wasn't* hallucinating, then that meant Jake Donovan and Ryan Donnelly were standing on her best friend's front porch.

She may have grown up in the upper-crust of Connecticut, and hockey may not have been the "approved" sport to watch, but she would have had to be living under a rock not to recognize the two athletes.

The two had already made a name for themselves as top players in the National Hockey League, both playing on the gold medal-winning Olympic team a few years back. They also graced more billboards and commercials than most other professional athletes. And they were both dead-ass sexy.

It made absolutely no sense for them to be here, but it was a better scenario than she'd envisioned, so she opened the door. Both hockey hunks smiled down at her from their nearly-a-foot-taller heights. The size difference caused Vince to jump to the forefront of her mind for what felt like the millionth time that morning.

She'd stood her ground and told him she wouldn't be

going out with him that evening but as much as she tried, she hadn't been able to banish him from her thoughts. That was information only she and her vibrator were privy to though. Because *hot damn,* the boy was spank bank material perfection.

"Umm...I don't remember entering any contest," she said to the NHL superstars.

"That's a bit random, but oh-kay." Ryan Donnelly sounded as confused as she felt.

Jake Donovan flashed her a smile that included the most perfect set of dimples she had ever seen. Vince's single dimple came to mind. That was Vince thought one million and one.

"We're here to help you move," Jake said.

"Not to sound rude or anything, but why in the world would you two"—she pointed at each of them—"be helping *me* move?"

"The Coven asked us to. And we've found life is much easier when we don't question them," Ryan said.

"Seriously...I need to meet this mystical Coven. I've heard them mentioned like a hundred times." It was an exaggeration but still.

Jake's brows furrowed. "What do you mean? Aren't we helping you move in to Beck and Gem's place?"

"Yes?" What did that have to do with the Coven?

"They're two of the founding members," Ryan said as he bent to lift her two large suitcases.

"And...they are your friends?"

"Yup," Jake said, draping the straps of the remaining duffles over his shoulders before walking to a black Escalade parked on the street.

Not one to look a gift horse in the mouth, she gathered up the last of her bags, grabbed her purse, and followed the hockey boys.

Vince took two steps back from the force of Griff's latest hit to his side. Sparring with the World Boxing Council's current heavyweight champ did wonders for his own boxing skills, but it was hell on the body. His bear-sized friend knocked him around like one of those weighted clown punching bags, pushing him back only to have him return for more.

"Vin, you're dropping your left shoulder, leaving yourself open for Griff's hit." His uncle Mick—the gym's boxing coach and a WBC champ back in his day—instructed from outside the boxing ring.

"Come on, Superman, you can do better than that," Griff taunted, knocking his red boxing gloves together.

Shaking off the most recent hit, he squared his shoulders, resuming his fighting stance and watching the position of his shoulder.

Growing up the nephew of a famed boxer, he was usually one of the MMA guys who could hold his own inside the ring, but his concentration was shot. The gray matter between his ears was consumed by the knowledge that Holly should be moving into the apartment across the hall from his. Becky had already left to be there for her arrival, and Gemma was working out of the apartment, meal prepping for him and whichever clients were on her list for the day.

Loving what he did for a living, the six hours he spent training five days a week usually flew by. Now, not so much. Holly may have turned down his date, but they would be spending the evening together, she just didn't know it yet.

"Watch the elbows, Vin," his uncle called out as he bobbed out of the way of Griff's latest jab.

He shuffled his feet, he and Griff dancing around the ring, toying with each other as they traded blows. Griff wasn't pulling his punches, making Vince especially grateful for the protective headgear. His family might be obsessed with the

Rocky franchise, but he didn't need to look like Balboa after fighting Apollo Creed. He wanted to look his best for Holly later, and a swollen eye just didn't scream pretty.

"Vin!" Mick yelled, exasperated. "Get your head out of your ass and stop leaving yourself open to a kidney shot." His hands slapped against the matted floor of the ring. "That's it...I can't take anymore. Go work with the speed bag."

Well, shit. Now he felt like a kid being sent to the principal's office.

Grabbing the towel hanging over the black ropes of the ring, he ran it vigorously over his head, then wiped the sweat from his bare chest and arms. He held the Velcro of his right glove in his teeth to unwind it before removing his left glove. Then he pulled off the bottom layer of cotton wraps and added them to the basket to be washed at the end of the day.

Rocky made her way over as he pulled out the gray Mexican-style hand wraps he preferred for speed bag work. She'd wrapped his hands long before becoming the gym's official physical therapist.

No words were needed as she slipped his thumb through its loop and set to work winding around his wrist, up his hand and through his fingers.

After both hands were wrapped, he flexed and stretched his fingers, clenching his fists, alternating knocking each against an open palm.

"Good?" she asked.

He nodded. "As always."

She gave him a smile, her matching gray eyes sparkling back at him as she unconsciously rubbed a hand over the small bump of her belly. She had a shirt with a cartoon baby wearing boxing gloves and a speech bubble above it saying, 'Who called my mommy fat?'

"You know," she said as she walked with him to the row of speed bags alongside the windows. "If you want me to keep being able to wrap your hands, you'll have to take a small hiatus after you bring home the belt to ring in the New Year."

He loved how confident she was in his abilities. Growing up, they had always been each other's greatest champions, her supporting his fighting career and him supporting her freaky smartness and her ridiculous number of certifications.

"I don't think that will be a problem. If I win this thing, I'll finally be able to sponsor that women's shelter. I'm sure that will keep me busy."

"When, Vin." She stopped him with a gentle hand on his arm. "*When* you win this thing." She stared him down until he agreed.

"Good. Now stop thinking about a certain pretty baker and get to work."

"I wasn't thi—"

She cut him off a with a look.

Damn.

She could read him like one of Maddey's books.

Chapter Thirteen

H olly couldn't believe the size of her new apartment. When Jake first pulled into the under-ground parking garage for the newer high-rise building, she thought there was no way they were in the right place.

Then she stepped through the doors to 12A and knew this couldn't be her new home. The apartment was huge—even split three ways, she didn't understand how it could be so affordable.

Both of her new roommates were in the kitchen when Jake walked in without knocking. Gemma was cooking something that smelled like heaven, and Becky hung out on one of the barstools. After a quick detour to give kisses hello, both guys disappeared down the hallway to the right with her stuff, clearly knowing which room was hers.

The main living space was made up of a huge open kitchen, dining room, and living room with hallways branching off on either side.

The hardwood floor shined, the kitchen was all granite countertops and stainless steel. She noted there were two refrigerators and remembered Gemma saying she was a personal chef and did meal preps for the fighters from the gym as well as a list of other clients.

Kyle and Lyle's place was decorated with an eclectic, modern feel, unsurprising considering how colorful Espresso Patronum was. This place was obviously a female domain, with the chrome and hot pink acrylic bar stools and pink and animal print throw pillows on the dove gray, tufted, microfiber sectional. The shaggy area rug, a few shades lighter than the couch, looked comfortable enough to stretch out on. And the white wood furniture and twinkle light accent wall lent to the feminine feel.

The best thing about the apartment, though, was that no matter how nicely it was decorated, it felt homey and like people *lived* in it. It was pretty much the exact opposite of her old life.

She loved it.

"Hey, girl," Becky greeted with a smile.

"Hey." She gave a small wave, then cursed herself for being awkward.

"Hungry? I have extra." Gemma held up a bowl.

These two women had been nothing but nice since they met, yet Holly couldn't help but feel intimated by them. Having grown up in a world where image was everything, being faced with these two effortless beauties made her feel like she didn't belong.

Gemma was mean-girl-from-a-teen-drama pretty, her messy bun stylish even leaning slightly to the left but it was most likely due to her tossing it up without a care, if the leggings and loose cotton tunic with the picture of a pizza cutter and the words 'This is how I cut carbs,' she wore were any indication. At least it seemed like she might be her funny t-shirt spirit sister.

Then there was Becky, with her fire engine red bob, green eyes that missed nothing, and the overall take charge person-ality you couldn't miss.

These girls knew their place in life, and it made her the tiniest bit—okay, North Pole sized—jealous. She wanted to be like them when she grew up. Maybe living with them would cause some of their awesomeness to rub off.

A girl could dream, right?

"Okay, you're all set, Hol," Ryan said as he and Jake reentered the kitchen, the casual nickname only Kyle and Lyle used catching her off guard. She had grown accustomed to the formality of her old life. "Oh, whatcha makin', Gem?" He reached out as if he was going to take some of the food she was preparing.

"Not for you." Gemma smacked his hand out of the way. "I'm prepping meals for your brother so Nick and Damon can drop it off for me when they go to the game later."

"This is Jase's?" Jake asked.

"Yup. So keep your grabby hands to yourself." Gemma leveled them both with a narrowed-eyed stare, pointing at them with her wooden spoon.

Unperturbed, Ryan wrapped a hand around the spoon, bringing it to his mouth while he took a selfie, Jake jumping into the background of the photo and miming maniacal laughter.

"You know Rock is going to be pissed you're messing with her bestie," Becky said dryly as they watched Ryan post the picture to Instagram.

@CaptainRyanDonnelly9:

Hey @EnforcedByJaseDonnelly13 me and @BrickWall-Donovan30 call dibs on this food @GemCooksForYou made. #SorryNotSorry #Nomnomnomnom #GetInMyBelly #Joey-Doesn'tShareFood

"Nah. Rock loves messing with him as much as I do," Ryan replied.

"I swear, there are times I think Sean is more mature than the lot of you." Gemma shook her head in disgust. "And he's *nine.*"

"Oh, and Jake," Becky called out before wrapping an arm around Holly's shoulders. "Your wife told us to tell you to drop the dogs off at your parents' because you guys are watching the game here tonight. Holly here needs a proper welcome party."

Holly was happy enough to have a new place to live, but now these people she barely knew wanted to celebrate her moving in, for no other reason than to make her feel welcomed. It was such a contrast to her old life.

"You don't have to do that. I'm probably going to spend most of the day unpacking and everything," she tried to beg off.

"Of course we do." Becky shot her an incredulous look. "Do you have any idea how long we looked for someone to fill Rocky's room after she ditched us for Gage?"

"True story," Gemma added.

"You're the first person we clicked with."

"You better hope your crazy doesn't scare her off." Ryan chortled.

"Don't start, Captain America." Becky gave him epic side-eye.

Holly snorted at the nickname, trying to cover it with a laugh. He did look a lot like the Marvel hero.

"Nah, man. She's gonna fit right in," Jake said, clapping him on the back.

After the guys were gone, Becky and Gemma gave her a tour of the apartment. Both of their rooms were down the left hallway while hers was to the right. Each room boasted its own attached bathroom with an additional powder room across the hall from her room.

Her bedroom was already furnished with a dresser, king-sized bed and matching end tables. How was rent so cheap? Yes, living here would get her out of her friends' guest room, but she didn't want a handout.

Both girls waved off her concern, saying that they actually

owned the apartment and when everything was split three ways, it really was that affordable.

Instead of getting hung up on the money, she decided to embrace her good fortune and got to work on settling into her new life. A life she controlled.

FOURTEEN

Coven Conversations

From the Group Message Thread of The Coven

PROTEIN PRINCESS: Is it wrong to have a crush on our new roommate?

PROTEIN PRINCESS: Asking for a friend.

YOU KNOW YOU WANNA: Fuck that. I have a HUGE lady boner for this chick. She rocks.

MOTHER OF DRAGONS: The boys got her all moved in?

YOU KNOW YOU WANNA: Oh yes. Your fine AF husband and brother were so efficient they only needed one trip to get all her stuff here.

. . .

MAKES BOYS CRY: I hope you put them to work while they were there.

PROTEIN PRINCESS: I fed them.

THE OG PITA: Gem you're such a softie.

QUEEN OF SMUT: Question?

QUEEN OF SMUT: Also asking for a friend…

QUEEN OF SMUT: Does she know Vince lives across the hall??

MOTHER OF DRAGONS: Book research?

QUEEN OF SMUT: Always. Neighbors/Roommates is one of my favorite tropes.

YOU KNOW YOU WANNA: No, she doesn't know.

PROTEIN PRINCESS: Should we tell her?

ALPHABET SOUP: NO

. . .

ALPHABET SOUP: WAY

ALPHABET SOUP: I NEED to be there for when this goes down.

QUEEN OF SMUT: OMG me too. I'll bring my laptop and take notes.

QUEEN OF SMUT: *GIF of Elle Woods taking notes in class*

THE OG PITA: *GIF of girl spitting water laughing*

THE OG PITA: ^^what you just made me do, Madz.

ALPHABET SOUP: Vin has been a MESS all day. Griff knocked him around the ring like Griff was Clubber Lang and Vin was Rocky in *Rocky III.*

YOU KNOW YOU WANNA: *facepalm emoji*

MAKES BOYS CRY: I smell a Coven meeting, as the boys would say.

MAKES BOYS CRY: *GIF of a girl rubbing her hands together*

. . .

MOTHER OF DRAGONS: This isn't *Gilmore Girls*. You can't smell a Coven meeting like Loralie smells snow.

MOTHER OF DRAGONS: *GIF of Loralie Gilmore saying "I smell snow"*

MAKES BOYS CRY: Shut up. You know what I mean.

THE OG PITA: Hell yeah we do. Guess we know where we're watching the Storm game tonight.

QUEEN OF SMUT: Fuck that. Who needs hockey when we have REAL LIFE drama to watch.

QUEEN OF SMUT: *GIF of a guy pulling a tub of popcorn off the floor and settling back onto a couch to watch*

Chapter Fifteen

Holly spent the rest of the afternoon unpacking and putting away her belongings. It was nice to feel completely settled in place for the first time since she made her escape. Even while staying with Kyle and Lyle, there had been a sense of limbo keeping her from truly unpacking—this was home.

She mentally added another checkmark to her list.

Escape the clutches of her family. Check.

Get a job. Check.

Find a place to live. Check.

Figure out a plan for the future. Yeah, that was the one she was still working on.

She got along with her new roommates like she'd known them forever. Gemma cranked up Bruno Mars to ear-splitting volume, all of them bobbing around as they lent a hand either with Gem's meal prepping or her own unpacking. When she questioned if they were worried about the neighbors complaining they told her it wasn't an issue—they knew everyone on the floor, and the people who lived above them were at work.

She'd never really had close girlfriends before. Hell, who

was she kidding? Aside from Kyle, she didn't have any *real* friends, regardless of their sex. The people from her old life would stab you in the back faster than you could blink if it meant elevating their social status.

Just the memory of how Gemma and Becky looked at her when she asked what she should wear for the party had her smiling.

"Why would you need to change?" Becky asked.

"You said it was a party. Shouldn't I be dressed for the occasion?"

"No way. Stay comfy. We're only going to be watching hockey. No need to be fancy," Gemma agreed.

True to their word, neither one changed.

The door to the apartment opened and she recognized the gorgeous, raven-haired woman who entered as Vince's sister, Rocky. A part of her perked up at seeing yet another person connected to Stud Muffin—the dumb part that was all for ignoring the smart thing to do in favor of getting naked with him.

"I don't know if I'm going to survive this pregnancy working in the gym," Rocky said, plopping down in one of the armchairs in the living room.

"Well, seeing as you still have to bake that baby for another six months or so, I would say that is something you need to figure out, Rock." Becky laughed as she entered the living room with glasses of wine for her and Holly.

"Do you have *any* idea how much my sense of smell is heightened right now?" Rocky scrunched her nose as if sniffing something pungent.

"I thought you said you liked the way Gage smells after a workout?" Gemma asked, carrying in trays of food to put on the coffee table.

"I do." Rocky's tone turned dreamy as she stared into space for a minute. "But having to be around the six of them as they train, not to mention anyone else in the gym, might just kill me."

"Could be worse. Jordan has to go into locker rooms," Becky reminded her.

"True." Rocky spotted Holly on the couch for the first time, her gray eyes widening when she did. "Oh my god. I forgot you were moving in today. Pregnancy brain is no joke. I'm Rocky—nice to officially meet you."

She shook her outstretched hand, returning the greeting and smiling at the way Rocky's words seemed to tumble out on top of each other.

"I guess I should thank you for moving out so I could have a place to live."

"Please, girl." Rocky pulled her feet underneath her, rubbing circles on the slight swell of her belly. "I pretty much moved down the hall a year ago. I was out *long* before I made it official."

Before she could learn more of that story, people started to trickle into the apartment. Leading the pack was a tall, pretty strawberry blonde in the middle of a conversation with another good-looking girl with light brown hair that faded into a rose gold ombre—*were all their friends attractive?*—carrying a baby who looked about a year old.

Behind them were Gage and someone he had to be related to based on the matching dark brown hair and bright blue eyes.

"Seriously, man. It's all your fault for bringing The Coven into my life," the shorter guy said to Gage. "You move out here, marry a girl, and now *I'm* the one who has to pose half naked for a charity calendar."

"Oh, puh-lease, Wyatt," the strawberry blonde said as she poured herself a glass of wine. "You and all the other guys at the firehouse were *vying* for one of the twelve spots we have open for the Men in Uniform charity calendar. *You* are lucky we picked you to represent the firefighter in it."

"Oh my god, is Wyatt *still* bitching about being objectified?" said a short blonde who walked in with Jake Donovan, two mini versions of her toddling ahead of them.

"Hi, I'm Skye," the strawberry blonde said with a wave toward Holly before turning back to the woman with Jake. "One hundred percent. Makes me rather work with Tucker's diva ass than have to listen to him complain."

"Oooh, no good, bro. Those are like fighting words coming from Skye." Jake laughed and dropped to the floor, dumping a box of blocks from one of the shelves onto the rug for the twins.

"I didn't miss it, did I?" A girl with a riot of blonde curls who was a regular at the coffee house asked breathlessly as she rushed inside.

"No, Madz, you're good," Becky answered as the blonde fell into a free corner of the sectional.

"If you guys aren't careful you're going to scare off Gem and Beck's new roommate," Ryan Donnelly chided, joining Jake on the floor.

Formal introductions were made, and Holly finally learned what, and who, The Coven was. Someone turned the television on, flipping through the channels until they found the channel for the NY Storm pregame show.

It amazed her how they all treated each other like family and how much they genuinely seemed to like each other. They made her feel like she'd always been part of their group so seamlessly she nearly started to believe it.

She learned that Jordan and Skye ran a public relations firm that specialized in athletes and they represented the hockey players there as well as the fighters from The Steele Maker. They congratulated Jake and Ryan on having their Instagram post from earlier trending.

For the first time in what felt like forever, Holly started to relax.

Then she heard *his* deep voice.

.   .   .

VINCE ASSUMED EVERYONE was already at the girls'
apartment by the time he finished his shower since both Ray
and Deck's doors were closed as he made his way to the
kitchen for one of Gem's protein shakes then searched the
freezer for an ice pack. He wasn't surprised they went across
the hall before him since he had to spend a few extra minutes
under the hot spray rubbing one out to ease the perpetual
state of blue balls he'd been in since Holly crashed into his life
earlier in the week.

Fuck.

The swiftness with which he got himself off to thoughts of
her was embarrassing. He needed a plan for when they
finally got naked together because he was more likely to
become Santa Claus à la Tim Allen style than last more than a
minute or two with her at this rate.

No ice packs in the utility closet either, and the cornucopia
of bruises Griff's beating inflicted were aching. He'd have to
get one from Rock.

But first…time to see Holly.

Not bothering with shoes, he strode across the hall
into 12A.

His gaze instantly locked on Holly sitting on the couch
when he entered the room. She looked so goddamn breath-
taking with her cognac and purple hair tied into a stubby
ponytail, leggings, fuzzy socks, and a loose cotton shirt,
sleeves pushed up around her elbows.

It wasn't her looks that got him though—hell, he was
surrounded by beautiful women every day between The
Coven and fighter groupies. No, it was the funny little flip his
heart did when he caught sight of her that told him *this one is
special.*

"Hey, Rock. Do you have any ice packs back at your
place?" He kept his eyes trained on Holly as spoke. The way

her eyes widened and the tempting O her berry mouth formed confirmed she wasn't expecting him.

Holly wasn't the only one to jerk to attention at the sound of his voice. Like always, the Donovan twins abandoned their blocks to run to him, squealing, "Bin, Bin, Bin," as they did.

He bent to scoop the girls up, breathing in the bubble gum scent of their shampoo. He could see why people chose to procreate. He was only a pseudo-uncle and they greeted him like a conquering hero every time they saw him. It made him feel like he could slay dragons.

He winced as Lacey's tiny fist—the earring trick was genius—connected with his bruised side. He walked them over to their dad and uncle, setting them down to resume building their epic tower of blocks.

"You sure you want to stop after this little guy?" he asked Jordan, placing a hand to her baby bump while dropping a kiss hello on her cheek. "I mean, I'd make an awesome godfather."

"No way. Jake is getting snipped after I pop this little guy out. No more pulling the goalie for him." She sent a wink to her husband. To Jake's credit, he didn't even wince at the mention of someone going near his balls with a scalpel, he only looked at his wife like she hung the moon.

"Besides," Skye cut in, "what makes you think you'd be fourth in line? I think Sammy would beat you out after Tucker for the title."

"That cuts deep, Skye." He mimed being stabbed in the heart.

She shrugged. "You could always try and knock Tucker from his post."

He sent Jordan a hopeful look, but she shook her head. "He's my BB3."

For as much as their friend was a playboy, prankster and a flirt, he had been a constant pillar of support for Jake and

Jordan. He'd declared himself her third big brother, or BB3, in college. *Can't compete with that.*

"Vin, chill. You know you're going to be godfather to this one. Stop being greedy." Rocky rolled her eyes at him, before narrowing them as if she had X-ray vision and could assess his injuries with a look. To be fair, she usually could. "What do you need ice for?"

He pulled his shirt over his head. It took everything in him not to smirk when he heard Holly hiss in a breath as his torso was bared. In his peripheral vision, he could see the way her eyes scanned him from head-to-toe. He looked good. He trained his ass off every day, earning each defined cut and ridge of muscle on his body. Now that he was cutting weight for a fight, those lines were only getting more pronounced.

It wasn't the lust in her eyes that stood out—he had seen that the other day before he kissed her—it was the way they softened in concern as she locked in on the giant bruise on his ribs.

"Damn, I got you *good*, pretty boy." Griff whistled in appreciation as he walked in from the hallway and took in his handy work.

"Yeah, well, I was a little distracted today." His eyes tracked back to Holly, as did every other set in the room.

Subtle, his friends were not.

"Whatever you say, Steele. You know I own your ass in the ring. Anyway"—Griff tossed his phone to him—"you left this back in the apartment. Jase has been blowing it up. Probably too late for him to see your response seeing as he's out on the ice. But at least this way he'll have them by the time the first intermission rolls around." He pointed to where the Storm/Bruisers game was about to start.

"Umm…" Holly's hesitant voice sounded, and he wasn't able to stop his smirk as he knew *exactly* what she was about to ask. "You live in this building too?"

"Sure do." His smile was full-on Big Bad Wolf. "Right

across the hall, in fact." He moved to her, bending to speak in her ear, inhaling the heady scent of sugar and vanilla on her skin. "You can run, Cupcake, but you can't hide."

She shuddered at his words. When he stood up, every one of his friends was staring.

Whatever.

He wanted Holly.

He would have her.

Case closed.

Holly had no idea how to start processing everything she had learned over the past week. There was meeting Vince, learning her friends were friends with professional athletes, finding a new place to live only to learn temptation incarnate lived across the hall, and her brain was flashing *not enough memory.*

She had made it through two periods of hockey so far, learning the basics of the game from this ragtag group of people that had already declared her a member of their squad.

Vince, however, had kept his distance after whispering his dark promise in her ear. And from his sinful lips it was definitely a promise, not a threat.

She made a valiant effort not to appear affected by his words, but by the dimple in his left cheek peeking out, she wasn't fooling him.

She wanted him—bad.

And the jerk knew it.

She was royally screwed.

In her attempt to ignore him and how goddamn sexy he was or how flipping adorable he was playing with the Donovan twins, she focused her attention on the third period of the game. It was a nail-biter, the two teams still scoreless.

There was a lot of colorful language each time Jase Donnelly went toe-to-toe with the Bruisers' enforcer, and he had spent his fair share of time in a timeout everyone called "the sin bin."

For as violent as the game had been, Jase looked no worse for wear as the camera panned over him bumping knuckles with two guys in Bruisers jerseys behind the glass.

"Sometimes you are just the best brother *ever* when you go all media darling on me," Jordan spoke to the TV like her twin could hear her.

"I resent that," Ryan said.

"Oh, shush."

"Umm…shouldn't he be doing that with Storm fans though?" Holly asked. She might be a hockey novice, but she knew the black and gold jerseys the fans wore were for the team from Boston and not the home team.

"Yeah. But those two guys are our friends. They played with us back at BTU," Jake explained.

"And those amazing boys managed to get a picture of the moment from someone sitting a few seats over from them. Let's get this bad boy trending," Skye said, tapping away on her phone. "I don't know, Cap, looks like you're falling down Jor's favorite brother scale."

"How quickly you forget my man and I were trending early today." Ryan clapped Jake on the shoulder.

"Uh-huh." Skye continued on her phone. "I wonder who will get more likes."

"Them be fighting words, Miss Masters," Ryan threatened.

"Whatever you say, Cap. Whatever you say."

"You know what? Fine." In a flash, Ryan was up from the floor and dropping down beside Maddey as she typed away on the MacBook Pro in her lap. "Say cheese, Madz." He held his phone out, the two of them mugging it up for the camera, posing like they were typing on the computer.

Phones around the room pinged with social media notifications after he posted the picture. Leaning to the left, Holly read the caption on Becky's screen.

@CaptainRyanDonnelly9: ***Broadening my horizons, jumping in as a co-author with @AuthorBelleWillis since she will no longer let me help her with the sexy times inspiration. #NewCareer #BestFriendsForever #TooMuchPower #Future-BestSeller #NotJustACoverModel***

She scanned the words once more, her gaze snapping to the pair as they registered. "*You're* Belle Willis?"

Lyle and Kyle were officially dead men. Not telling her one of her favorite authors was not only their friend but worked out of their coffee shop most days of the week…it was unforgivable.

"That would be me," Maddey answered.

"Those Samson men are dead," she deadpanned. "I *love* your books. Like *seriously* love them," she fangirled.

How did she not recognize Maddey sooner? She internet stalked the woman on all her social media accounts and was an active member in her reader group on Facebook. It must have been the name that prevented her from seeing something right in front of her face.

"Wait a second." She held up her hands in a T shape. "Are you writing one of your books *right* now?"

"Yup. I'm working on the tenth book in my hockey boys series."

"But you only just released book eight a week ago." She'd devoured it the day it hit her Kindle.

"I'm always a book or two ahead when I release. It helps keep the stress of deadlines to a minimum, but it doesn't always work out that way."

For the next twenty minutes, all thoughts of hockey games or too-sexy-for-their-own-good fighters were forgotten as she got to live every romance junkie's dream of getting a behind-the-scenes look at what was in the works for one of her favorite cast of characters.

It wasn't until she stepped out of her bedroom after making a pitstop to use the restroom that she was reminded of the allure of Vince Steele. There was no way to avoid it when she bounced off his hard-as-steel—yes, pun intended—chest, then backed inside her room.

He kicked the door shut with his heel.

Gulp.

Chapter Sixteen

Holly stared into eyes the color of rolling thunder clouds, lightning sparking as Vince ran his sizzling gaze over her face, locking onto her lips.

Holy talking snowman, Frosty. The guy had smoldering down to a T.

With only a look, he managed to make her feel kissed breathless. Lord help her when he finally put his lips on her again. The first two times he had, she barely managed to keep her clothes on, and she knew what they said about the third time.

"Howdy, neighbor." He was pure swagger, the left side of his mouth hitching up enough for his dimple to make an appearance. That little skin imperfection was dangerous. It was a good thing he didn't have a matching set like Jake because they would be straight-up lethal. Her panties wouldn't stand a chance.

"Ne-neighbor?" she stuttered out, unable to articulate anything else thanks to the lust coursing through her body.

His only response was to pull the other side of his mouth up into a predatory smile. That was exactly what she was —prey.

She was so damn screwed.

Potentially in the literal sense, if his expression was anything to go by.

Wordlessly, he bent toward her, his nose dragging along the bump of collarbone exposed by the loose collar of her shirt, skimming up the pounding pulse point of her throat, his tongue peeking out to lick the sensitive spot behind her ear before sucking her lobe into his hot mouth.

A startled gasp escaped her, and when he bit into the flesh, her knees buckled. Like, they literally gave way and her chest smashed against his as she collapsed in his hold. She didn't think that was actually a thing that happened to people outside of reading it in one of her books.

With a manly chuckle, he adjusted his hold around her body, moving them until he had her braced against her dresser.

"Fuck." His words vibrated through her as he spoke against her skin. "I'm addicted to your scent."

The feeling is mutual, buddy. She caught a hint of pine lingering from whatever soap he used.

"I'm going to need to check into rehab after I get a whiff between your legs."

"Oh, god." Her head tipped down, and she buried her face in the soft cotton of his shirt as her cheeks flamed from his dirty words.

He stepped farther into her personal space, her knees spreading to allow him to do so. He was so much larger than she was, but not once did he use his size to intimidate her. Instead it was like he made it his mission to show her how capable he was of keeping her safe.

If only he knew how much she needed that to be true.

"Feel what you do to me, Cupcake?" Thanks to her position on the edge of the dresser, their lower bodies were in perfect alignment for his erection to bump against her throbbing clit.

"Muf—" The words faded into a moan as the head of his cock dragged along where her clit was trying to come out to play, the thin layer of her leggings and his sweatpants barely forming a barrier between them.

"Don't go calling me, Muffin, Cupcake. Because right now, *all* I want to do is find out how *your* muffin tastes."

She wanted that too.

She couldn't.

She shouldn't.

But she did.

She really, really did.

"Yes."

HE WAS MOVING too fast.

He should woo her.

He should take her on a proper date first.

But whenever Vince got within five feet of Holly, there was a driving *need* to claim her. To show her how great they would be together.

With the softness of her breasts pillowed against his chest, the scent of baked goods invading his senses, her knees intermittently squeezing his sides, he was a *goner*.

He.

Needed.

Her.

He wrapped his hands around the back of her neck, his thumbs dragging along her jaw line, over her plump bottom lip then pulling it down.

She sighed, and he was done.

He crashed his mouth to hers, swallowing down her squeak of surprise. The sweetness of the wine she'd drunk lingered on her tongue.

He slid one hand down the line of her spine to her ass,

giving it a squeeze before continuing to her thighs, digging his fingers into the muscled flesh.

She hummed in the back of her throat when his thumbs stroked the juncture where her thighs and hips met.

As much as he wanted to, he couldn't fuck her now. But he needed a taste. An appetizer to tide him over until they could get to the main course.

He abandoned her mouth, trailing biting kisses down the column of her pale throat, across her shoulder, skirting the line of pressure of leaving a mark, only to back off on the suction before he left any evidence.

He could have her leggings stripped away before he could blink, but if he did that, he wouldn't stop until he was buried balls deep inside her. They needed to stay on.

However, that didn't mean he couldn't get her off.

He curled an arm around her hip, palming her ass to anchor her to him. With his free hand, he cupped her pussy, the heat of her center radiating through her leggings. He found the line of her slit through the cotton, pushing his finger until he felt her lips part beneath it.

"Oh, god." She clutched his shirt in her hands, her nails digging into his flesh.

Somewhere in the back of his mind, it registered that there was a room full of his friends and family who would notice their absence if he took too long. Quick and dirty it would have to be.

He found the hard pearl of her clit, setting a punishing pace while she writhed against him.

"*Vince.*"

Nothing had ever sounded as good as his name falling from her lips in a broken plea.

Her hips rocked on the edge of the dresser.

Sealing his mouth over hers, he swallowed her moans as she exploded from his touch. Gradually he slowed the pace of his finger until she came down from her high.

Unable to resist sampling what was sure to be the sweetest dessert, he snaked his hand beneath the elastic band of her leggings, dragging a finger through the wetness between her legs, before bringing it to his mouth to suck clean.

She tasted like pure honey.

There was the barest hint of whiskey visible in her eyes as she tracked the path of his hand. Her breath hitched again at his *mmm* of approval while he savored the taste of her on his tongue.

He placed a gentle kiss on her forehead. "Tomorrow, Cupcake." Another kiss, and he pulled back. "You let me take you out."

Then he turned on his heel and left the room.

Chapter Seventeen

The next morning Holly slept in, needing the extra hours to help sleep off the orgasm hangover. Every time she said she would keep her distance from Vince, he managed to find a way to sneak past her defenses like smoke.

She had a hard enough time avoiding him while working across the street from him, now that they were neighbors she was screwed, and not in the way she almost was against her dresser.

God, all he did was touch her over her clothes and she came harder than she ever had. Angels sang and sugar plums danced as she exploded beneath his skilled fingers.

And now he thought they would be going on a date.

Again.

Time to hide out at Espresso Patronum while coming up with a game plan to get out of it. Vincent Steele was not a complication she expected or needed in her life at the moment. What she needed was to shut it down—now.

Good thing she had a few hundred cookies to bake and decorate. That was one way to keep her mind occupied for most of the day.

As promised, a set of car keys waited for her on the kitchen island. Already her new roommates were proving to be better friends than the majority of people she grew up with. Lyle had mentioned that she didn't have a car, so Becky told her to feel free to use hers since she carpooled with any number of their friends who lived in the building.

After seeing them in action, she immediately understood The Coven reference and had to agree, they were some of the coolest chicks she had ever met. There was absolutely no pretense, and they loved fiercely and unconditionally. She had learned more about them in one evening together than she had most of the people she'd spent thirteen years in school with.

Stepping inside EP, she spotted Maddey in her usual corner, typing away on her laptop, Mickey Mouse Beats headphones holding back her blonde curls. As if knowing she was thinking of her, her favorite author lifted her head and waved.

Lyle wouldn't meet her eyes as she made her way around the counter toward the kitchen. She would deal with him and his scheming husband later—right now, she had cookies to bake.

Shedding her coat and tying her bandana around her head, she pulled up Christina Aguilera's "Merry Christmas, Baby," on her playlist and set to work gathering the ingredients she needed for her cookies.

She set out the different KitchenAid mixers: one for dry ingredients, one for wet, and one to use for once everything was combined.

Cups of flour.

Vince backing her against the dresser.

Baking powder.

The way he growled her name before biting down on her neck.

Salt.

The feel of his tongue stroking against hers.

Softened butter.

How easily he maneuvered her into position so he could be between her legs.

Almond extract.

The way he owned *her body's response with the drag of his thumb.*

Sugar.

The way he stuck a hand down her pants and licked her from his fingers.

A piece of eggshell cracked into her mixture when she was distracted by how utterly *carnal* that particular move was.

"I know you like your modern version of Christmas music, but I didn't think they had cursing in them," Lyle said, entering the kitchen.

"*You,*" she hissed, leveling him with a narrowed-eyed stare so fierce he held his hands up in surrender.

"What did my darling husband do now?" Kyle asked, draping an arm around Lyle's shoulders.

"Oh, don't think *you're* innocent in all this. You *both* knew who lived across the hall from my new place and *neglected* to tell me."

The whirl of the mixers was the only sound in the room as one song ended and another began, both men looking properly chastised as she stared them down.

"What? We didn't think you'd have a problem with it since we caught the two of you fucking each other's mouths back here."

Shit. She couldn't deny that. It was *exactly* what had gone down. Thank god, they didn't know what went down in her bedroom.

"Still." She ran a frustrated hand through her hair. "It would have been good information to have."

"You say that like you wouldn't have moved in with the girls. And we all know *that* isn't true," Kyle stated.

It was true. Already she felt like she had been friends with them for years and not hours. The Coven was life, and she *desperately* wanted to be a part of it. To have a squad of her own, to know there were people to call on who wouldn't question. Kyle had been the only constant like that in her life, and for years even that had been from a distance.

"That's not the point." She slapped the counter, the sound ringing out in the room. "Vince keeps trying to get me to go on a *date* with him." She spat the word date like a curse.

"I don't see the problem here, Sweets," Lyle said, coming around her workspace to pull her into a side hug. "Vince is sex-on-legs." He sent a look of apology to his husband. "Sorry, babe."

Kyle waved him off. "No worries. It's true."

"So…I don't get the problem here, Sweets."

She hung her head, letting out a sigh of defeat. "I need to figure out how to stand on my own. I've always been Holly Vanderbuilt, this is the first time in twenty-three years I've ever gotten to be"—she released a heavy sigh—"Holly."

The two men nodded in understanding. They were the only ones who knew the details of her previous life.

They let the subject drop. With a kiss on the cheek, they retreated from the kitchen, allowing her to get lost in the task of creating her cookies for the next eight hours.

Training camp was a delicate balance of going full steam ahead while trying not burn out before the actual fight, especially when a fighter needed to cut weight to be eligible to fight in a particular weight class.

Monday through Friday, Vince trained hard. He dedicated a full day to each discipline in his repertoire—boxing, judo, Muay Thai, Brazilian jiujitsu and wrestling, as well as a day for cardio. Some of them overlapped as they used similar techniques, but thanks to both his father's and uncle's histories and his own background as a high school wrestler, he was one of the most diverse and well-rounded fighters in the league.

Saturday mornings had been for yoga for as long as he could remember. It originated with the Covenettes going, eventually growing by them bringing whichever of the guys they were able to talk into it until the law was laid down that the fighters had to practice as part of their training. Every Saturday morning, whoever was in town met at The Steele Maker for yoga class.

After a round of goodbyes that always seemed to take at least ten minutes, he headed for the sauna to shed a few pounds. Skirting the line of dehydration was a technique he could only apply on days he didn't train.

Inside the locker room, he stripped down completely, wrapped himself in a towel and headed for the private sauna reserved for the full-time fighters of the gym. Since they didn't officially train on the weekends, he would have the place to himself.

Scooping two ladles of water onto the hot stones, he settled back on the upper bench in the corner, spreading his knees and letting his head fall back to thunk against one of the cedar-lined walls of the room.

During camp, weekends were for recovery. First the yoga, now the sauna and on Sundays he had a session with a massage therapist.

He expanded his lungs fully, breathing in the thick, soupy air. Though the sauna used eucalyptus oil, the only scent he was able to detect was vanilla and sugar as Holly worked her way to the forefront of his brain.

She hadn't been far from his thoughts since the moment he laid eyes on her singing and dancing in the kitchen of Espresso Patronum. Recognition of his missing half hit him like a roundhouse kick to the heart less than a week ago. *Had it really been less than a week? Fuck. I really am like one of Maddey's goddamn books.*

He wanted to shake off the thoughts, tell himself they were crazy, that there was no such thing as love at first sight. Sure, there was lust at first sight, which he one hundred percent felt for Holly, but deep down he knew it was more than that. Lust didn't explain how he yearned to know everything about her. Her hopes, her dreams, what made her tick, and how she came to be here now, baking at Espresso Patronum.

There was something else though. Something she wasn't telling him. It didn't happen often, but every now and then he got a glimpse of shadows lurking behind her soulful eyes.

A lesser man might give up—especially given that she'd blown him off once already—but he literally fought for a living. He stepped inside a seven hundred and fifty square foot octagon to face down guys whose sole intention was to knock his ass out. A rocky past wasn't anything that would have him running away or screaming for his mommy.

He was preparing for the most important fight of his entire career as a professional MMA fighter, but he had a feeling that fight would have nothing on what he would have to face to win her heart.

He had been hooked from only a few lingering kisses and some verbal sparring, but now that he knew what it was like to hold her in his arms while in the throes of passion, he was done. Knocked to the mat, count to ten, raise his opponent's arm, done.

He felt his dick stir underneath the soft terry cloth of his towel. Not surprising since his body reacted *anytime* he thought of Holly.

He'd jerked off to thoughts of her so many times over the past week it was a miracle his hand wasn't blistered. But it wasn't going to stop him from partaking in another self-love session to his tasty Cupcake.

He ran a hand over his abs to pull the knot of the towel loose. Peeling the terry cloth open, he let each end fall to the side while he spread his knees farther apart, slouching down more on the bench and getting comfortable.

Another deep inhale, followed by a forceful exhale. His hand wrapped around his dick at the base, stroking it from root to tip and back again as he thought of the way she shuddered against him when he kissed the soft spot behind her ear.

His palm glided across the pre-cum leaking from the tip, using both it and the sweat the steam room created to lubricate the up and down jerks.

A groan escaped as he remembered the way her legs squeezed him and how she rubbed herself against him when he had her pinned against the oven.

Up.

Down.

A twist of his wrist.

A flash of the way her eyes sparkled as she tried to tell him he wasn't her type, when the entire time he could see the pebbled tips of her nipples giving her away.

He increased the pressure on his dick as his thoughts turned to the night before. She was so fucking responsive he could barely handle it. He wanted to learn *all* the ways he could get that pretty blush to spread across her chest.

Up, down.

Up, down.

His speed increased as last night played like a movie reel.

Each breathy sigh.

Each bit back moan.

The way his name sounded falling from her sweet lips as she tipped over the edge in ecstasy.

Faster and faster his hand moved until he exploded across his belly at the same time Holly came in his memory.

His chest heaved as he came down from his release. He'd

only gotten the briefest sample of her sweet flavor and already he was addicted. He planned on devoting *hours* getting his fill between her legs once he got her naked and spread out beneath him. There was a chance he'd develop diabetes, but it was a risk he was willing to take.

Chapter Eighteen

Vince spent the next few hours adulting, taking care of the tedious task of doing laundry and the even worse one of actually folding and putting it away. The struggle was real. The only saving grace was they had a washer and dryer inside the apartment, so he was able to kick back and watch the afternoon Lions game with Gage in between loads.

His brother-in-law was a cool dude. Vince liked to pride himself on being an integral part of Gage and Rocky getting together. Gage had almost let his own jealousy get in the way of being with her. It wasn't until Vince had broken down the group's history that Gage started to understand and move past his jealousy of Rocky's previous relationship with Jase.

Was it a little unconventional for people to remain friends —best friends, in fact—with their exes? Yeah maybe, but their crew was anything but normal.

"You feeling good about the fight?" Gage asked, keeping an eye on the hockey game.

"Yup," he said while drinking Gemma's protein shake. "I've seen O'Doyle fight throughout his career, and we all know Rocky has made me watch countless hours of film. I'll keep doing what we've been doing…you know, me kicking your ass around the gym."

Gage guffawed deep and loud. "In your dreams, pretty boy. I'll give you this…we *are* the most evenly matched at the gym, but I can still take you. You can't compete with these guns." He flexed his left arm, making the octopus tattoo winding its way down to his wrist dance.

"Whatever helps you sleep at night. But don't forget, old man, you're getting up there in the age department."

"You just wait. I'll show you who's old on Monday. You're going to be crying for your mommy, or I guess your sister in this case."

"Bring it on, James."

Gage shrugged him off, cheering when his team scored a goal. A quick glance at the television showed the goal scorer was BTU alum Wade Tanner.

"Whatever, bro, it's a win-win for me. Either I kick your ass and get bragging rights for the day. Or you get in some good shots, and Rocky kisses my boo-boos all better." The smirk gracing Gage's lips was the first clue Vince wouldn't like what he said next. "And to be honest, I'm almost hoping for the latter because the things your sis—"

"Whoa!" He held up both hands. "Do. Not. Finish that sentence. I *beg* you." He clasped his hands in front of his chest. "Rock and I are close, but *not that* close."

Gage's laughter followed him as he got ready for his date with Holly.

Becky whistled in approval when she caught sight of him dressed. "Where are you going all cleaned up?"

"Wouldn't you like to know, Beck?" He waggled his eyebrows.

"Yeah. I would. So spill. The Lions are on now, we have the Blizzards to watch later. So please, tell me where you are going that isn't with us?" She circled her finger to include the full room. His roommates, sister, and the other full-time fighters were spread out around his apartment.

He was setting himself up for endless commentary, but there was no avoiding the truth. Holly was their roommate. Might as well get it over with.

"I'm taking Holly out on a date."

"Whoa, bro, really?" Nick wore a look of shock.

"I thought you didn't 'date' on account of your mom wanting to marry you off to the first nice girl you bring home?" Damon said.

"It's a date, not a family dinner." He suppressed a shudder at the thought of the infamous Steele family dinners. He was developing deep feelings for Holly—a fact that made no sense with how little he knew her—but family dinner was an entirely different weight class.

"Ummm." Gemma chewed on the corner of her thumb the way she did whenever she was nervous or uncertain. "Does *she* know about the date?"

He was taken aback by the question. Of course Holly knew, he'd asked her the night before. Okay, so more like he *told* her instead of asking, but potato, vodka. It was all the same.

"Uh, yeah. Why would you ask that?"

"Well…you seem ready to go. And she's still working?" Her inflection said the words she didn't—*duh, dumbass.*

If that wasn't a hit below the belt, he didn't know what was. *Whatever.* He shook it off. It was a minor setback, he would just have to pick her up at Espresso Patronum, no big deal.

"Guess I'm picking her up." He grabbed his keys and phone. "Don't wait up, kids," he called over his shoulder as he went to get his girl.

For hours and hours, Holly lost herself in the act of baking and decorating. She refused to look at the clock on the wall, not wanting to calculate how late she would have to stay before Vince wouldn't be waiting to take her out.

Was it right to ghost him? Was it really ghosting or was she just standing him up? She wasn't sure which term to use. She did know that neither was the *right* thing to do, but if she saw him, the resolve she was barely hanging on to would break.

It had been proven on three separate occasions that she was unable to resist the pull he had on her.

Complete avoidance was the only way to keep her distance—a feat to accomplish with him living across the freaking hall. She needed new friends because the match-making twins were clearly too blinded by the hearts in their eyes to appreciate her situation.

"You know…it's a good thing I have a healthy ego, other-wise I might start to get a complex with how much you're trying to avoid going on a date with me, Cupcake."

She closed her eyes as his deep voice washed over her. She wanted to say she was surprised he showed up, but deep down a part of her was expecting him.

She took a moment to steel herself. He was more tempting to her than cookies were to Santa.

With another deep breath, she turned to the doorway, gripping the counter behind her in an attempt to prevent herself from walking to him.

Damn, he looked good. The messy way his hair was styled made her wonder if that's what it would look like after a night spent running her hands through it in bed. *Shit, Hol. Do not think about sex with him.*

She couldn't help but appreciate the way the waffle weave of his henley hugged the bulges of muscles under it, or the way his forearm porn-worthy arms looked with the sleeves pushed up to the elbows. She could see the colorful ink decorating his right arm, but was too far away to make out the details.

As she continued her inspection of his body, her gaze lingered on the bulge behind his zipper, the one she knew was like one of those giant candy canes filled with Hershey's Kisses, having had it ground against her in only a pair of loose sweatpants last night. And don't even get her started on how his thighs filled out the denim encasing them.

Fuck a duck, she didn't stand a chance.

"I—" Her voice cracked, so she stopped to clear her throat before trying again. "I told you. I can't go out with you. It's not the right time for me."

VINCE WATCHED HOLLY from his spot leaning against the doorjamb. He honestly couldn't think of anything cuter than the sight of her bopping around to Christmas music as she baked. Not even the annoyance of her trying to avoid him could detract from how enchanting she was to watch in her element.

As she blew him off for the second time in as many days, he was able to read all the things she didn't say lurking in her eyes—fear.

He'd worked with enough women in the self-defense classes to spot a woman who was spooked. And Holly fit the mold to a T. What was she afraid of?

"I hear the words you're saying…I really do," he said, asking himself if he should crowd her or not. If he was to have a shot with her, she needed to be comfortable around him. Carefully he closed the distance between them.

"But there's something *you're* not getting when it comes to us." His finger hooked under her chin to tilt her head back enough to see her eyes. "And it's kinda a biggie."

She visibly swallowed but leaned into his touch.

"Wh-What's that?"

The golds and browns in her eyes swirled with emotion as she met his stare, a piece of him breaking at all the things they said that her words didn't. Someone had hurt her, and when he found out who and how, they were dead.

"You and me, Cupcake." His other hand came up to stroke a finger across her cheek before cupping it. "We're inevitable."

She stilled at his words. She stopped breathing, and he was pretty sure if she could do it, her heart probably would have stopped beating as well, *that's* how still she went.

"You know it. I know it. All you have to do is stop denying it and let me in." He gently touched her head, then rested his hand over her heart. "I'm not the only one who feels it."

Her heartbeat pounded under his palm. She cupped her hand over his.

"But I'm a patient guy. I can wait for you to be ready." He bent to her ear. "Just know I'm not going to make it easy for you."

"Vince—"

"Tomorrow," he cut off the objection before she could voice it.

"What about tomorrow?" She stepped away from his touch, but let her soft hand trail off his slowly. "I'm not going to change my mind about the date overnight."

"We'll circle back to that."

"Anyone ever tell you you're kinda cocky?"

"Daily." Her eyes moved to his dimple. "Still doesn't change the fact that we'll be seeing each other tomorrow."

"We live across the hall from each other, of course we'll *see* each other. But I'm still not going to go on a date with you."

"We'll work our way up to that." He crossed his arms to keep from reaching for her. "Which brings us back to tomorrow."

She arched a brow, remaining silent.

He dropped a kiss to his favorite spot behind her ear then walked from the room without looking back.

She had no idea what was coming for her.

He was like a dog with a bone. When he wanted something, he didn't stop until he got it. It was one of the reasons he was fighting for the title belt next month.

But as hungry as he was to be the next light heavyweight champ, it had *nothing* on the craving he had for her.

Chapter Nineteen

H olly woke up stressed.

Drank her coffee stressed.

Ate breakfast—you guessed it—stressed.

Each time the apartment door opened she tensed.

Vince hadn't given her any details. All he said was *tomorrow* and, well, it was tomorrow.

He'd relented on the date issue, but other than that she had no idea what to expect.

"Go get dressed," Becky said, startling her.

"Dressed?"

"Yup. Wear something to work out in. We leave in five." She pulled two reusable water bottles from a cabinet.

"Leave?"

"For The Steele Maker." The bottles went into a bag.

"The gym?"

"Yup." Becky took her by the shoulders, pushing her toward her room. Her mind was having a hard time catching up.

Where was Vince?

"Hurry up, slowpoke."

Holly did as she was told, dressed in black leggings and a sports bra and pulled on her loose 'Let's take an #Elfie' t-shirt.

She glanced at Vince's front door when they stepped into the hall, but it was closed.

Becky was unusually quiet and remained that way the entire ride to the gym.

Vince wished he had wrapped his hands if for no other reason than to have something to fiddle with while he stared at the gym's front door. The longer he waited, the more he questioned if using Becky was the right plan.

His hope was Holly wouldn't say no to her roommate, and he could convince her to stay once they arrived.

"You're playing with fire, man," Gage cautioned, stepping next to him.

"With Holly?"

"No." He scoffed. "With your sister. Pissing off Steele women first thing in the morning is *not* the best game plan, even if she's a James now."

Vince looked to the back hallway Rocky's office was in. He hadn't expected her to be here on their day off, but surprise surprise.

"Dude." He clapped Gage on the back. "Aren't you supposed to keep your Covenette too satisfied to worry about the rest of us?"

"Oh, Blue is satisfied all right." A pleased expression overtook Gage's face. "But both she and Jordan have some sort of superpower that allows them to think even after an orgasm—at least from what Jake has told me about his wife—but if you want me to go into detail of the way me and your sister fu—"

"Uncle! Uncle!" He waved his arms in a panic. He *so* didn't need to know about his sister's sex life.

"You're too easy, Vin."

The door opened.

Holly was here.

It went against every instinct to not go to her the moment she stepped inside the gym, but his sneakers were firmly planted to the padded floor.

He needed her trust.

The first step to earning it was not forcing himself into her space.

She saw him and stopped. Becky turned around to say something he was too far away to hear, but whatever it was it was enough to get her moving.

"Vinny-boy." Becky smirked, smacking him on the shoulder as she walked past.

"Trouble," he said, but his eyes never left Holly.

"Vince?" There was uncertainty in her voice as she said his name.

"Cupcake."

Her head was on a swivel as she looked around the gym. "Wh-What am I doing here?"

"Well." His hands clenched with the need to touch her. "Since you're determined to crush my fragile ego by refusing to go on a date with me—"

"*Fragile*." She snorted.

"Oooh, she already knows you well, Vinny-boy." Becky laughed with Gage.

"You know I *hate* being called that," he growled.

"Why do you think I do it?"

He rolled his eyes.

"I need new friends," he groaned.

"Hey." She held her hands up in surrender. "*You* invited *me*."

"A grave miscalculation on my part."

"Oooh, am I missing pick on Vince time?" Rocky asked as she moved to her husband's side, Gage's hand falling to rest on her small baby bump.

Vince groaned. This was a mistake. Granted, he couldn't get Holly to agree to be with him one-on-one. But his family? Big, *big* mistake.

He gave them the side-eye and stretched a hand out to Holly. "Come with me?"

She hesitated, eyes bouncing from his hand to his face and back.

He held his breath. Moment of truth time.

"COME WITH ME?"

Those three words held so much more weight than the ten letters they were comprised of. Holly had lost count of the number of times she had heard them in her life.

Except…

Vince wasn't commanding her, he was asking. Giving her the option and allowing her to make the decision if she wanted to or not.

That was why she placed her hand in his, the massive paw swallowing hers in a gentle grip. That was also different.

She wasn't pulled or tugged. Instead his hand rotated to thread his fingers with hers and waited for her to walk with him.

This was a side of him she hadn't seen before, and if she were honest with herself, it was just as dangerous—if not more so—to her heart as the dominating one. She was fucked in the head.

He led her to a room, holding the door open for her to step inside. There was a desk and two low-backed padded chairs, and based on the connected treatment room, she assumed they were in Rocky's office.

He gestured for her to take one of the chairs while he took the other.

She mirrored his posture, leaning forward to rest her elbows on her knees. There was a seriousness in his expression she'd never seen before. Gone was the playful jokester who crashed her kitchen to kiss her senseless. In his place was the one she expected stepped into the octagon.

It was fierce. Intimidating. Sexy.

"I'm going to ask you something," he said.

"Okay..."

"Who hurt you?"

She froze.

How to answer? She didn't want to lie to him, but she didn't want to tell him. It was embarrassing. The only person she'd ever told was Kyle and even that was just admitting the truth when he saw the evidence hidden under her clothes.

She couldn't breathe. Panic was overtaking her senses.

Why? Why of all the things he could've asked did it have to be *that*?

"Hey." His hand cupped her knee and squeezed, bringing her back to earth.

She couldn't speak over the lump in her throat.

"You're safe here. I'm not going to let anything hurt you, Holly."

It was his use of her real name that broke her from her stupor.

"How—" She swallowed, then swallowed again. "How did you know?"

She was sick of playing the victim. For too long she'd let others control her, keep her down. She was told she had no options, that her degree was worthless, nothing more than a vanity diploma to make her more appealing as a potential partner. The worst part—she believed them.

"I teach self-defense to survivors of domestic abuse."

She noticed he said survivors not victims. That...that meant—*something*.

"And what? You think just because you spend an hour or two a week with these women that you can decide I'm a battered woman?"

"First off." He shifted closer, and his knees brushed hers. "I never said anything about *battered*." His eyes were harder than granite. "And second, my work with the survivors has become a passion project of mine. The purse from my fight is going to be used to fund a new women's shelter."

Really? He wasn't hot enough, he had to go and have a heart under all that swagger?

"So...yes. There were certain signs I've picked up on with you. Now answer the question. Who hurt you?"

"It doesn't matter."

"The *fuck* it doesn't." His tone was lethal.

"No, Muffin. It doesn't." His eyes softened at the nickname. "What *does* matter is I got out and I'm safe."

He studied her a beat longer. He was so much bigger than those who had hurt her. He wielded the power to do so much more damage than anyone else, yet everything about his presence gave her a sense of peace.

"And we're gonna keep you that way. Which brings us to why we're here."

"In your sister's office." She pointed to the ground.

"No, smartass." He chuckled, the creases bracketing his mouth softening. "At the gym."

She arched a brow.

"I'm going to teach you self-defense." He held a hand up when she tried to object. "All the Covenettes have learned. You're not the only one with a history."

Chapter Twenty

Holly was on a hunt for coffee. It had been a long day baking, and she still had a self-defense lesson with Vince to get through. Part of her cursed the people-pleasing engrained part of her for participating—he essentially told her they were doing them instead of asking—but even she had to admit they were a good idea.

"Hey, Sweets," Lyle said as she stepped behind the counter and blew him a kiss. "You heading out to see your man?"

Coffee pot in hand she froze. Looking over her shoulder, she leveled him with major side-eye.

"He's *not* my man."

"Oh, Sweets." Lyle chuckled.

She bristled. She'd spent way too many years being patronized, and it needed to end.

"Sammy," Lyle greeted the newest customer, shooting her a knowing wink. He reached a hand across the counter to exchange a complicated handshake with the copper-haired hottie.

"Hey, Ly, how's it going?" He had one of those blinding

smiles that drew a person in and made them want to be friends.

"Can't complain, can't complain."

"Staying out of trouble?"

Holly snorted. *Yeah, right.* Lyle's middle name was trouble.

Eyes the color of melted caramel turned her way, and damn, did her friends have some hot as hell friends.

"Hol, this is Sammy." Lyle was quick to make introductions. "Sammy, this is Holly. She's taken over all the baking for the shop."

Sammy's eyes brightened. "Oh, so you're the one my best friend curses for needing to log extra hours in the gym."

"Excuse me?" She was a little taken aback by the accusation. "I don't even know you, let alone your best friend."

He laughed, the sound warm and endearing, easing her prickly feathers. "No, no, no," he quickly backpedaled. "It's the highest of compliments. Maddey raves about your blueberry crumbles and red velvet scones."

"You should see her cookies," Lyle boasted.

"Why does that sound dirty?" she deadpanned.

Her friends had rubbed off on her considering how much time her mind spent in the gutter lately. Ha—*rubbed off.*

"Part of me wants to say you're exaggerating, but Maddey has come into my kitchen looking for treats on multiple occasions."

"You want the usual?" Lyle asked, falling back to the espresso machine.

"Yeah and Jam's too."

"Where is your better half?"

"He was spotted." Sammy pointed a long arm at the shop's glass wall. Outside a group of people were taking selfies with a tall guy in a baseball hat and sunglasses.

"He's gonna need a better disguise than that," Lyle said.

"First world problems," Sammy said with a shrug.

"Go on." Lyle nodded his head toward the back of the

shop. "Go to, Madz. I'll bring your drinks when they're ready."

Lyle made the drinks, and Holly watched the guy outside finally extricate himself from the small group of people surrounding him to enter the café.

"Hey, Jame." He reached out and did the same handshake thing with the new arrival as he did with Sammy.

"Hey, Ly." He removed his sunglasses, tucking them into the collar of his white t-shirt.

Holy shit. That's Jamie Hawke.

Her hand beat a quick staccato of backhands against Lyle's chest as she stared wide-eyed at the rockstar.

Lyle wrapped a hand around hers to halt the attack.

"How about you *not* beat me up, Hol?"

"Umm…how about *you* explain to me how you never mentioned you knew Jamie-*freaking*-Hawke," she countered.

"It never came up." He shrugged.

"This is *not* the type of information you wait to come up in casual conversation. I have half a mind to tell Ky not to give it up to you."

"*Pfft*…you know he is too hot for me to resist this." He waved a hand down the length his body. Damn him for being right. Kyle had it *bad* for his tatted-up husband.

"Hate you." There was no heat in her words.

"No, you don't. You love me."

"Damn, I hate that you're right."

A musical chuckle reminded her there was a rockstar standing in front of her.

"Hi. I'm Jamie." He reached a hand out for her to shake as if she didn't know who he was.

Proper etiquette had her taking the outstretched hand even as she stood gawking at the front man for her favorite band. Even under the Yankees hat he used as part of his "disguise," everything about him *screamed* bad boy rocker.

"This is Holly. She grew up with Kyle, and now that she's

escaped from...*Connecticut*"— Lyle shuddered as he said it— "she's overhauling the bakery side of the business." Thank goodness he spoke for her since she was standing there mute.

Jamie's violet eyes widened in surprise. "You're the one responsible for all the cool shit being posted on EP's Insta?"

She nodded, then cleared her throat to finally speak. "You follow us on Instagram?"

"Fuck yeah," he said enthusiastically. "That Baby Groot cake you made last week looked so real I was waiting for it to actually dance."

The coffee shop's bakery items were her daily work, but cakes, cupcakes, and cookies were where she really shined. It took her three days to make the Guardians of the Galaxy cake, but the final product was absolute perfection. Every insult and criticism she'd faced from her family through the years melted away as the superstar in front of her sang her praises.

"Yeah, that was a fun one to make, for sure."

Before Jamie could respond, she heard a familiar voice.

"Cupcake."

As a group, they turned to see Vince standing at the entrance, cold air blowing through the open door.

"Umm...what are you doing here?"

"Just making sure you weren't blowing me off again."

He spotted Jamie, and they exchanged *hey, man*s and a bro-hug, then he offered her his hand. "Ready?"

Nope.

She didn't think she'd ever be *ready* for him, but took his hand anyway.

When Holly was late for their second self-defense lesson, Vince was done letting her stand him up. This wasn't like the date he still wanted—though both were equally important to him—this was about making sure she knew how to defend herself if the need arose.

He'd been surprised to see that she was waylaid by Jamie Hawke at EP rather than just ignoring him.

He rewrapped his hands as she used the locker room to change. He had taken a quick shower after his training, wanting to be fresh and not a sweaty, stinky mess after the punishing workout. He was trying to impress the girl, not repulse her.

She eyed him warily as she made her way across the gym to him. That needed to change.

He bent for the hand wraps he'd ordered specifically for her. Their first session had been spent teaching her how to get out of an attacker's hold and blocking hits. Now it was time for her to learn how to hit. The best defense was a good offense, after all.

"Give me your hand." He held out one of his own for her.

She hesitated, then did as he asked.

He peeled open the Velcro strap, letting the cupcake printed material unspool to the floor. He stroked his thumb along the sensitive skin on the inside of her wrist, feeling her pulse flutter like a hummingbird under his touch. He loved the way her body reacted to his touch.

Slipping the thumb loop over her finger, he set to work, making sure she was properly protected.

"What's all this?" She held up her wrapped hand.

"The wraps add a layer of support for your wrist as well as cushion for your knuckles when you hit."

"And what am I hitting?" She sounded skeptical.

"Me," he answered and dropped the other completed hand.

"You?"

"Yup." He bounced on the balls of his feet.

"I'm *not* hitting you."

"Sure, you are."

"No, I'm not." Her eyes narrowed, her shoulders pressed back. He adored when she got feisty.

"It's not like you're gonna hurt me, Cupcake."

Her eyes flashed at the challenge.

Bring it on, baby.

"Muffin," she warned.

"Cupcake." He smirked, showing his dimple, her eyes automatically going to it.

"I'm not—" Her words cut off as she balled her fists. "Wait…are those cupcakes?"

"Of course. I needed to get cupcakes for my Cupcake."

"You're a dork." He shrugged. "Are yours muffins?"

"Nope." He held up his hands. "Superman for me."

She rolled her eyes but cracked a smile.

"Okay now, time to get serious."

At their last lesson, he had shown her a basic fight stance, but now that he was actually teaching her how to hit, he wanted to make sure she had it perfect.

He circled, checking her posture. In a normal class, he wouldn't touch his students, but with Holly he couldn't resist the urge. He wanted her to be comfortable with him in her personal space.

In a move that could backfire, he stepped in close, his front brushing her back as he placed a foot between hers to widen her stance. He skimmed his fingertips along her triceps, raising her left arm up, and bent to breathe in her sugary scent.

She didn't pull away. Instead her head canted to the side as the tip of his nose brushed the soft spot behind her ear.

"Looking good." He circled back to her front.

"Shouldn't you be teaching me, *not* hitting on me?"

"Oh, Cupcake." He shook his head. "I'll *always* hit on you." His expression sobered. "But I'll *never* hit you."

The unease left her, and the crinkles around her eyes weren't as deep as he stayed silent, letting his words sink in.

"Now." He curled a hand around her fist. "The most important thing to remember with a punch is not to tuck your thumb." He freed the digit, placing it on top of her fingers.

"Why?"

"Lessens the chance of breaking it."

She nodded.

"Another mistake people make is only using their arms."

"Yeah? And what else do you use? Your legs?"

His lips twitched at the heavy sarcasm.

"Yes, smartass. Your legs, your hips, hell, your entire body should be used. It increases the force of your strike, no matter how much smaller you are than your opponent."

Her brow scrunched, taking in the information.

"Now, hit me."

Holly didn't move.

"Come on, Cupcake. Hit me." He tapped his chest.

She did as he asked, bumping one pec with a lackluster punch.

"You can do better than that."

Another swing, this one a bit stronger.

"Not great, but better. This time swivel your hips with the movement."

Swack.

"Again."

Swack.

"Again."

SWACK.

That one had him rubbing his chest.

There was his little fighter. Nice to see her show up.

Chapter Twenty-One

Holly sang along with Kelly Clarkson's "Wrapped in Red" as she put the finishing touches on the brown sugar topping to the blueberry crumbles that had become a fan favorite at EP. Though she loved Halloween—all holidays were meant to be celebrated in the fullest, in her book—she couldn't wait for the day the calendar flipped to November first, and it became sociably acceptable for her to crank up the yuletide tunes.

In her old life, she only ever got to listen to the contemporary pop and rock versions of the classics when she had her earbuds in. *God forbid* she played anything other than the sleep-inducing, old school originals, and don't even get her started on putting the volume dial anywhere above a four. Blasphemy.

"You really do love your pop Christmas music don't you?" Vince spoke from the doorway. He might as well put a plaque on the wall since he'd stood there every day that week.

"It makes me happy." She shrugged.

"I can see that."

Hello there, Mr. Dimple. Can you be a dear and go away before you make me stupid?

"Plus, I never really got to blast these versions...before..." She trailed off, but Vince picked up on what she didn't say.

They hadn't talked much about her life in Connecticut, but she'd shared enough for him to know when she was enjoying little freedoms her new situation afforded her.

"I swear, if there was music for *every* holiday, you would make a playlist for it," Kyle said as he walked into the kitchen.

She finished off the last crumble before turning to face her best friend, hands on hips. "You know, Ky, I thought we were friends."

A crinkle formed between his blond brows. "We are. You're my bestie."

A small part of her got all squishy at the affection in the words. In the mean-girl social strata of private schools, it had been difficult to make true friends. Finding someone who didn't judge her by how her last name could boost their own status was hard enough. But it was even tougher to hold on to the good ones if her family didn't deem them *appropriate* to associate with.

Her father worked hard to keep her under his thumb. Kyle was the *only* friend he didn't throw out of her life like last season's designer duds, and that didn't last once Kyle became open about his sexuality.

"Okay, *bestie*." She leveled him with her fiercest look, which lost its effectiveness when he reached out to brush some of the crumble mixture from her nose. She seriously had no idea how she managed it. "Why didn't you tell me that *Jamie Hawke* frequents your shop?"

The rockstar and his husband were once again having coffee at EP.

"It never came up." Kyle pinched some of the crumble topping between his fingers with a shrug.

"Oh, really?" She crossed her arms over her chest. "Not *once* in, oh, about the bajillion conversations we've had did you *ever* get the opportunity to relay this information?"

"Glad to see I'm not the only one you give a hard time, Cupcake." Vince chuckled, still looking too hot for his own good in his gym shorts, BTU hoodie and backward cap.

Every day he said they were going on a date.

And every day she informed him they weren't.

Instead he resorted to trying to drive her insane with sexual tension. So potent he could do it from across the room.

"Don't even start, Muffin." She held up a finger in warning.

He said nothing, only smirking more, dimple deepening.

That was what he did.

He didn't pressure her or drag her into a closet—or bedroom—to have his wicked way with her, but he was always *there.*

Always watching.

Looking hot AF.

Radiating his alphaness like the sun did its rays.

She was gradually losing her mind, one naughty look and teasing touch at a time.

"Wait a second." Kyle swung a finger between her and Vince. "Why are you all the way over there? Afraid if you get too close you two will start going at it like bunnies?"

"No," she said at the same time Vince said, "Yes."

"Interesting," Kyle mused.

Before she could debate the status of her "relationship" with Vince, Jamie burst into the room, hugging the wall.

"Jamie?" Vince said.

The singer whipped around but relaxed when he saw it was Vince. "Hey, Vin."

"Whatcha doing?"

"Jam?" Sammy's voice called out before he could answer.

"In here," Jamie called back.

"You good?" Sammy asked as he came in the kitchen door and looked him over with a critical eye.

"Yeah, Spins. Stop worrying."

"Can't help it." Sammy still watched Jamie closely, as if evaluating the truth of his words. Holly got the feeling he wasn't a person you wanted to cross.

"You know," a deep voice called out as yet another hot guy stepped into the room. What did they put in the water in this state? "Just because you're practically my brother-in-law doesn't mean your skinny ass gets preferential treatment."

"Look, I may not be an ex-frogman like yourself, Just, but my ass is *anything* but skinny." Jamie grabbed a butt cheek in each of his hands. "I do my squats."

"You're a prima donna, Hawke."

"*Pfft*. Furthest thing from it, McClain."

"Talk all the shit you want, Just. You know Maddey was the one to call you, not us. And we *all* know none of us turn down a request from a Covenette," Sammy said.

Holly snorted. The Covenettes were quickly becoming her favorite people in life. It was highly entertaining how much power they wielded. They were the standard she aspired to for her new life.

Light green eyes tracked to her immediately from mister hot cop. "Well, *hello* there." He reached out, taking one of her smaller hands in his much larger ones. "Who might you be, beautiful?" His eyes shifted over to Kyle standing next to her. "And why do you keep this one hidden in the back?"

She felt her cheeks heat in a blush. "I'm Holly."

"Justin." The smile he sent her way dripped with charm.

"Justin," Vince said, moving to her free side.

He didn't grab her or tug her away from Justin like she expected, but it was still a possessive move. One Justin noted based on the way his eyes widened and the slight nod he gave.

"Now," Justin clapped Jamie on the shoulder. "How about

we get your ass out of here before the small club out there turns into a mob?"

"Aww, do you have a crush on me, McClain?" Jamie batted his eyelashes playfully. "That's the second time you've brought up my ass in as many minutes. I'm sorry to break it to you, but I'm a happily married man."

"McClain?" Holly asked.

"Maddey's oldest brother," Vince said as they watched the others banter.

"Why did I leave the Navy and come home? No respect." Justin tilted his face to the ceiling as if speaking directly to God.

"You know, for a guy who made it through BUD/S, you sure are a pussy," Sammy said with a laugh as everyone but Vince exited the kitchen.

"So…" he said, shifting to lean against the counter. "Where do you want to go to dinner tonight?"

"Dinner?" she asked, putting the finishing touches on the crumbles and loading them into the oven.

"Yeah, for our date." He moved, this time staying close. "It will have to be late. I have a meeting with the director of the women's shelter after training, and I'm not sure how long that will be."

He was persistent, she'd give him that.

"Well, *I'll*"—she pointed to her chest—"be having dinner with my roommates tonight, seeing as I'm *not* going on a date with you."

"Come on, Cupcake. Don't leave me hanging. I'm always jazzed after these meetings."

"No." Her tone was firm, her resolve not so much.

"Cupcake." He pouted, and it was annoyingly adorable on him.

"Not happening." She sucked in a breath as he brushed something from her cheek.

"Buzzkill."

She shrugged. "Tell me why you'll be jazzed."

He resumed his perch against the counter, arms and ankles crossed. "It's exciting to see my plans come to fruition. This new shelter has been a dream of mine for a few years now. I can't believe I'm finally in the position to make it a reality."

She paused, measuring cup of flour held in the air as she took a moment to study this enigma of a man in front of her. There was a depth to him she didn't think many people outside his circle got to see.

"You weren't kidding when you called it a passion project, were you?"

He spoke with such fervor anytime the subject came up.

"I may have originally gotten involved with everything because of JD and her ex, but meeting these women, learning their struggles, and watching them overcome them has been one of the most inspiring things I have ever witnessed. The system itself is flawed, but I'm in a place—at least I will be after this fight—to help tip the scales in their favor."

Oh, my heart.

"I may not know your whole story." He placed a finger over her lips when she started to reply. "And one day, you'll trust me enough to tell me. But I want to help the people who don't have a Kyle in their life."

"Vince."

"I know, babe."

What did he know? She didn't even know what she meant, how could he?

The meaningful expression transformed back to the cocky one he usually wore before he bent to kiss her hard and swift.

"I should start taking bets on if that will happen before or after you finally go on a date with me."

With that, he was gone, leaving her more confused than if she were hit by one of Hermione's Confundus Charms.

Chapter Twenty-Two

Another day, another visit from Vince, another date rejection from Holly.

He was persistent, and she was waffling.

Thank god for lunch break time restrictions. She wasn't sure if he would ever leave if he didn't.

The biggest problem? *She* wasn't sure she wanted him to.

"Hey, Sweets," Lyle said as she stepped behind the counter after walking Vince out.

"Hey, Fiddler."

His brow furrowed. "Fiddler?"

"Yeah, you know. Like *Fiddler on the Roof.* Seeing as you and my so-called best friend keep going all 'Matchmaker, matchmaker, make me a match,' on me, I figured it was appropriate."

"Oooh...you have jokes now. I'll remember that." He tapped his temple with a finger.

She pointed to the front display case. "Anything specific you need me to whip up?"

"Nope. You're off the clock for the next few hours."

She looked at the Deathly Hallows-shaped clock on the wall. Her shift wasn't over yet.

"You have plans. And I know you don't have any pending bakery orders, so you are dismissed for the day." He waved a hand in front of him. "Ah, your chariot awaits."

She followed the line of his arm. Maddey stood, laptop bag slung over her shoulder, beaming at them.

"Come on, girl. Get your stuff. You're coming with us."

"Us?" she questioned.

"Yup, us. Time for you to come out with The Coven. We have an appointment for manis and pedis."

No female in her right mind would turn down mani-pedis. She mentally patted herself on the back for shaving the day before. When the weather turned cold it was always a crapshoot if she did. The fact that her legs didn't resemble the long weeds of the wild had everything to do with her keeping up her personal grooming and nothing to do with wanting to be prepared should a certain Dauntless-looking male manage to get her out of her clothes. No. Nope. That was her story, and she was sticking to it.

Hell, who was she kidding? It had *everything* to do with him.

The nail salon was two blocks down from Espresso Patronum, and the rest of the girls were already picking their colors when they arrived.

OPI's Samurai Breaks a Nail—a bright, pretty purple—in hand, she toed off her pink Chucks, rolled up her leggings, and settled into a chair between Rocky and Maddey. Becky finished off their row and Jordan, Skye, Gemma and Beth were across from them.

"God, I love half days." Beth sighed, melting into her massage chair.

"I don't know how you teach, B. I would end up killing the first hormonal teenager who got on my bad side," Skye said.

"You figure it out." Beth shrugged. "Besides, it's not much different keeping the athletes you represent in line."

"This is true," Jordan agreed. "Some of the guys can be *real* divas."

"Truth. Managing fragile male egos is more of a full-time job then running The Steele Maker," Becky added.

"Well, from everything I've witnessed, you all call the shots," Holly said as the nail tech rubbed her calf with an exfoliating scrub. "I heard of The Coven long before I even knew what it was."

She was so appreciative of how they made her feel included, not once treating her like a newcomer to the group. What she found hardest to wrap her head around was how down to earth and genuine they were. With sports contracts and endorsement deals being public record, she knew most of them were connected to people with some serious money, yet they acted *nothing* like her family.

"So, Hol." Maddey shifted in her seat to see her better. "Give us all the deets on what Kyle was like growing up."

"Well." She took a moment to gather her thoughts in a way that wouldn't give too much of her own history away. "Honestly he was pretty much exactly how you know him now, except *closeted,* I guess."

"He really didn't come out until he brought Lyle home?" Skye's eyes widened.

"That would be a hard no."

"His family disowned him over it?" Maddey's question came out as a whisper. Holly knew Sammy had been her best friend growing up, but with a much different support system when he came out. As in, he actually had one.

"Oh, yeah. It was *ugly.* But I was so proud of him. He stayed eerily calm the whole time, and when they threatened to disown him and cut him off if he didn't drop Lyle and marry a *proper* lady, he walked out of there with his head held high. He's pretty much my hero."

That day was filled with so much ugly and ignorance, it

still baffled her how people could think, let alone say, some of the things the Huntingtons had.

The Huntingtons and the Vanderbuilts were cut from the same hand-spun silk cloth. Kyle's family even encouraged him to date her since they had always been close and she came from the "right" bloodlines.

Their families didn't understand that their blood was as red as everyone else's.

Saying Kyle was her hero wasn't an exaggeration. The resilience he presented that day to not only come out, but to stand his ground, not crumbling under the weight of the silver spoon he was born with, took Herculean strength.

It took her four more years before she finally found the fortitude to do the same.

"I didn't think people actually disowned other people," Rocky said.

"Oh, yeah. Happens all the time in our world. It was the oldest trick in the book to get a child to fall in line before their trust fund kicked in."

"What was it like?" Gemma asked.

"Have you guys ever watched *Gossip Girl* or *Gilmore Girls*?" Seven heads nodded. "So it was like the uppity, DAR world of Chilton and Emily Gilmore, with the over-the-top, spoiled, entitled feel of *Gossip Girl*. Parties like the ones Chuck Bass would have were a real thing most weekends. I'm glad Kyle left when he did. What are your families like?"

She changed the subject, not wanting to risk them digging deeper, and the ladies followed her lead. Topics switched at a rapid pace after that, some serious, some ridiculous and some just straight-up weird.

So this is what it's like to have girlfriends?

Chapter Twenty-Three

V ince and his roommates made their way across the hall to 12A to find its three occupants in the kitchen. Holly fit in seamlessly. It looked like there was another Covenette in the making. *Just my luck.*

"You ate?" Gemma asked the moment she spotted him, his nutrition drill sergeant.

"Yes, ma'am." He snapped his heels together at attention and gave her a salute.

"Mock me all you want, smartass. But not *once* since I took over managing your culinary needs have you actually *felt* like you were cutting weight before a fight. So don't play."

The was no arguing that fact. Even before Gemma had officially graduated from BTU with a degree in nutrition, she had managed all his meal planning and prep. His weight, even when not officially training for a fight, had been more consistent, making him stronger when it came time for weight cuts.

Gemma pulled pre-made parfaits of Greek yogurt, fresh fruit and her custom-blended granola and passed them out to Deck and Ray, leaving a third on the counter for Gage's arrival.

"Seriously, Gem." Deck spoke around a heaping spoonful. "Marry me."

"Oh, Deck." She patted his face patronizingly. "I told you…if you *ever* want me to take you seriously, the proposal needs to come when my food isn't involved."

"You never learn, Deck," Becky added.

"She's so mean to me, Beck." He wrapped himself around her from behind and rested his head on her shoulder with a pout.

"I know, buddy." She reached around to stroke his hair. "It's not your fault. You've taken one too many hits to the head. It affects your ability to think straight."

Deck reared back in offense. "Cold, Beck. Stone cold."

"What did Deck do now?" Rocky asked as she and Gage entered the apartment.

Using the momentary distraction of the new arrivals, Vince made his way over to Holly. His leg brushed the outside of her thigh as he leaned back against the counter on his elbows.

His height gave him a prime view of the way her spectacular cleavage rose as she sucked in a harsh breath. He didn't crowd her, but he was close enough for her to feel his body heat.

"Morning, Cupcake."

She hit him with some major side-eye as she returned his greeting with a stilted, "Stud Muffin."

Yet her whiskey eyes darkened the longer she looked up at him.

He worked to chip away a piece of her resolve against him daily. Every day he left Espresso Patronum grinning like a fool because their time together while she worked was the best part of his day.

They could be so much more than friends if only she gave them a chance. All he needed was an opening to prove it. If using sexual tension got it done, so be it.

He kept his distance physically for the most part. When he couldn't fight it, he made sure to linger and used his eyes to telegraph each filthy promise he thought of.

Doing so may have left him with balls so blue he was afraid he was becoming part Smurf, but he knew the belt at the end of the fight would be more than worth it.

"We good to go?" Rocky asked the room.

Everyone was dressed casually in either jeans or leggings for Sean and Carlee's NJ Blizzards Youth Hockey League game. Vince noticed Holly was the only one without any Blizzards attire and ran back to his place to grab one of the other hoodies hanging in his closet.

"Here, wear this." He held out the navy hooded sweatshirt for her to take.

Her eyes studied him until they crinkled in the corners with her smile. "Is this your way of trying to mark your territory by getting me to wear your clothes?"

Her feistiness was one of his favorite things about her.

"No, this is me not wanting you to be left out." Her eyes softened at his words, another baby step forward for him.

By the time she switched tops, they were the last ones inside the apartment. Taking advantage of the rare moment of privacy, he backed her against the wall, caging her in with a hand on either side of her head.

It was a bold move, a risk even, but he thought she'd let him.

"When I mark my territory, it will be with a *hell* of a lot more than a simple piece of clothing." He bent to place his lips against the fluttering pulse in her neck. "No. When I finally get you to give in to your feelings for me"—he spoke against her dessert-scented skin—"you'll be *wearing* hickies for days. Right here." He kissed the spot with the gentlest of sucks.

"Vince." His name was a broken plea.

"Don't worry, Cupcake." His thumb brushed away the last

of the sting, her skin already returning to its usual creamy complexion. "I won't do it till you *beg* me for it."

His hand skimmed along the length of her arm until his fingers threaded their way through hers. With a gentle tug, he led her out of the apartment so they could meet up with the rest of their friends.

She wasn't ready for him yet.

But soon.

Holly followed the stream of people into the sports complex that housed all the NJ Blizzards Youth Hockey League's home games, impressed with how nice the building was. The entrance was a wide-open space that flowed into a decently sized concession area.

Vince walked the entire way from the car with his arm casually draped across her shoulders. When she tried to shake him off, the jerk had the audacity to laugh.

She wanted to be mad, to say she didn't like how touchy-feely he was with her, she really did. But she couldn't. There was a pull, a draw he had that had her longing to be close that far surpassed the attraction between them. That was the thing that scared her.

They bypassed the concession area, heading directly for the rink. Seated behind the team benches was everyone else. Jake and Jordan were there with their girls and introduced her to both sets of their parents, each grandmother holding a twin also decked out in miniature Blizzards hoodies.

She saw Skye sitting with Sammy and Jamie, while Maddey was in a heated discussion with Ryan. She also recognized the other fighters from the gym who did not live in their building sitting with Beth and her husband Wyatt, their own child already reaching her pudgy arms out toward Gage.

Done resisting, she let Vince lead her to the open seats next to Maddey and Ryan, his arm only leaving her body to greet the guy she recognized as Jase Donnelly in a handshake, back-slapping bro-hug.

"Bro, your fight with Bishop was epic. It's rare to see you throw down like that in a game," Vince said in greeting.

Jase gave a sheepish grin. "Yeah, well I can't fucking *stand* the guy."

"Jason!" His mother scolded. "Little ears."

"Sorry, Mom."

"Relax, Mama D," Jake turned to his mother-in-law. "They hear worse from their mama here."

Jordan backhanded him on the chest. "Oh, yeah, because when you and the guys get together you're *so* much better."

He kissed her temple, and Holly was mildly jealous of the easy affection between the two.

Except for Vince, her own experience with love was much different.

Not that she was in love with him or anything.

He was the first person she was comfortable letting into her personal space. A fact she'd worry about analyzing another day.

"This the newest member?" Jase asked Vince, nodding in her direction.

"Member?" She pushed down the bottom of her seat so she could sit.

"Yup," Vince replied, throwing his arm back around her. "Jase this is Holly. Cupcake, this is Jase, JD's twin brother."

"And best-looking brother." Jase winked. She blushed under the attention of the guy who looked like he could be related to the Hemsworths.

Snorts and scoffs rang out through the group.

"Yeah, yeah, yeah. Yuck it up, assholes. You know it's true."

"Asshole," a high-pitched voice said, and all heads turned to look at the Donovan twin who spoke.

"Asshole." The other twin parroted before both girls volleyed the word back and forth between them, their mom facepalming herself in resignation.

"Thanks a lot, bro," Jake failed to bite back his laughter.

Once they'd gotten their own hysterics under control, Holly repeated her question.

"What *exactly* am I a member of? I don't remember drinking any Kool-Aid, so it can't be a cult."

Jase shared a knowing look with Vince before returning his attention to her after Vince's nod.

"Nah, The Coven isn't a cult. It is its own entity."

"Me?" She pointed a finger to her chest.

Jase gave her a quizzical look. "Wait." He shifted in his seat to face everyone. "Did you guys *not* tell her?" His tone was incredulous.

"There's no formal ceremony or anything." Skye held up a hand as if to say *are you for real right now?*

"This is true," Jordan agreed. "It's really only you two idiots that are obsessed with calling us The Coven."

"We just roll with it," Rocky added.

"You wanna do the honors since she's your girl?" Jase asked Vince.

She didn't get the chance to correct Jase on her being Vince's girl before he was agreeing.

"Absolutely," Vince said, then focused all his attention on her.

She squirmed in her seat as his gray eyes locked onto hers intently.

"Cupcake." He cuffed her under the chin, his thumb stretching out to stroke across her bottom lip and setting off starbursts in its wake. "We'd like to *formally*"—that was pointed—"induct you into The Coven."

Her heart turned over, exposing its soft underbelly. As

much as the guys joked about The Coven, she had learned exactly how important each member was to the whole group. She didn't think they handed out "membership" lightly. Easy acceptance into a clique wasn't something she had experience with.

"Hell yeah!" Becky cheered.

"Someone get this girl a text handle," Rocky declared.

As she listened to the buzz of those around her, she got lost in the unfamiliar feeling of acceptance radiating through her.

Did she really just find her squad for the first time in twenty-three years?

THERE WAS NOTHING more competitive than a group of athletes, especially professionals—they took *all* sporting events seriously, even youth hockey. The passel of nine- and ten-year-olds on the ice were already getting big cheers from their section and it was only warmups. Things would only escalate once the game got underway. He was pretty sure the coaches hated all the extra "bench coaches" in the stands.

Along with their standard squad, it wasn't out of the norm for other players from the Blizzards to catch a game to support their Captain's younger brother.

"I'm serious, Madz. You should say something to Just. It's a little weird." Vince heard Ryan say. The two had been in a heated debate since they'd arrived.

"No way." Maddey shook her head vehemently.

"Madison." Ryan's tone grew serious.

"Don't you *Madison* me, Ryan Donnelly." The barely-five-foot blonde got all up in the giant hockey player's face. It was interesting to watch them interact. They loved each other fiercely, even without the diamond ring connecting them anymore. "You make even the *briefest* of mentions of this to my brother, and I'll write you into one of my books with a micro-penis and erectile dysfunction so bad not even Viagra can help."

A look of horror washed over Ryan's face as the rest of the males sucked in a collective breath at the threat. *No one* wanted to be immortalized in one of her best-sellers in a negative way. Their pixie friend had an evil streak in her longer than the Mississippi.

"You kids play nice now," Vince teased.

He had no clue what the drama was about and more than happy to remain in the dark. Instead, he lifted a hand to play with the purple tips of Holly's hair. Her eyes flashed his way, but she didn't pull away from his touch. *Progress.*

"Don't even start with me, *Vincent*." Maddey was practically spitting fire.

He jumped into Jase's lap, wrapping his arms around his friend. "Save me, Jase. Your triplet is being mean."

Jase played right along, circling his own arms around Vince's body, holding his fingers out in a cross gesture as if to ward off evil. "Back. Back, I tell you."

Maddey's stern expression softened before finally giving way to a smile. "You two are stooopid."

"You love us," Jase countered.

"Only because you're both related to my best friends."

"You ever been to a hockey game?" Vince asked Holly as he shifted off of Jase's lap.

"No." Holly looked down at the rink.

"Really?"

"Yeah. I'd never even watched a game until the night of my welcome party," she said sheepishly.

"Looks like I get to be your tutor." He rubbed his hands together.

"Umm…shouldn't that job go to one of the many professional players here?" She circled a finger in the air.

"Fuck that," he spat.

She laughed. The devilish twinkle in her eye told him he reacted like she thought he would.

When the referee's whistle rang out and the puck dropped, everyone turned their attention to the action down on the ice.

Holly's lack of knowledge of the sport allowed him to linger anytime he leaned in to explain what was happening or how the rules differed for youth hockey versus the pros.

Sean took a shot on goal, the puck hitting the post with a *ping* and ricocheting over the boards.

"What's with the cooler?" she asked as one of the referees retrieved a fresh puck.

"They keep the pucks on ice. When the rubber gets too warm, it tends to bounce." His lips brushed her earlobe, leaving behind another secret kiss to the soft skin. "Kind of like your knee is doing now." He cupped the joint in his hand, giving it a squeeze.

"Vince." His name a warning.

"I told you, baby—inevitable." He reached up to brush the hair that fell in her face as her head listed forward, her breath hitching, eyes widening as he tucked it safely behind her ear.

"Vince," she tried again.

His thumb caressed her cheek as he pressed his forehead to hers, effectively closing them in their own private bubble.

"I keep telling you." He stretched his thumb out to stroke across her bottom lip, groaning as her tongue brushed it. "All you have to do is let me in."

Her eyes flared, the moment growing heavy.

Not wanting it to scare her, his mouth hitched into one of his signature smirks, popping out the dimple in his left cheek. "Then you can start to fall in love with me."

Just because he used a joking tone didn't take away from how much he meant it, but it was enough to have Holly releasing a small giggle.

His free hand traveled down her arm, linking their fingers together.

Each and every time they touched, her body responded beautifully.

Even now, he could feel the twitch of muscle as his thumb stretched out to trace patterns on her thigh. His fingers itched to explore higher, having firsthand knowledge of just how quick he could bring her to screaming release through her clothes.

He had to shift in his seat to hide the evidence of how much the memory of her coming against him affected him. The people around them were his family, both by blood and by choice, they did not need to witness the steel rod pressing against his zipper.

"Come on, Sean, check his ass." Chance Jenson, one of Ryan and Jake's teammates, yelled, popping their bubble like a needle.

Vince faced the ice again, looking down to where Sean was battling it out for control of the puck along the boards

"Umm…I'm not sure how youth hockey works back in *Canada*"—Gemma's tone bespoke of the animosity the two shared—"but here in America, there's no checking."

"I *know* that, Princess. I'm just cheering our boy on," Chance retorted.

"Whatever you say, Rookie."

No one knew why the two of them were so hostile, but whenever they were within five feet of each other, they got along like oil and water. Or more like a match to kerosene.

"Go, go, go," Jake cheered as Sean got a breakaway and headed for the other team's net.

"Pass it to Carlee," Ryan yelled. "Pass it."

Without looking, Sean deftly passed the puck to where Carlee waited to the left of the net, earning himself an assist as Carlee lit the lamp with a goal.

Their entire section was on their feet, cheering like it was the game-winning goal of game seven of the Stanley Cup.

During the first intermission, the girls went on a hot chocolate run.

"So that's her, huh?" Jase nodded toward the doors the Covenettes disappeared through.

Vince followed his line of sight as if he could see Holly on the other side of the concrete wall.

"Yup."

"Still no progress on the date front?"

"Not an inch." He ran a hand through his hair in frustration, adding to the messy style. "I know it has nothing to do with attraction. We have that in spades...it's just..." He tried to find the right words to explain. "She's scared."

They watched the Zamboni clean the ice for the second period.

"I think you're right." Jase's voice broke him out of the hypnotic trance of watching the ice resurfacers drive in calculated circles. "She definitely *wants* you. But sometimes that's not enough." He leveled him with a look. "You know what you have to do, right?"

He shook his head. Of course he didn't. If he did, they would already be dating.

"You're gonna have to call in reinforcements."

Jase's eyes tipped up with his smile as he watched the realization of his words sink in.

Sonofabitch. He meant The Coven.

"Time to bend the knee, bro."

It took everything in him to remember this was his best friend and it wasn't his fault he was right. If anyone could help him convince Holly to agree to a date, it would be the girls and whatever voodoo magic he swore they used to get people to do what they wanted.

They'd earned their name for a reason.

They were going to give him so much shit.

Sonofabitch.

Chapter Twenty-Four

Another week passed, and Vince was still dateless.

He saw her daily at EP. They talked. They joked. They had bi-weekly self-defense lessons.

If they were out with the squad, they sat together, his thigh pressed to hers or his arm around her. Still—no date.

With the calendar creeping closer to Thanksgiving every day, he thought it might finally be time for him to take his best friend's advice and seek out help from The Coven.

Just the thought of humbling himself to some of the most important women in his life made him drop his head on the matted floor underneath him while he cranked out a super-set of pushups.

They were *never* going to let him live this down.

He knew from talking to his sister earlier that Holly wouldn't be joining them for their girls' night because she already had plans with Kyle and Lyle.

Chest burning, arms shaking, he pushed through the last hundred pushups in the set, mentally working out his strategy for winning them over to his side and praying to God, or whoever was listening, that whatever he came up with worked better than what he had when it came to Holly.

When his arms felt like overcooked fettuccine—no spaghetti references for these guns—he dropped to the mat, rolling onto his back to stare into the ceiling lights as he caught his breath. It didn't matter how in shape you were, super-sets were built to kick your ass. If you weren't completely gassed by the end, you were doing it wrong.

"Vin, don't just lay there. Get your ass up and stretch out those muscles before they get cold." His sister, ladies and gentlemen, always pushing him farther.

Because he wasn't an idiot, and because he didn't need any of the Covenettes mad at him before he threw himself at their mercy, he did what he was told. Clasping his hands behind his back, he pressed his palms together, straightening his arms until he felt the pull across his pectoral muscles.

With training done for the day, he and his two roommates, Ray and Deck, drove back to The Hightower. Since his meals were regimented down to the hour, he opened the fridge for a container of the venison chili Gemma and his Aunt Hope were famous for, along with a portion of brown rice. While his meal heated, he munched on pre-cut veggies. Gemma made sure their meals were as grab-and-go as possible.

Once he was showered, dressed and fed, he headed out with the same trepidation one would feel when preparing to face the firing squad.

Okay, so yeah, he was being dramatic. The Convenettes were amazing, and after they spent an appropriate amount of time giving him the shit he probably deserved, they would bend over backward to help him get the girl. Especially since they more than approved of the one he wanted.

Holy shit, did he *want* Holly.

She was funny. And spunky. She never shied away from giving him shit and putting him in his place. The only time she struggled to do so was whenever he purposely tried to ramp up her libido.

She always smelled like dessert. He never really had a problem sticking to a meal plan, but one whiff of her sugary scent and he wanted to gorge himself on sweets. Specifically the sweetness between her legs.

She was also one of the most down-to-earth people he had ever met.

Waving hello to Jimmy, the owner of The Ring, he made his way to the back of the restaurant where he knew the ladies tended to spend most of their time playing pool.

He cringed as he overheard the conversation going between his sister and Jordan.

"Hell no. I don't care what anyone says, you want the epidural. Did you really think I was pushing two kids back-to-back out of my hoohah without drugs? *Girl*, you know me better than that," Jordan advised with a laugh.

"Oh, no. I want the drugs. Give me all the drugs. Have you seen the size of my husband? I'm not trying to push out a mini Kraken without the aid of good pharmaceuticals," Rocky answered.

"And *what-ev-er* you do, *don't* use a mirror to check out the sitch down there after." Jordan feigned disgust. "Your lady bits will look like your namesake at the end of the first movie when Rocky loses to Creed. Full-on, swollen-shut eye."

"Soooo not something I needed to know, JD," Vince said, stepping up to their table.

This.

This was why the guys didn't attend Coven meetings. There were just some things men *did not* need to know about the women in their lives.

"Well, well, well, ladies," Becky called out when she spotted him. "Looks like we got ourselves a party crasher."

"What's up, Vinny-boy?" Beth asked around a swallow of beer.

He *hated* being called Vinny. He went by Vince for a

reason, damn it. But since the schoolteacher called her own cousin-in-law Dumbass on the reg, he had no hope of her *not* using the dreaded nickname.

"Ladies." He dropped a kiss on each of their cheeks, starting with his sister and Jordan.

"To what do we owe the *honor* of your company?" Skye leaned on her pool stick.

Yeah, sarcasm was strong with his friends.

"I've come to fall on my sword and throw myself at the mercy of the court, seeking parley."

See? He could play with the best of them.

"I'm pretty sure you're mixing up your idioms." Maddey looked like she was itching to take notes at his expense.

"Whatever, Tink. You're the writer of the group." He ran both his hands over his head, gripping his skull over the fitted material of his backward hat. This was even harder than he thought it would be. "I…need…your help," he finally managed to choke out.

Seven sets of eyes stared at him, blinking, no one saying a word for what felt like hours but was barely a minute, before they bent over laughing at his expense.

"Oh—my—god." Jordan got out the words in between laughs, holding the volleyball-sized bump under her shirt. "Great. Now I have to pee. Do *not* say a word until I get back." She pointed a finger at him while she made her directive, then hurried off.

He pulled out one of the empty bar chairs and settled in while the ladies went back to their pool game.

"Okay, you were saying," Jordan reclaimed her own chair a few minutes later, making a *go on* gesture with her hand.

"Like I said. I need your help."

"When you say *your*, you mean one of us individually or do you actually mean you"—his sister pointed at him—"Vincent Steele, has come to seek help from *The Coven*." She whispered the last two words as she circled a finger around to include the other six.

He took a deep breath, reminding himself he'd expected this. Hell, he deserved it, he did name them after all.

"Yes," he gritted out reluctantly.

"Wow," Rocky breathed.

"Never thought I'd see the day." Becky finished his sister's sentence like she always did. The two of them had some kind of psychic connection almost as strong as Jordan and Jase's with their freaky twin ESP stuff.

Don't even try to tell him that wasn't a real thing because he had witnessed it too many times not to believe in it.

"So, Vin...what could you possibly need help from little ol' us for?" Gemma asked with a hand on her chest.

Sometimes he hated being so close to his family. They were assholes.

Okay, they weren't, but you knew what he meant.

"Holly."

No one was surprised by his admission.

"And what is the problem with the pretty baker?" Beth asked, sarcasm dripping from her words. She was a dangerous addition to the group. *Damn Gage*. "She not giving you her cookie?"

"The only *cookie* of hers he better be trying to get is her vagina. He's on a strict diet otherwise." Gemma laid down the law.

"Calm your tits, Gem. Pussy is calorie-free," Becky said with an eyebrow waggle.

And people said guys were worse than girls?

"She won't go out on a date with me."

"You mean you finally met a woman who didn't fall at your Theo James-looking feet the moment you flashed her that dimple in your cheek?" Maddey dug a finger into the spot where his dimple popped out when he smiled. He wasn't smiling at the moment.

"It's because he only has one and not a matching set." Jordan winked. He'd overheard more than one conversation where she had gotten naked thanks to nothing more than a flash of her husband's perfect set of dimples. Not really a conversation he wanted to hear. No, more like wanting to bleach his brain so he could forget it.

"Can we *please* be serious for like five minutes?"

"Oooh. *Serious* Vince is here to play," Skye sing-songed. "I don't think I've *ever* seen him outside of the cage."

"You guys got jokes," he deadpanned.

"Payback's a bitch, huh?" Gray eyes that matched his own sparkled at him as his sister mimicked his tone.

"Alright. Let's play nice." Jordan brought them around, the eternal mother of the group.

"Question." Beth raised a hand like one of her students. "Have you tried *asking* her on a date?"

He nodded. "Yeah. A lot. Every time she's bugged off. She's scared, and it's keeping her from saying yes, even when I can tell she wants to."

"So cocky," Skye tossed out, earning herself an elbow from her best friend.

"What do you mean you think she's scared?" Jordan asked.

He shrugged.

"I take it if you're coming to us, you want her for more than a night or two?" Maddey asked.

Now for the crazy part.

Was he really about to admit his feelings out loud? As he took in the expectant faces surrounding him, he made the decision, that yes, yes he was.

"Yeah...I was thinking more along the lines of forever."

And it's all your fault for filling my head with all your romantic mumbo jumbo, he thought as he watched Maddey's ice blue eyes widen so far they were at risk of falling out of her head.

The girls did that thing where they communicated with each other silently before turning to face him again.

"We'll convince her to go out with you tomorrow night. You just worry about how you're gonna woo your girl."

His girl.

He liked the sound of that. He liked it a lot.

TWENTY-FIVE

Coven Conversations

From the Group Message Thread of The Coven

YOU KNOW YOU WANNA: YO! Roomie…you've been holding out on us.

YOU KNOW YOU WANNA: *GIF of Ricky Ricardo saying "You got some splainin' to do" to Lucy*

PROTEIN PRINCESS: Seriously…you HAVE been holding out on us.

MAKES BOYS CRY: I need ALL the information.

MOTHER OF DRAGONS: *GIF of girl crying out "TELL ME"*

THE OG PITA: Don't hold back.

• • •

QUEEN OF SMUT: The dirtier the better.

ALPHABET SOUP: Well maybe not TOO dirty. It is my brother after all. I don't want to have to bleach my eyeballs.

ALPHABET SOUP: *GIF of Phoebe Buffay saying "OH! MY EYES!! MY EYES!!!"*

YOU KNOW YOU WANNA: Party pooper.

MOTHER OF DRAGONS: *GIF of Steve Buscemi toasting with a teacup "I hear you, sister"*

SANTA'S COOKIE SUPPLIER (Holly): Do I even want to ask what the hell you guys are talking about??

YOU KNOW YOU WANNA: Ummm…about you and Vince.

SANTA'S COOKIE SUPPLIER: What about me and Vince?

MAKES BOYS CRY: *finger point emoji* *ok sign emoji* *eggplant emoji* *donut emoji*

• • •

MOTHER OF DRAGONS: *facepalm emoji* Can't take you ANYWHERE Skye.

SANTA'S COOKIE SUPPLIER: I AM NOT having sex with Vince.

THE OG PITA: Why not? Have you seen him?

THE OG PITA: *GIF of Theo James looking broody*

THE OG PITA: *GIF from a promo shoot of Vince smirking while hooking his thumbs in tiny fighting shorts*

YOU KNOW YOU WANNA: If the guy wasn't practically my brother I'd climb that boy like a monkey does a tree.

ALPHABET SOUP: Really Beck?! Do I need to leave this conversation?

PROTEIN PRINCESS: *string of squirrel emojis*

MOTHER OF DRAGONS: Gem is right. Can we focus on the topic at hand before I have to pee again for like the 92708364892376 time today?

ALPHABET SOUP: *GIF of girl saying "Girl, same"*

. . .

MAKES BOYS CRY: I'm never getting pregnant. So NOT glamorous *praise hands emoji* thank you IUD *praise hands emoji*

MOTHER OF DRAGONS: Famous last words Skye.

MAKES BOYS CRY: I think you've more than covered procreation in our friendship for the time being bestie of mine.

MOTHER OF DRAGONS: Damn my husband for being so hot and making such cute babies.

PROTEIN PRINCESS: Can we focus here people? Holly still has to tell us why she WON'T go on a date with our boy.

QUEEN OF SMUT: Don't even try to say you're NOT attracted to him. Because girl...we could ALL get pregnant from the sexual tension surrounding you both when you are together.

QUEEN OF SMUT: *GIF of girl going to sit in a refrigerator to cool off*

SANTA'S COOKIE SUPPLIER: ...

YOU KNOW YOU WANNA: Oh no you don't.

PROTEIN PRINCESS: Anyone else in the mood for coffee?

Chapter Twenty-Six

Holly ran a hand over her hair, smoothing out any flyaways before continuing on to do the same to her top, wondering how she let the girls talk her into actually accepting Vince's date invitation.

This was a mistake.

A big, seven-tiered wedding cake mistake.

She'd been doing a piss-poor job of keeping her distance. She couldn't even keep him out of her kitchen, how the hell was she supposed keep him out of her heart?

She blamed Beth and that damn GIF she sent of Vince in all his fighter glory for finally giving in and accepting the date.

Those oiled-up muscles.

The full arm sleeve of tattoos.

The way his thumb tugged on the waistband of those tiny fighting shorts, teasing the viewer into thinking they would get a peek at what he had going on below the belt. It was a lot. She'd felt it pressed against her numerous times.

Then there was that devil-may-care smirk he gave the camera.

And finally, that dimple.

That *goddamn* dimple.

There was a better chance of Santa giving up milk and cookies than there was of getting her to admit how much time she spent watching the three-second clip since it was sent.

When the girls finally left her in peace after convincing her to agree to *one* date, her first response was to think up ways to get out of it. She was so far away from being in the place where she should be dating that her internal GPS couldn't find a signal.

But before she could power up the shields around her heart, Vince was there, leaning against the doorjamb like always, arms crossed, sweaty t-shirt clinging to his body, illustrating every one of the lickable muscles underneath.

How the hell he managed to look like sex-on-legs in the middle of what had to be a grueling workout, she had no idea. All she knew was seeing him there, gray eyes shining like silver, both that smirk and dimple out and proud, her clit was jumping up and down in her pants like Buddy The Elf yelling "Santa! I know him."

She had a *Frozen* cake to finish, and he had to adhere to Gemma's regimented meal plan, so a casual night out of drinks was the plan.

Casual was good.

There wasn't as much pressure with casual.

Yet things with Vince felt anything but casual.

If they really were casual, why did she spend so much time stressing over what to wear? Raised by people where the word *casual* was considered more offensive than certain four-letter words, cocktail dresses and high heels were the standard.

She tugged the hem of the white silk shirt layered underneath a thin, black, three-quarter-length sleeved sweater, thinking if her mother could only see her now, preparing to go out on date in leather leggings and classic black and white Chucks—Xanax would be needed.

Fiddling with her shirt, she moved to leave only to find Vince watching her from the doorway.

Her panties nearly caught fire from the molten look in his mercurial eyes as they ran down her body in a slow perusal of appreciation.

"Hi." Her voice squeaked like a prepubescent boy.

It was almost indecent how he filled out the dark jeans, or how he took a simple henley shirt and made himself the poster child for forearm porn with the sleeves pushed up to his elbows. And that backward hat.

Oh, Christmas tree, he's gorgeous. Oh, you wanted my panties? Here just take them, my bad boy.

"Hey, Cupcake."

Gah! Why did the nickname sound so filthy coming from his mouth?

"Are you ready?" He didn't move from his perch in the doorway.

"Yup." She studied him carefully. "I just have to grab my purse. Did you want to come in?" She waved a hand, indicating the bedroom.

He shook his head.

"Why not?" She tilted her head.

"Holly, if I take one step inside this room, I will be spending the night buried so deep inside you, you won't know where you end and I begin." His voice was guttural. "As much fun as that *will be*." His cocky swagger should grate, but it didn't. Like usual, all it did was turn her on more. "I'd rather spend the night getting to know you, and *not* in the biblical sense."

Ever the gentleman, Vince held the car door open, taking her hand in his as they walked inside The Ring. He wanted somewhere they could talk without the pressure of sitting across from each other while making idle conversation.

They were met with a wall of sound as they stepped inside the main dining area, the entirety of the left side taken over by a massive oak bar with a crazy number of beer taps and a wall of liquor bottles stacked taller than she was. There had to be over a dozen sixty-five inch TVs in the main room alone, all either playing a hockey or basketball game.

They continued past booths and tables, through a room with four billiards tables, and into a sectioned-off back room with a wall dominated by a movie theater-sized projection screen and spaces for air hockey, foosball and darts.

It was love at first sight. This was the type of place she should have been spending her early twenties in, not the country club she used to frequent on a weekly basis.

"Pick your poison." Vince gestured to the games around them.

"Poison? Isn't that what you usually say when asking someone what they want to drink, not what game they want to play?" They shed their coats, Vince hanging them on a hook on the wall.

"It is." His arm went around her shoulders, pulling her into his side as they made their way over to the open air hockey table she indicated, the smell of fresh soap and pine making her heady. "But you may get venomous when I kick your ass."

"Oh, so sure of yourself, Muffin." He let out a snort. "How do you know I'm not an air hockey savant?"

"Are you?" One black brow lifted.

"No." Her palm wrapped around the nub of the striker, her fingers curling under the protective plastic ridge on the sides. "But doesn't mean I'm going to *let* you win."

Feeding quarters into the game, the air blew out of the tiny holes along the surface of the table, the plastic disk dropped down, and the battle was on. The first game Vince crushed her, throwing his arms up in victory, running around the table in celebration in a very unsportsmanlike manner.

She was rolling her eyes at his ridiculous celebration when he hooked an arm around her middle, pulling her in for a quick but thorough kiss.

While they played, they talked. It amazed her that they still had things to learn about each other after hanging out almost every day.

It was a night of random facts.

He and Jase were the reigning hot dog eating champions in the group's Fourth of July competition, and she knew the episode names for all two hundred and thirty-six episodes of *Friends*.

They jumped right in to game two but were interrupted periodically by people stopping by for an autograph or a selfie with Vince.

"I'm sorry." He was adorable, grabbing the back of his neck, looking down and toeing the floor with his gray sneaker. She should be focused on his apology but she was distracted by the popping biceps against the seam of his shirt.

"Huh?" she asked in a lust-dazed stupor.

"I said I was sorry about all the interruptions. When I planned tonight, I was thinking more of how low-key this place is, but forgot about how I sometimes get recognized more when I have an upcoming fight."

He wasn't bragging. If he had been, she would have been turned off, but he spoke as if stating a simple fact.

"It was actually fun to watch you interact with most of them. You're really good with people." With his personable demeanor, it didn't come as much of a surprise to see he was a natural with his fans.

"Thanks." Again he grabbed the back of his neck as he gave her a sheepish grin. "It doesn't get old. I'll never forget the first time I was recognized, it was so fucking cool."

"Tell me about it?"

"It was here." He pushed in the quarters needed to start their third game. "We were sitting over there." He pointed to a section of pub tables across the room. "I had graduated a few months before and started doing the fighting thing full-time."

He dropped the plastic disc on the table and sent it sailing in her direction, using the conversation to distract her from defending.

She huffed as she retrieved it from the slot on her side of the table. Not wanting to give up any more gimmes, she held onto it while motioning for him to continue.

"It was Ryan's first season with the Blizzards. We were all here to watch one of his away games." His eyes got a faraway look in them as he got lost in the memory. "So this guy—Eddie was his name—comes up to us, looking so green I thought he was going to puke."

"Nerves?" She couldn't hold back a giggle at the picture he painted.

"Yup." He flashed that damn smirk as he nodded. "To be fair, we were here with like *half* the Titan hockey team, so we made for an intimidating group."

She could understand that. But within five minutes of a person talking to any of them, all those feelings melted away. They were quickly becoming the family she never felt she had.

"So, my man Eddie goes, *Are you Vince Steele* and I'm like *yes*, all questioning and skeptical like."

"You mean you were sarcastic? *Gah,* that's *so* hard to believe."

"You're one to talk you know that right, Cupcake?"

Why do I like it when he calls me that so much?

After staring moony-eyed at each other too long, he gestured for her to drop the disc.

"What happened after you tried to kill Eddie with sarcasm?"

"Hi, Pot. I'm Kettle." Vince stretched his hand across the table.

It was this, his goofiness and ability to not take things too seriously that made the crushing weight of her family, their expectations, their demands lift.

"But let's see…oh, yeah." He snapped his fingers with the memory. "So Eddie is still standing there, staring, not saying a word. And I'm like, *Spit it out, bro, I don't bite.*" He braced himself on the edge of the table, those drool-worthy forearms flexing. "But, for you, Cupcake." He leveled her with a searing look. "I can't make the same promise."

Sweet reindeer games, that smile spells trouble.

"Eventually, Eddie told us how he recognized me from one of my undercard fights—fucking surreal."

"Did you offer to give him an autograph?"

"No." His response surprised her. It didn't fit with the humble man he'd been all night. "Wait—I mean I *did* give him an autograph. But the first thing I did was hug him. Almost took him to the ground I was so enthusiastic."

Now that was the Vince she knew.

The focus shifted back to their game where he kicked her butt again.

"I still say you cheat." She pouted as he looped his arms around her middle, crossed his hands at the wrists, resting them on the top curve of her ass.

"How's that, Cupcake?"

"You're best friends with a hockey player. He must have rubbed off on you or something."

There were the tiniest flecks of blue that sparkled in his eyes when he laughed. His deep chuckle rumbled through where their bodies touched.

"Oh, honey. I can gua-ran-damn-tee that neither Jase nor *any* of the other puck heads have *rubbed* off on me."

"Eww." She thunked her head against his chest. His rock-hard, *can I lick one of your toffee colored nipples* chest. "*So* not what I meant."

"I know. Besides…" He bent to speak in her ear. His warm breath sent a fresh bolt of electricity down her spine. "I'd much rather rub against you, seeing as it was so much fun the first time."

Her entire body flushed at the memory.

"Come on, Cupcake. Let's see if you're any better at darts than you are at air hockey."

VINCE STOPPED to grab a set of darts from behind the bar, before rejoining Holly in the alcove by the boards. With her back to him, he took a moment to admire the way her legs looked encased in her leather leggings, a little disappointed her shirt got in the way of him paying proper respect to her spectacular ass.

Only a few hours into their date, everything he had been feeling had been confirmed and solidified. It might be a cliche and it made him feel like one of Maddey's romance heroes in real life, but he was falling hard and fast for the pretty baker.

Turned out, finding a woman he wanted to bring home for family dinner wasn't the hard part. No, it was actually convincing her they were meant to be.

Good thing he never backed down from a challenge.

Ever.

"All right, Cupcake." He spoke as he came up behind her, wrapping an arm around her body to bring her back flush to his front. He was so much larger that when he spread his hand, it covered her entire stomach. "Let's see how good your aim is."

Over the course of their time together, he had gradually ramped up the amount of physical contact they had. With her history, he knew he pushed her limits, but she never shied away.

She tipped her head back onto his chest, her cognac and purple hair fanning out as she tried to meet his eyes over her shoulder.

She was so fucking beautiful he could look at her all night without saying a word.

"You're a *real* charmer, Muffin. Did you know that?"

God, the mouth on her. It was witty and delicious and looked like it was made to be wrapped around a dick. His dick in particular. That precise fantasy practically played on a loop while he had daily dates with Handgela since he found her hiding out in the EP kitchen.

"You're really gonna hurt my street cred calling me Muffin, babe."

"Would you rather I call you Stud?" Her lips pursed at the end of the question, and every good intention he had of waiting until the end of the night to *really* lay one on her flew out the window.

His hand coasted up her body, his palm brushing against her erect nipples on the way to cupping the side of her face. His thumb hooked across her chin, while his other four fingers wrapped around the back of her neck, keeping her in place for his mouth to drop onto hers.

She sighed at the contact, her tongue brushing along his. Everything else around him faded out of focus as he got lost in the tartness he could taste left over from the lime in her club soda. She had chosen to abstain since he didn't drink during camp.

He was on the verge of tossing her over his shoulder and carrying her back to their building like a caveman to have his wicked way. Knowing they had already skipped ahead a few rounds in their relationship a few weeks ago, he pulled away before acting on those animalistic urges. He couldn't take her to bed until he knew she was on the same page as him. Because he was in—all in.

Between the last few hours of their date, as well as the

time they'd spent recently, he had learned a lot about her. But there was still this niggling sense she was holding something back.

Something big.

Though she told stories of her and Kyle growing up, she barely mentioned the five years since they separated for college—Kyle to Princeton and her to The Institute of Culinary Education.

There was a burning desire to know all of her secrets, but he didn't want to spoil the best date he had ever been on by probing. It was a conversation meant for a later date.

They broke apart, both their breaths labored as she looked at him with the same dazed expression he was sure he wore. Not once had he experienced this raging inferno of desire for a woman, especially after just a kiss. If he burned any hotter, he'd combust on the spot.

Like a bucket of cold water, someone behind him asked if he was in fact Vince Steele. Externally he smiled and was pleasant while internally he cursed himself for coming to The Ring. Jimmy hosted fight nights whenever the UFC had a fight, he should have known there was a good chance he'd be recognized with all the promotion both the UFC and ATS had him doing to generate buzz.

It was on the tip of his tongue to apologize to Holly again, but she waved him off before he could speak, offering to take the picture so the guy and all his buddies could be in the shot.

"I appreciate the support, guys," he said as she handed back the phone. "Now you have a good night. It's time for me to school my girl in darts."

"YOUR GIRL?" HOLLY arched a brow as a shit-eating grin, dimple and all, spread across Vince's too handsome face.

"Oh, Cupcake. You know it's true. You've been mine since

the day you saved me from my sister's pregnancy cravings. Even if you haven't admitted it to yourself yet."

She swooned when he said things like that. He was so... confident. She shouldn't want him. The last thing she needed was yet another person telling her what to do.

But that was the thing about Vince. Whenever he went full-on alpha on her, she felt wanted, protected—never controlled.

And worse, he wasn't wrong. She was having so much fun on the date that she was starting to forget why she ever tried getting out of it.

Luckily, she did have experience playing darts. They settled on playing Cricket, a game focused on closing out the numbers fifteen through twenty on the board, as well as the bullseye, by hitting them three times. A player could finish a number faster by landing their dart in the double or triple lines circling the numbers on the board.

For most of the game, they were evenly matched...until Vince started playing dirty.

She lined up her next shot. She only had to hit the bullseye and the number eighteen, and the game would be hers. Then she felt the heat of Vince's body behind her, not too close, only the barest brush of fabric as he leaned down to speak against the nape of her neck.

"Don't miss, Hol." A butterfly-soft kiss. "I only have one number to close out and I win."

"Ye-Yeah...but you need all three hits of seventeen to win," she stuttered out as her eyelids lowered, luxuriating in the brief touch of his sinful lips.

"Oh, baby." His mouth tracked up to her ear. "One thing you should know about me." His hips moved in to cradle her. "*Multiples* are my specialty." A familiar bulge pressed into the cleft of her ass. "I can hit doubles and triples with you all night."

It was officially Niagara Falls in her panties.

"You talk a big game." She swallowed down the cupcake-sized ball of lust in her throat. "But it makes me wonder...is that all it is...*talk*?"

He made tsking noises with his tongue.

"Oh, Cupcake." His chuckle was pure swagger. "The *millisecond* you admit you're mine as much as I am yours, it's on."

Chapter Twenty-Seven

Holly crooned along with Rascal Flatts as they sang about being home for Christmas while putting the finishing touches on the last of the Thanksgiving orders. The cookie turkeys, pilgrim hats, pumpkins, and fall leaves had become a fixture inside the kitchen.

Vince continued his daily visits as well as her self-defense lessons. The only change to their relationship since their date was the nights they hung out together. He teased her mercilessly, whispering dirty promises of what he would do to her once she agreed to be his girlfriend.

The funny thing was, if he just *asked* her to be his girlfriend instead of *telling* her, she would accept. Like with their date, he'd yet to figure it out.

She was supposed to be keeping her distance, focusing on figuring out who she was as an individual—then maybe her future—but she couldn't stay away. He was the Santa to her Mrs. Claus, the top hat to her Frosty, bringing a sense of magic to her life she didn't think existed outside of the romance novels she loved.

"Mmm," Vince said into the curve of her neck as he wrapped

his arms around her from behind. Since their date, he took this position more than the one by the door. "Smells so good. You have no idea how bad I want to eat one of your cookies."

"Now…when you say cookie"—she picked up one of the turkeys and waved it near his nose—"do you mean one of these or do you mean my *cookie*?"

"Fuck, Cupcake." His teeth bit into the skin of her shoulder. "I get so hard when you talk dirty to me." To prove his point, he ground the rolling pin in his pants against her, making her moan in appreciation. He was an expert level tease.

He had drawn a metaphorical line in the icing on anything past second base, but damn if the guy wasn't playing jump rope with it when he teased her.

"Vince." His name was a breathy plea as her head tipped back onto his chest. The paintbrush she used for detailing clattered onto the counter.

"Oh my god. You guys really *do* have kitchen sex back here." Maddey's voice melted the sexual tension around them like a snowman in Hawaii. "Just try and keep it off the scones I love, and we'll be okay."

"Maddey!" she screeched. Of course they had never been caught *actually* having sex, but she lost count of the number of times they'd been caught canoodling.

"Madz." Vince chuckled. *He* thought it was hilarious when people caught them. "To what do we owe the pleasure?"

"I needed someplace private for my Skype call." She pointed to the open laptop in her hands as the telltale ring sounded from it. The biggest smile Holly had ever seen bloomed across Maddey's face. "What's up, losers?"

"Tink!" a chorus of deep male voices bellowed from the speakers.

"Ohmygodthisissoawesome." Maddey's words bled

together in excitement. "I *never* get to talk to all of you at the same time."

Holly pointed to a clear spot on the counter for Maddey to set her Mac on, kicking over a stool to sit on. As she did, she caught sight of three good-looking guys dressed in desert uniforms.

"Seriously, what the *hell* do you guys put in the water in this state? I don't think I've met one person you guys know or are related to that isn't hot," she observed as all three sets of eyes on the screen tracked to where she stood inside the camera's sight lines.

"Well, *hello,* beautiful," a guy with brown hair and green eyes said to her. He had to be one of Maddey's brothers because he looked a lot like Justin.

Was that a growl? She whipped around to face Vince as he stalked to her. His gray eyes were stormy as someone tried to move in on his territory. Boys could be so dumb at times.

"Guys, this is Holly. Holly, these are my brothers, Tyler and Connor, and our friend Dex," Maddey said.

"Back off, Con," Vince said to the guy on the screen, wrapping his arms around her. "This one's taken."

"Vin. Dude. Shouldn't you be training so you can kick some major ass next month?"

"Guy's gotta eat. You know Gem is just as strict as my dad is. Can't be slacking on nutrition."

"Nope. No way." Maddey waggled a finger back and forth in a no-no gesture. "You are not bogarting my phone call with my brothers. Uh-uh." She shooed him with her hands. "Go away. Go back to sexing up your girlfriend. I *never* get them all in one place and I'm taking full advantage."

For once, Vince didn't take the opening, instead keeping them so they could be part of the conversation. Maddey rolled her eyes but turned back to her computer screen, shit-eating grin still in place.

"So when do you idiots get leave again?"

Holly had a feeling her friend had more than platonic feelings for Dex. It was a hunch based on some of her books.

"I should be home sometime after the holidays," Connor said.

"Not sure when we're up. But shit can't come soon enough," Tyler answered.

"So…you going to tell us about your new friend?" Connor asked, clearly trying to get under Vince's skin. Boys were definitely dumb.

"If she's with Vince she's gotta be a member of The Coven, right?" Dex asked in a rumbly voice.

"Yup. Holly's revamping the bakery side of the business at EP and she is *ah-may-zing*," Maddey gushed, reaching for one of the discarded cookies set off to the side and taking an exaggerated bite. "*Mmm. Soooo good.*"

The guys visibly drooled.

"You're just mean, Tink." Dex's words came out as a pained moan.

"You used to be my favorite sister," Tyler complained.

"I'm your only sister, you dork. So I'm *pretty* sure I'm safe in that department."

Maddey settled in to talk with her guys, and Vince dropped a kiss on Holly's head before returning to The Steele Maker. She had to choke back laughter on more than one occasion while sorting out the last of the cookies. Her friend was a sassy one.

Before Maddey left, she confirmed Holly would still be joining the other Covenettes for the Blizzards game that night.

Who knew having friends could be so entertaining.

Holly had never been to a professional hockey game before. Her mother would say such a violent sport didn't befit her upbringing. Oh, what she wouldn't give to be able to witness

Mother Dearest's reaction when she found out her daughter was dating a professional fighter. Okay, not really, because that would mean she would have to *see* her family, but she knew it would be something like—"Oh, the *horror*."

She took immense pleasure sitting in a seat next to the boards, Jake Donovan jersey on, cold beer in one hand, a hot pretzel in the other as they waited for the puck to drop.

Heaven.

She was in heaven.

After the national anthem, Jordan and Maddey, each holding a twin, stood to have the girls stand on the ledge along the outside of the boards. She watched as Jordan and her girls shared a knuckle bump through the glass with Ryan and a kiss with Jake.

She was pretty sure the arena sighed at the adorable display.

Everyone retook their seats as the players on the ice lined up, with Ryan in the center waiting to face off for the puck drop.

Since moving in with Beck and Gem, she had watched a lot of hockey on TV, but nothing could have prepared her for what it was like to experience it in person.

It was fast. She could barely keep track of the puck as it glided across the ice, losing it more times than she wanted to admit.

It was loud. The cheers of the fans and the sound of bodies hitting each other or the crack of them slamming into the plexiglass.

It was flipping exhilarating.

Jordan's season tickets butted against the Blizzards bench, so they had a front-row seat for whenever the players jumped over the half wall of boards separating the bench from the ice.

When Ryan took a nasty hit while battling it out for the puck in the corner, Jordan, Maddey and Skye were on their feet, banging their fists against the glass. She snorted her beer through her nose at the spectacle of two girls barely over five feet totting toddlers on their hips, cursing a blue streak at the refs missing the call.

"Are you blind?"

"What the fuck was that?"

"Open your eyes, zebra."

Play stopped after the hit without a penalty being called, and Ryan skated back to the bench, one arm wrapped around his middle.

At the next face-off, Chance Jenson dropped his gloves to fight the guy from Philly who gave the dirty hit. This time all of them were on their feet, cheering him on while he grabbed the guy by the front of his jersey, laying out a quick series of punches.

"Come on, Chance."

"Knock his teeth out."

"Fight, fight."

"School his ass."

"Lay him out."

"Kick his ass."

"Yeah, Jenson."

When the referees finally broke up the fight, both players headed back to their teams' locker rooms instead of sitting in the penalty box to serve their major penalty, since there were less than five minutes left in the period.

"At least Rookie is good for something." Gemma sat down, taking a sip of her beer.

"I take it you don't like the guy?" Holly asked her roommate.

"Yeah, not so much."

"I keep telling her to just do him already. A good hate-fuck will clear him out of her system," Becky chimed in.

"Yeah...*so* not gonna happen." Gemma's tone was monotone, but there was a slight blush staining her cheeks. *Interesting.*

"I never understood why you guys butt heads so much. Chance is a good guy," Jordan said.

"Yeah, he's Canadian. It's like written in their constitution or something that they have to be nice," Skye added.

Gemma chose to ignore them, chugging the remainder of her beer instead.

"Who cares about Chance and Gem. They're old news." Rocky shifted in her seat, eyes locking onto Holly, and the glint in her eye spelled trouble. "What I really want to know is…what *exactly* is going on with you and my brother?"

She knew the question was coming. If she were honest, she was mildly impressed by their restraint. She'd half expected them to be waiting for her in the kitchen the morning after the first official date.

"We're dating?" She should maybe be more confident in that statement.

"Why don't you sound sure of the fact?"

She blew out a breath, trying to marshal her thoughts. "What I mean is…he treats me like a girlfriend and he calls me his. But…" She scowled at her beer bottle, not sure if she wanted to admit the next part or not.

"But…" Rocky prodded when she stayed silent.

"Buthewon'tsleepwithmeuntilwe'reofficial." Her words came out in a rush of embarrassment.

Her friends collectively lost their shit. Doubling over in guffaws of laughter, wiping tears from under their eyes, both Rocky and Jordan claiming they now needed to pee. When they finally managed to compose themselves, conversation resumed.

"Oh, Vin." Rocky shook her head. "What does that mean? Official."

"I guess he's waiting for me to say I'm his girlfriend."

"Wait," Rocky held up a hand. "I thought you said he calls you *his*?"

"He does."

"Doesn't that make you his girlfriend?"

"No," Holly stated.

"Why not?"

"Because." Now she was the one chugging her beer. "He hasn't actually asked me. He's *told* me I'm his girlfriend, but he hasn't asked."

"Oh, Vin."

"Boys are dumb," Becky declared.

"Amen," Holly agreed. "Still, I'm the one who gets teased and turned on, only to be left hanging."

"Ahh," Rocky said knowingly. "He's leaving you with blue clit."

"Blue clit?"

"Oh, yeah. It's a thing. Guys like to think they're the only ones who can suffer from the affliction, but it's not true. They have blue balls, we have blue clit."

"I love it." She nodded enthusiastically. "But, yup, blue clit is a daily occurrence for me. I've gotten to know the shower massager in your old shower *really* well," she admitted.

"Girl, I feel you." Maddey held out her beer to toast.

"If he's drawn it out this long, I think he needs to ask you in a big way. Like…promposal big," Skye said.

"Oh my god." Rocky facepalmed. "Don't go giving him *any* ideas. You know he, Jase and Tucker would take the idea and run with it. They'd end up going viral."

"It'd be good PR," Skye said offhandedly.

Like a can of worms being opened, the debate continued with topics tumbling over each other as they changed.

Girls nights were the best.

Chapter Twenty-Eight

T hanksgiving was one of Vince's favorite holidays. It was a day dedicated to eating and watching football —what wasn't to love about that? Nothing.

But...

Since he was in the middle of *the* most important training camp of his career, he had to abstain from most of the goodies he usually gorged himself on if he wanted to make weight in six weeks. Yeah, first world problems, cry him a river and all that.

Aside from forgoing his favorite pies, the day at his parents was fun as always. Both Gage's and Wyatt's parents flew in from California to join them, and the Jameses rounded out the Steele/Reese crew perfectly. His sister really did good in her choice of life partner.

He'd debated inviting Holly to join them but ultimately didn't. The Steele family dinner he knew was in their future would be bad enough, he didn't need the added pressure of a holiday.

Instead he let his girl spend the day with the Samsons, settling for picking her up on the way home. And, yes, she was his girl—if only he could get her to admit it.

"You guys ready to go?" he asked Gemma and Becky. They would be riding back with him to The Hightower, while Rocky and Gage hung back to spend more time with the Jameses.

"Yup," Gemma answered cheerily.

"Take us home, driver." Becky placed a chauffeur hat on his head. Where the fuck did she get it? It was no surprise they called her Trouble.

It was another ten minutes before they were done saying their goodbyes and could leave, him proudly wearing his hat as the ladies sat in the backseat for the drive to the Samsons.

Holly would get a kick out of the hat, so he left it on, angling the brim to sit off-center.

Lyle's turquoise eyes were a bit glazed when he opened the door. "Well, *heelllloooo* there, handsome." His words had the barest hint of a slur to them.

"Hey, Ly. Happy Thanksgiving." They shared their standard complicated handshake as he tried to peer around Lyle's shoulder. "My girl ready?"

"*Oooooh,* I *love* hearing you call our Sweets *your girl.* Give me a minute while I swoon over here." He fanned himself with a flourish.

"Muffin!" Holly cried when she spotted him in the entryway, throwing herself at him and wrapping her arms around him in a tight hug. Thank god for his fast reflexes, otherwise her very nice ass would have been on the ground. "Happy Turkey Day."

He assessed her, the whiskey hue of her eyes swirling.

"Hey, Cupcake." His lips tipped up as he took in her 'Finish the turkey and bring on the fat man' sweater. The cartoon drawing of a turkey dinner wearing a Santa hat was so her.

"I like your hat." She flicked the brim.

"Thanks. I wore it just for you."

"Really? You did?"

He didn't, but the way her eyes lit up at the thought, fuck if he wasn't taking the credit for Becky being a smartass.

"Of course." He looped his arms around her, keeping her close. "Anything to see my girl smile."

She pulled back so she could look him in the eye. "Am I?"

"Are you what?" He wasn't following her tipsy logic.

"Your girl?"

"I told you, baby. You've been mine since that first day at EP."

Thinking she was too cute for school when her face scrunched in confusion, he knew he was further gone for her than even he realized.

"But…I'm *not* your girlfriend."

"Of course you are. *You're* the only one who refuses to use the label."

"You never *asked*." She attempted to level him with a hard stare, and the glazed look in her eyes lessened the impact of it, but not the words. *Shit.* Was that the issue?

"Are you telling me this last week was because of semantics?"

She stepped back, folding her arms over her chest. "It may be semantics to you, but to me it's important. I've spent my whole life having—and letting—people tell me what to do. I'm done with being bossed around."

There was a dirty comment in there. Thankfully, his common sense kicked in before he made it.

"So you're saying"—he reached out to smooth the little v that formed between her brows—"if I had said, *Hey, Cupcake. Will you be my girlfriend?* You would have said…"

"Yes, you big idiot."

He cleared his throat. "Hey, Cupcake. Will you be my girlfriend?"

"See…was that really that hard?"

"I'll show you hard." He couldn't resist that one. "But you didn't answer the question."

"Yes." Then softer, "You big idiot," and buried herself against his chest.

"Oh, shoot." Lyle's voice broke in, reminding him they had an audience. "I should have been filming that. You two are rom-com gold."

"Ly," Kyle admonished, coming down the hall. "Leave the kids alone."

He accepted Holly's wool peacoat from Kyle and helped her slip into it, tugging the lapels up to protect her neck from the cold front that had moved in. They said their goodbyes, and with his girlfriend tucked under his arm, he ushered her to the car.

Tickled by the chauffeur facade, Holly ignored the front seat and settled herself in the back to the great delight of the two delinquents he already escorted.

If the strength of his feelings wasn't enough to tell him she was made for him, the way she clicked into The Coven like the missing puzzle piece would have sealed the deal.

The girls sang along with the Christmas music playing on the radio, even carrying on the last lines of "Jingle Bells" when the *Glee* cast was silenced as he turned the car off.

"Come on, ladies." He chuckled as he herded his tipsy charges to the elevator, content to listen to them babble while holding his girl.

The elevator took them to the twelfth floor without making any stops, and he was back to prodding the chattering females along.

The boisterous laughter cut off when they noticed the door to 12A was cracked open. Though they tended to have an open-door policy when they were all home, they locked up when not.

"Stay here." His voice brooked no room for argument as he went to the door to his own apartment, hoping Deck was home and that was the reason their door was open.

He tried the handle—locked. Keys in hand, he unlocked the door, calling out for Deck, only to be met with silence.

"Get in here and wait for me to check out your place." He was quick to shut down any argument, the subject not up for debate. The hell he would allow them into the apartment until he knew it was free of intruders, and there was also no way he was leaving them out in the hall where they would be vulnerable.

Once he had the girls safely tucked into his apartment— behind a locked door—he slowly eased open 12A, every defensive instinct on alert.

Nothing seemed out of place, the open concept layout allowing him to see the kitchen, dining room and living room in one sweep.

Stepping inside, he started with the closets closest to the door. He might be paranoid, but the apartment was home to some of the most important women in his life. There was a better chance of Gemma letting him eat an entire pumpkin pie than there was of him allowing them to step one toe inside without him checking every nook and cranny.

He checked Gem and Beck's rooms before moving toward Holly's down the opposite hall. Nothing odd stood out.

When he stepped out of her ensuite, he noticed the bushel of holly in the middle of the bed.

She gave a whole new meaning to the Christmas spirit.

Chapter Twenty-Nine

There was a pit the size of Connecticut in Holly's stomach as they waited for Vince to get back from checking out 12A. She wanted to believe—like Tinkerbell needed viewers to believe to live—that one of them just didn't shut the door all the way when they left that morning, but she knew for a fact they had not only shut it, but locked it.

For the first time, the three of them sat together without saying a word. The anxiety in the room was palpable.

What felt like hours but was probably only minutes later, the door opened, and Vince stepped inside.

"Vin? Everything check out okay?" Gemma asked.

Without a word, he stalked across the hardwood, squeezing the breath from her lungs as he lifted her from her seat and pressed her tightly to his body. His warm, hard, shaking with lingering tension body.

"Buffen." His nickname came out all garbled with her face buried between his pecs.

She didn't feel him relax until he buried his face in the crook of her neck and inhaled a deep lungful of her scent.

"Is everything okay?" she asked when he let go.

"It is. I just need a minute after..." His words trailed off as they let the heavy go.

"Okay then." Becky clapped her hands and jumped from her stool. "More wine."

"Because you didn't have enough earlier?" Vince finally grinned.

"Never!" All three girls echoed together.

"You know." He shifted them back to the island but kept an arm around her waist. "You really do take your Christmas cheer to levels even I didn't realize."

"What do you mean?" Holly asked.

"You keep your namesake in your room."

"My namesake?"

Maybe she shouldn't have any more wine because he wasn't making any sense.

"The bushel of holly on your bed, and Christmas season doesn't even officially start until tomorrow."

Everything inside her froze at the words.

They found her.

It was a warning.

Without a doubt, Vince was going to have questions. Questions she didn't want to answer.

"What did you say?" Her voice went as cold as the ice flooding her veins.

"No offense, babe. I just think it's funny, it's a little hotelish—you know, flowers on the bed and stuff."

"Holly?"

"Yeah. That was a cute touch. Though I thought the berries were red? I've never seen it with the white ones before."

White berries?

White berries.

Mistletoe.

It was worse than she thought.

This wasn't a warning, it was an outright threat.

Mistletoe was poisonous to animals. She'd learned that the last time she tried to stand up to her father and her dog paid the price.

No, she wouldn't think about that now.

Leaving something behind delivered the message that they knew where she was. That something being mistletoe was their twisted way to let her know the lengths they would go to if she didn't do what they wanted.

Vince's arms turned to steel bands around her the longer she stayed silent. His eyes were the color of rolling thunder clouds in a storm as he watched her. He could probably tell something wasn't right.

"Umm...what's wrong?" Deck asked as he entered the apartment.

"Someone broke into our place."

"What?" Deck asked.

"Hold on. What?" Vince asked.

"I don't keep holly—or in this case, mistletoe—on my bed. Someone put it there."

Vince reared back, and her body instantly chilled from the loss of his touch.

"It's fine, Vince."

"The *fuck* it is." He raked a hand through his hair, sending the blue-black strands in a million chaotic directions. "Someone *broke into* your apartment and left mistletoe on your bed. That is the *opposite* of *fine*."

If she thought he was shaking earlier, he was practically vibrating now. She'd witnessed his alpha side more times than she could count. This was something different.

Something primal.

"Please." She wanted to reason with him.

His tumultuous thoughts were written clearly across his handsome face. It almost made her break, but this was too important to allow that to happen.

. . .

VINCE HAD NO idea how to even begin to process this information. Holly's tone lacked any emotion, like she was shutting herself behind every one of the walls he had managed to break down brick-by-brick.

How was she so calm? She had just told them someone broke into her place like she would say it was raining outside.

Needing her to anchor him through the torrent of emotions rocking through him, he looped his arm around her middle, pulling her into his side. The thought of an intruder in her home enraged him.

"I think it's time to talk to about that stuff you've been avoiding," he said.

The five of them spread out in the living room. Vince pulled Holly onto one of the leather recliners, keeping her tucked tight against him. He rubbed her thigh with one hand, the back and forth motion meant to soothe the nerves radiating off her body, while playing with the ends of her purple-tipped hair with the other.

"Cupcake." He was the first to break the heavy silence of the room, his heart cracking at the fear swimming in her honey-colored eyes. "Talk to us."

She shook her head vehemently.

He thumbed away the lone tear leaking from her eye, leaving his hand there to cup her face. She nuzzled against it, seeking comfort in his touch.

"Baby." He switched from his usual playful nickname, hoping it would show her how seriously he took the situation. "You're going to have to let us in if we're going to help."

It was like her entire body collapsed under the weight of her sigh. No one spoke as they waited for her to find the resolve to give them a peek behind her curtain.

"How much do you guys know about Kyle and his family?" Her question was not what he expected.

"About as much as we know about yours," Becky

answered. "That you both come from wealthy families, with big wallets and small minds."

Holly's lips tipped up, giving the first hint of a smile.

"Yeah, that's a pretty accurate description actually." Another heavy exhale. "Kyle's full name is Kyle Samuel Huntington the Third."

"Huntington?" Gemma asked.

"Like the hotel chain?" Deck added in the question.

"Yup," Holly nodded glumly. "Before he was disowned for falling in love with a man"—she rolled her eyes—"he was the heir to the Huntington Hotels fortune."

"Holy shit," Becky breathed out.

"That's some serious coin to walk away from," Deck said.

"Yup." Again it was like Holly's answers were on autopilot.

"Okay." He squeezed her side. "But what about *your* family?"

He hadn't pushed her to tell him to tell about her past, though he wanted to learn everything about her. He had a hard enough time convincing her to actually date him, he wasn't risking his chance at building a relationship with her by pushing too hard. It was a testament to his self-control because his instincts had screamed at him to find out more about who abused her.

"So…umm…Kyle and I became friends because our families obviously run in the same circles." Her gaze dropped to her lap, staring blankly at where she systemically cracked each of her knuckles. The *pop-pop* rang out like gunshots in the eerily still room. "My name isn't Holly Vander," she said and quickly backtracked. "Well, it is, but…my full legal name is Holly Meredith Vanderbuilt."

"As in Vanderbuilt Pharmaceuticals?" Vince asked.

"The one and the same." Her voice was small, almost like a wounded animal.

"Okay." Becky made a rolling motion with her hands.

"Help me out here. What's the connection to"—she circled a finger—"all this?"

"My father…is…controlling. He will do *whatever* it takes to get his way."

Vince didn't like this—at *all*. He came from a family that loved and supported each other in all things. They would die to protect each other, so it was hard to fathom a parent *purposely* hurting their child.

"The mistletoe is his sick way to ruin my favorite holiday. He's showing me he knows where I am and that he can get to me anytime he wants. But he wants to play with me first. Mind games are his specialty."

"What aren't you saying, Hol?" He needed all the information if he was going to keep her away from those trying to hurt her and where she belonged— by his side.

"About a month ago…I…ran away. Packed my car with whatever it could hold and drove away."

"But you don't have a car," Becky pointed out.

"No, not anymore." Holly continued to speak without making eye contact with any of them. Looking at the floor, the wall, anything but them. "When I left…I drove to straight to Philly. Kyle and Lyle met me there, loaded my stuff in their car, helped me arrange a tow truck to send my car back, and brought me home with them."

"Why Philly?" Gemma asked.

"I didn't want to run the risk of them tracking me here through the GPS in the car. I even sent my phone back with my car when I ditched it. Fat lot of good it did though, since they obviously found me. Not sure how much longer I'll be able to stay before they come to bring me back themselves."

She slumped in his arms like the plug was pulled on one of those blow-up Christmas lawn decorations, resigned to her fate.

Fuck that.

"You're not going *anywhere*." His words were guttural.

"This is your home. You belong here." He hooked a finger under her chin, pulling her face around until her eyes met his again. "Baking at EP. Hanging out with your fellow Covenettes. And most importantly"—his thumb ran back and forth across her bottom lip that was swollen from her biting it —"*with* me."

Holly was *his*. He'd be damned if he'd let anything or anyone hurt her.

Her family fucked with the wrong person. He didn't earn a reputation for being one of the toughest fighters to step inside the octagon by being a quitter.

He was a fighter. He protected the ones he loved.

And Holly.

She was quickly becoming the thing he loved above all else.

No touching the gloves here.

This was a good old-fashioned cage match.

Bring it on.

Chapter Thirty

When the unexpected drama of the night wound down, Vince knew there wasn't a chance in hell he was letting Holly out of his sight for the fore-seeable future.

Now to broach the topic of her staying at his place for the night—their first *ever* sleepover. He didn't want *any* of the girls sleeping across the hall.

"Why don't you girls stay here for the night."

"Yeah, we didn't think Holly would be staying in her room," Gemma said. "But we'll get together for breakfast in the morning. We have some serious online shopping to do if we want to take advantage of Black Friday deals."

"No, Gem." He wasn't sure if his cousin misunderstood what he was saying or if she was being purposely obtuse. "I mean all *three* of you should stay here for the night. Ray's gone for the weekend, so you two"—he pointed to both her and Becky—"can share his bed."

"Oh, Vin." Becky walked over to pat him on the chest patronizingly. "This whole alpha thing you have going on lately might work with your girlfriend"—her green eyes flicked to Holly before returning to him—"but it doesn't fly with us."

He shared a knowing look with Deck, grinding his molars. *Why couldn't they* ever *make things easy?*

"Hey, Hol," Deck said to gain her attention. "Would it be cool if I crashed in your room tonight?"

He had never been more grateful for the decades' worth of friendship and the ability to read each other's minds. As nice as it was going to be to hold Holly in his arms all night, a part of him would have been worried if the others stayed by themselves across the hall. He didn't want anything getting in the way of his first sleepover with his girl. He wanted to be fully present in the moment, not stressed over if his loved ones were safe.

"You guys are ridiculous you know that, right?" Becky said as Deck put his arm around her shoulders and headed for the door.

"Humor us, Beck. Besides...I've always wanted to be invited to a slumber party." He caught his friend waggling his eyebrows suggestively, not surprised in the least when Becky elbowed him in the gut.

"Does that mean we get to paint your nails?" Becky batted her eyelashes at Deck.

"Whatever you want, Beck." It was the last thing they heard behind the snick of the door shutting.

He strode to the door, flipped the lock, and followed with the deadbolt for good measure. He'd lock the door to his bedroom too, but the best protection if anyone tried anything would be him. His hands were literally registered as lethal weapons.

"Come on, Cupcake. I think we've had enough excitement for the day. Time to Netflix and chill."

Some of the sparkle had returned to her eyes when she peeked from underneath his arm. "Does that mean you're finally going to make good on all those promises you've been making?"

"We'll get there, baby. But I meant it more in the literal sense for tonight. You and I both need some time to decompress after everything, and I can't think of any way better than holding you in my arms while binge-watching some mindless TV."

He meant every word. Plus it wasn't like it would be a hardship to have her soft curves pressed against him.

Once they were locked securely inside his room, he pulled one of his old BTU t-shirts from a drawer, the cotton soft and well-worn, and flicked on the television screen hidden inside the mirror on the wall above the dresser.

"Do you want a pair of sweats or anything?" He handed over the shirt he was sure she'd be swimming in.

"No. This is fine." Then, in a move he wasn't expecting, her arms crossed at the waist, lifting her sweater up so inch-by-inch the creamy skin of her torso was revealed, before neatly folding the garment and placing it on the dresser.

She calmly went through the motions, as if she were getting ready for bed any other night. He stood there trying to not swallow his damn tongue as her fingers flicked open the button on her skinny jeans, peeling them down her legs, uncovering the panties that matched the deep plum bra barely restraining the generous globes of her breasts. His mouth watered at the absolute perfection standing before him.

Unaware of how his dick now wore the imprint of his zipper, she pulled his shirt over her head, the hem of it falling past mid-thigh. Enthralled, he didn't move an inch as both arms went behind her back, unclasping her bra, and pulling it free from her body through the armhole of the shirt. Jesus, that move was incredibly sexy.

"Do you have a side of the bed you prefer to sleep on?" she asked as if she didn't strip mostly bare in front of him.

"You take the right side." His voice was gruff when he shook himself from his lust-filled stupor. He usually slept on the right, but he'd be damned if he wouldn't be the one closest to the door.

He pointed to the slim black remote on the nightstand. "Why don't you find us something to watch while I get ready for bed."

He disappeared into his bathroom, needing a minute, or ten, to get his dick under control so he wouldn't be popping a tent worthy of Woodstock when he came out in his boxer briefs ready for bed.

THE ADRENALINE FROM finding out her family had discovered her location was mixing with the raging case of lust Vince inspired whenever he was near, coming together in a volatile mixture.

Holly had never really be an overtly sexual person, yet the primary fantasy running on a loop in her brain was what *could* have happened if they weren't interrupted the day they were caught dry humping against the oven in the kitchen.

Vince was turning out to be the complete opposite of everything she'd been conditioned for her entire life.

He was a genuinely happy person. He never put on airs or faked his affections. If he liked a person you knew it, and if he didn't, there was no hiding it.

He was big and strong yet never used his size to hurt or intimidate. Not once did he make her feel small or like she was less than him. She only ever felt protected in his presence.

He was quick to lay claim to her, but it wasn't as if she were a trophy or used as a method of control. Whenever he called her his, it was with a tone of pride rather than possession. He also didn't hesitate in declaring he was as much hers and she was his.

Remote in hand, she slid between the cool—*are those Batman?*—sheets, and scrolled through the Netflix app for some mindless television. Spotting *Friends* in his continue watching queue, she pulled up her favorite sitcom, knowing the show so well it'd be easy to block out when things took a turn for the naughty. Because she had *zero* intention of actually chilling in a bed with Vincent Steele.

Hell to the no.

The faint sounds of running water cut off, and she lifted her eyes to watch the closed door, waiting for him to reappear. Thoughts of what he wore to sleep ran the gamut from a pair of adult-sized footie pajamas to his birthday suit, and she hoped it would end on the more naked end of the spectrum.

So when his form filled the doorway clad in only a pair of Superman boxer briefs, it came as no surprise that her lady parts stood up and cheered. She swore her nipples waved themselves like maracas and her clit pounded out a beat like a bass drum. The GIF of him in his fighting shorts and the countless other images she brought up on Google had *nothing* on Vince Steele in person.

Every.

Single.

Inch.

Of.

Cut.

Male.

Perfection.

On.

Display.

She wanted to slather him in frosting just to lick it off each bump and ridge of defined muscle.

"How are you real?" she asked as he continued to stand there, letting her take her fill.

"*Whatever* do you mean, Cupcake?" Mr. Funny Man

smirked, popping out his dimple, knowing exactly what she meant.

"It's like you're a real-life Photoshop image."

She couldn't see one flaw on his entire six-foot four-inch frame. From the top of his messy blue-black hair to the tips of his sexy bare feet—yes, even his feet were sexy, that's how flipping good looking he was—he was the epitome of male perfection.

Why he wanted her, a runaway debutante baker who couldn't cook without wearing half the ingredients, when he could have any girl he wanted by simply breathing, she had no idea, but you weren't going to hear any complaints.

"You really know how to stroke a guy's ego, babe." He lifted the covers, slid in next to her, reaching to cuddle.

She didn't give him what he wanted. Instead, she shifted to the side, sitting cross-legged on the bed, peeling back the covers until they rested at his hips, eyeing up his sculpted torso. From what she understood, he still needed to cut weight to be eligible for his fight, but she couldn't see a spare ounce of fat on his body.

His six-pack was so defined it looked like one of those plastic ones costume stores sold for Halloween when people wanted to be dressed like muscled superheroes. Then there was her, a girl who never met a cookie or cupcake she didn't like. Her stomach was flat and she knew the curves she did have looked fabulous in haute couture, but she didn't have *muscles*.

She walked her fingers up the length of his arm, tracing along the outlines of the superhero emblems on her trip up to the ball of his shoulder. Each inch of his skin from wrist to shoulder was covered in colorful ink, the most prominent piece being the Superman "S"-shaped crest at the top of his arm. Each symbol inked onto his skin was made to look like it was pushing its way out of his body, tearing through his flesh to be seen.

It fascinated her to no end how much a guy who had such a brutish profession was such a kid at heart.

He didn't limit himself to only the male heroes either. Mixed in with the famous bat and spider symbols, was the double W representing Wonder Woman as well as the star and banner of Captain Marvel. Then again, he was one of the guys proudest to admit the Convenettes were the leaders of the pack.

"You really have a thing for my ink, huh?" His eyes tracked the movement of her roaming fingers.

"Do any of you not have ink?" she asked, thinking of all the tattoos she had seen on her friends. Most of them had large pieces decorating their bodies.

"Hmm," he paused in thought. "For awhile Jake didn't have any, but that changed after the Olympics. Now they all have the rings across their inner arms." He lifted her right arm and stroked a finger along the spot he mentioned, the light touch tickling the sensitive skin where her biceps and triceps met.

"Isn't that a painful spot?"

"Oh, yeah." He gave a rueful grin. "The arm in general is painful. Most people don't realize it, but there are a lot of nerves that, even when the needle isn't directly on them, can radiate the pain elsewhere."

"But your *whole* arm is done." Her eyes went wide as she scanned over the ink again.

"It's 'cause I'm a badass, babe."

"And so humble."

Gah! How did he manage to be both boyishly charming and panty-meltingly smoldering? It was completely unfair to the entire female population.

"Then as you know, all the ladies have the mark of The Coven." His thumb ghosted over the spot where her wrist met her hand under her thumb, the same area the girls had a miniature witch hat tattooed. It was their own version of a best friends necklace.

A part of her wondered what it was like growing up with so much support, in both the form of the family by blood and the family they chose. The only person she ever had that she could rely on was Kyle, and for the last five years, she'd even lost a bit of that. Her friend really had earned a permanent spot on Santa's Nice List by dropping everything and helping her get away from her father.

"You're not scared of needles, are you?" His question caught her off guard.

"No why?"

"Because needles are how they do tattoos. So if you were afraid it would make things way more complicated when you go to get your own hat."

Her heart skipped a beat at the thought of being a permanent member of The Coven. She wanted it more than she wanted anything else in her life—current half-naked man excluded—unfortunately, it wasn't in the cards for her. As made evident earlier, her past had come a-knocking. It would only be a matter of time before it came barreling back in like a battering ram.

"Hey." He pushed up onto an elbow, his thirty-seven abdominal muscles rippling with the action, as he stretched a hand out to push her hair behind her ear. "Where'd you just go?"

She let out a breath, shoving those thoughts away to deal with another time.

"Nowhere. Long day, I guess."

"Well, then. Lay down and let's watch some *Friends*."

That wasn't the activity she had in mind. Unsure how long she'd be able to keep him, she wasn't going to waste another second not making the most of their time together.

"No. That's not what I want to do."

"Oh-kay." He drew out the word, confused. "You picked

Friends, but we can watch something else if you want." He spoke like a man used to dealing with impulsive women in his life. And she guessed he did.

She cast a glance at the sitcom playing on the flat screen. The episode was one of her favorites, where the girls lost their apartment to the guys on a bet, but she was sure the cast of six wouldn't hold a candle to Vince on top of her—naked.

"What I meant was...I don't want to watch TV. There's something else I'd much rather do in this bed right now."

The silver of his eyes darkened to a deep charcoal at her words. Then without giving him a chance to argue, she gripped the hem of the t-shirt she wore, pulled it from her body and dropped it off the side of the bed.

Chapter Thirty-One

Vince's eyes instantly went to Holly's boobs.
Seriously, could you blame him?

One, they were boobs.

Two, the movement from removing his shirt caused them to jiggle.

And three, they were boobs.

Okay sure he was repeating himself on the last one, but he was a guy and well—boobs.

He wanted to reach for her.

Hell, he *needed* to reach for her.

To pull her against him.

To roll her beneath him.

To taste every inch of her mouth-watering body.

To discover if every part of her tasted as good as the sample he had weeks ago in her bedroom.

The same bedroom where her own *fucking* family left a threat. Because that's precisely what it was. A threat.

And threats toward the woman he was falling in love with, well…that was *unacceptable*.

This was what had him holding back from acting on his

impulses. She'd faced one hell of a shock, and he didn't want to take advantage of her in a vulnerable state.

But...*fuck* if it wasn't hard, and he wasn't talking about the steel rod in his boxer briefs. Haha. See what he did there? So punny.

For real though, she was the most gorgeous thing he'd ever laid eyes on. Her skin was creamy white, a contrast to his own darker olive complexion, with freckles and the larger and darker beauty marks decorating the canvas of her body, tempting him into playing connect the dots with his tongue.

Those breasts he couldn't take his eyes off of were enough to fill his bear paw-sized hands and were topped by pale, petal pink nipples. Nipples currently standing at attention, begging for him to suck.

She still wore her plum-colored panties, the lace cover teasing him with only the barest glimpses of her sweet center. One he quickly discovered was waxed bare, and he wanted the chance to spend *hours* dining on all things Holly.

His Holly.

His girlfriend.

His Cupcake.

She claimed he was Photoshopped, but she was the one without flaws. His hands had the scars every fighter bore from hours upon hours of hitting things. There were other professional scars decorating his body, and his left ear had the mildest case of cauliflower ear from his years wrestling, the cartilage at the top folded over ever so slightly.

But Holly—she could have stepped off of the pages of any centerfold. The way her hips flared out from her narrow waist made him want to flip her over, grab on and bury himself balls deep from behind. Her ass was perfection. He could spend all day watching it as she wiggled it to and fro dancing around and baking. And if he didn't have to train, that's exactly how he would spend his days.

By the time his eyes made it back to her face, she was worrying her bottom lip between her teeth. That would not do.

"You…are the most beautiful thing I have *ever* laid eyes on." He pushed up, looping an arm around her waist, pulled so her nipples kissed his as he pressed their bodies together. "I could look at you all day and never get bored."

"You can't mean that." She looked down.

"The *fuck* I can't," he growled. No one. Not. One. Single. Person. Would put her down. Not even herself. "You are perfect for me, so that makes you perfect. Don't *ever* doubt that."

HOLLY BLINKED, TAKEN aback by the ferociousness of Vince's words. The gruff way he spoke them lent a seriousness, but it was the molten look in his gray eyes that broke the last of the walls she kept between them.

She was done.

The last thing she needed was another man in her life to tell her what to do, yet here she was, falling in love with Mr. Alpha himself.

She'd tried.

She'd tried so damn hard to keep him away and keep her heart safe.

That was an epic fail.

Because the longer she looked into those irises that swirled like a hurricane, she was pretty sure she was tipping over the edge from falling into fallen.

She was so screwed.

Hopefully more than just a figure of speech.

They leaned in, mouths meeting in a heated kiss, his tongue wasting no time tangling with hers. His hand pressed her side, and she straddled his lap, lining up her cha-chaing clit to ride along the erection poking out of the top band of his boxer briefs.

She ground down, the lace of her panties a useless barrier between them, her lips parted to hug his cock. Pleasure sparked through every cell of her body as she dry humped him like it was an Olympic sport.

Her eyes fluttered shut, and she tangled her hands in his messy mop of hair, as he raked his teeth down the side of her neck, across her collarbone, before *finally* tracking lower to suck a nipple into his wet mouth.

His hands coasted down her body, coming to a stop at her breasts, cupping each one in his massive hands, fingering the nipple not currently in his mouth with his thumb.

"*Vince.*" His name a broken plea as her head fell forward to rest against his. He moved from one nipple to the other.

"You taste so fucking good, Cupcake." His words sent another arrow of pleasure through her body as they vibrated around her nipple.

Back and forth, she rolled her hips.

The mushroom cap-shaped head of his dick was almost purple as it leaked pre-cum onto the bottom packs of his abs. The confirmation of his pleasure was all it took to push her over the cliff into her first orgasm.

"That's it, baby. Let go." He released her nipple with an audible pop, swallowing her moans as he crushed their mouths back together.

While she rode the wave of orgasm, he flipped their positions as easily as he would roll over in bed, and not at all like he was supporting her full weight. His strength was a major turn-on. Then again, *everything* about him seemed to turn her on.

"That was one," he said, holding himself above her with his elbow. His fingers curled around her head, the tender way he touched her at odds with the carnal need pulsing between them. "Now let me show you what I can do when there's not a pair of leggings between us."

The sheets rustled as he moved down her body, tracing the map laid out on her torso to the lacy edge of her panties. Panties he would find completely drenched.

"These are pretty," he said before the sound of fabric tearing filled the room as he ripped them from her.

"Vince," she cried.

"Sorry, baby, but I need your cunt right *fucking* now, and they were in my way."

She *hated* the "C" word but forgot all about it when he traced the seam of her lips with his fingers before plunging two inside.

Her back bowed off the bed, and another moan rang out.

"That's it, baby. *God,* you're fucking tight."

She clutched the sheets as he worked her over hard and fast with his fingers.

In.

Out.

His thumb moved to bump her clit with every thrust into her.

In.

Out.

Swirl over her clit.

In.

Out.

He hit her clit once more, and she was on orgasm number two, more intense than the first.

She tried to muffle the sound of her cries with her hand, but Vince was quick to pull her hand away. "Hell no, Cupcake. I want *all* your pleasure. No one else is here to hear you. Don't deprive me of your sweet sounds."

Without warning, he adjusted himself further down the bed and buried his face between her legs.

The fingers that had stilled while remaining buried inside her resumed their pumping as he sucked her clit into his mouth, dipping into her pussy like it was the most delicious pie.

"Fuck, you taste even better than I remember."

And holy shit, his tongue was as wicked eating her out as it was at tossing out dirty talk.

She grabbed his hair, taking fistfuls of it until she was screaming out in orgasm number three.

"Holy shit." She breathed out as he kissed his way back up her body.

"I'm not done with you yet, Cupcake."

Was this guy for real? She didn't think it was possible for her body to handle any more pleasure. She was boneless.

"I-I don't think I can come again, Muffin."

"Oh, yes, you can." His lascivious smile promised more than his words. "I'm not from the hockey camp. I don't stop at the hat trick."

He slid until he was off the bed, hooked his thumbs in the waistband of his boxer briefs, dropped them, and wrapped his hands around her ankles to pull her toward him.

"Now, it's time for me to show you why there's a Stud before my Muffin."

Holy hell. If the three-peat of orgasms didn't already prove it, there was a good chance she wasn't going to survive the night.

But what a way to go.

THE TASTE VINCE had gotten of the nectar between Holly's legs weeks ago was nothing compared to drinking directly from the source. She was so fucking sweet she should probably be banned from his meal plan.

Like he'd ever let *that* happen. He planned on feasting on her as often as she let him—preferably daily.

He had her with his fingers, his mouth, now time to fuck her the way he'd been fantasizing about since that first day at Espresso Patronum.

He had her off the bed, in his arms, legs wrapped around him, and pressed against his bedroom wall in seconds. He couldn't remember anything feeling as good as his dick sliding through her wetness as she ground against him, and he wasn't even inside her yet.

As his eyes closed in an effort to not come like he was fifteen again, he was struck by *why* it felt so good. She wasn't the only one bare. He had forgotten to grab a condom. *Shit.*

"Shit." He thunked his head onto the wall beside her.

"What's wrong?" Concern laced her tone. "Am I too heavy? Shit, I don't want to hurt you while you're in training. Put me down." She smacked him on the shoulder repeatedly.

She was hilarious.

"Yeah, it's not that, Cupcake. You're barely my warmup weight." He couldn't help but chuckle. He had a naked woman in his arms, wrapped around him, pressed against a wall, dick zeroing in on the landing zone, and he was laughing. Only his Cupcake could do that to him.

"Then what's wrong?"

"I forgot to grab a condom."

Her eyes widened as if only realizing it herself. Her lower lip turned white as her teeth bit into it. He used his thumb to free the abused flesh from her worrying.

"Hold on." He repositioned his arms around her to carry her with him.

"No, wait." She placed a hand on his chest to stop him. He raised a questioning brow. "I…" She hesitated. "I have an IUD, and"—he watched as her throat moved with her swallow—"and I'm clean. I've been tested."

Shock almost had him dropping her. That was *not* what he was expecting. At all.

He'd never been inside a woman without a rubber before.

One, not ever really dating anyone seriously, he would never take the risk. Two, piggybacking off of reason one, it was hard to trust that a girl wasn't trying to trap him into a free ride. He may not be a champion yet, but Jordan and Skye had certainly made sure he was the highest-grossing non-title-holder in the UFC. And third, he'd never wanted to, but, *fuck*, did he want to with Holly.

"Are you sure?" He had to ask.

"Yes."

"I mean, I'm clean too. I've never *not* used one, and fighters have to get tested all the time with how bloody the sport can be."

"Vin." Her hands came up to cup his face between them, her thumbs tracing figure eights along his cheekbones.

And yes, he had cheekbones, and they were fucking fantastic, thank you very much.

"Do you honestly think I'd even be considering this if you weren't? Not once since I've met you have you ever done anything to put me at risk. Why would I think this would be any different?"

She killed him. Her unadulterated trust almost brought him to his knees.

He shifted so her shoulders were anchored to the wall while her weight rested on his lower body. He buried both hands in the waves of her hair, fingers tangling in the strands, and claimed her mouth the way she claimed his heart.

With a swivel of his hips, his now weeping dick slid through her slickness and pressed its way home inside her. She was tight. So tight if he hadn't stretched her out with his fingers he'd be worried he was hurting her.

He pulled back slightly before pressing in a few more inches.

Again he pulled away until only the tip was inside, plunging back in, not stopping until he was seated inside her to the hilt, using gravity to aid his progress.

The breath whooshed from his lungs like he'd just taken a hit in the ring.

Her pussy gripped him like a vise, barely letting him pull out enough for his thrusts. He felt each ridge and vein of his cock drag along her inner walls.

Her head fell back as he pushed back inside, his mouth automatically finding the soft spot where her neck met her shoulder, sucking and biting her skin as he pumped inside her.

In.

Out.

A suck and a bite.

In.

Out.

Her moan.

His groan.

In.

Out.

Her pulse pounded like a drum as he continued to lave attention against the pulse point. He was sure her pale skin would easily bruise, and his inner gorilla beat his chest like he was Tarzan thinking of her walking around with *his* mark on her.

In.

Out.

"Fuck, Cupcake. I'm gonna come," he growled into her neck.

"*Vince.*" His name was a keening cry, and he felt the telltale flutters of her pussy as she came around him, soaking his balls as they emptied themselves inside her.

Wall sex. A good idea? Yes.

Wall sex. A bad idea? Also yes.

Why, you ask?

Well, he came so hard his knees were weak—which he'd

never thought was really a thing—and he also felt like he was about to blackout from acute pleasure.

Sex. Had. Never. Felt. Like. That. Before.

Only with Holly.

His Cupcake.

Fuck if he wasn't going to marry the girl someday.

Chapter Thirty-Two

Vince woke up before his alarm like every day during training camp. It was both a blessing and a curse.

With his arms wrapped tightly around Holly, he took a moment to inhale the sugary scent he'd come to crave. He forced his mind to stay in the moment and enjoy the feel of the warm, naked woman in his arms rather than think about what happened or what he learned last night.

Right now, all that mattered was Holly was there and officially his. He'd claimed both her mind and body, now all he needed was to claim her soul. Not in a creepy, *sell your soul to the devil* sort of way, but in the way she had claimed his. She was his soulmate, and it was time to prove he was hers.

He eased his arm from beneath her body, and gingerly made his way out of bed, slipping into a pair of basketball shorts, then headed to the living room.

Though it wasn't an official training day, thanks to the holiday, he didn't have any true days off during camp.

A few sun salutations to warm up, and he grabbed the jump rope from the storage cube in their entertainment center.

Earbuds in, he started with an easy pace, steadily hopping heel-to-heel as he lazily spun the rope around his body, keeping it steady for the almost seven minutes of Ed Sheeran's "Make It Rain" before increasing his tempo when it switched to 5SOS's "Youngblood."

Flick-flick-flick went his wrist as he whipped the vinyl cord faster and faster around his body.

No more easy heel taps, instead his toes barely touched the ground before lifting into his next quick jump.

Jump-jump-jump-jump.

Faster and faster.

Sweat coated his bare chest as he increased his speed.

Whip-whip-whip.

He reached the peak of his workout, the rope slicing around twice before his feet touched the ground. The song came to an end, the rope halted, and he paced in a small circle to bring his heart rate down from the pounding staccato he'd worked it into.

Movement in his peripheral caught his attention, and he whipped around, still on high alert from the night before, only to relax when he saw Holly watching him from the hallway.

Dressed in his BTU t-shirt.

Only his BTU t-shirt.

Bare legs on display.

Lust filled her eyes as they greedily scanned him from head to toe. His cock stirred awake at her inspection, rising to full mast when her tongue peeked out to swipe across her bottom lip.

He pulled out his earbuds.

"Morning, Cupcake."

"Morning, Stud Muffin."

He crossed the room, pulling her in, not giving one fuck that he was a sweaty mess. He'd clean her off *real* good in the shower. "Ooooh, full title this morning." He bent to drop a quick kiss on her mouth.

Her lips lingered in their pucker for a few seconds after he pulled away, tempting him to go in for another.

"I think after last night, you earned it…at least for today." Her tone was confident, but she blushed.

Damn right. He made her come eight times last night.

"I'll take it." He kissed the tip of her nose. Nudging her back toward his bedroom, the sound of a key turning in the front door had them both spinning around.

His muscles tensed and she went rigid as they waited to see who it was, last night's events still fresh in their minds. He shifted around, shielding Holly with his body. Any threat would have to go through him.

As if in slow motion, the door pushed open, and the breath he wasn't aware of holding whooshed from his lungs as his sister strode into the apartment still in her Ninja Turtle pajamas.

The door remained open, and like clowns exiting a clown car, the rest of his friends filed in behind Rocky. Gage first, never far from his pregnant wife, then the girls from across the hall and Deck. He was surprised—not sure why given how close they all were—to see the rest of the Covenettes closing out the parade of their squad.

So much for spending a quiet morning alone with my girl.

Like they did every time they saw him, the Donovan twins ran straight for him cheering "Bin, Bin, Bin, Bin" on the way. He loved those girls something fierce.

"Olly," they both squealed, each having trouble pronouncing the H in his girl's name. Lucy attempted to kamikaze dive out of his arms to Holly, his quick reflexes the only thing keeping her from taking a header and him having to face the wrath of her dad.

"Hey, Lu." Holly beamed as she reached to take the child

from his arms, mouthing the word *earrings* when he arched a brow at her knowing who she was taking.

"Bin ucky." Lacey smacked a hand to his sweaty chest, shaking it in the air, face scrunched up in disgust.

"No, Lay. Not yucky, it's awesome." He blew a raspberry against her neck.

"Ucky, ucky," Lacey screeched, pushing to get his sweaty head out of her face. He might cringe at how his mom asked him *all the time* when he was going to settle down and give her grandbabies, but he sure as shit loved kids.

Holly was in the middle of listening to an intense story about crime-fighting turkeys—almost-two-year-olds and their imaginations—and it was the first time the thought of a family dinner was something to look forward to. Because let's be honest, he knew there was a Steele family dinner on the horizon.

"Lu, Lay," Jordan called out to her kids. "Come here so Uncle Vin can get ungross and Aunt Holly can put some pants on."

Holly blushed at the reminder of her half-naked state. "Aunt Holly?" Her voice strangled with emotion.

Jordan gave her a *do you even have to ask* look. "Yup. All Covenettes are aunts. You're part of the family. Sorry to tell you this, but you're stuck with us for life."

"Yeah, no take-backs," Rocky agreed, and if he didn't already love his sister with all his heart, that right there would have done it. She was speaking for so much more than just The Coven, she was doing it for the Steeles as well.

Now to prove to Holly he was also playing for keeps.

After the fastest shower known to man, Vince found Holly waiting for him in his bedroom, looking adorable swallowed up in his shirt and joggers. She needed to roll the waistband over more than once to keep from walking all over them.

"Do you have any idea how beautiful you are, Cupcake?" He didn't miss the way her eyes tracked over his bare chest and down to the white towel knotted around his waist.

The way she looked at him made him grateful for every minute he logged training at The Steele Maker.

"Umm...I have bedhead, no makeup, and I'm swimming in your clothes...yeah." She made a scoffing sound in the back of her throat. "Real beautiful."

It killed him how she couldn't see she was perfection, absolute perfection, and it had nothing to do with her looks. He closed the distance between them, cupped her face between his hands and brought his forehead down to touch hers.

"If I can only accomplish one more thing this year, it wouldn't be winning the belt next month." He shook his head. "No...it would be proving to you once and for all how utterly perfect you are in my eyes. Anyone who doesn't agree can go fuck themselves because they are *wrong*." His eyes bore into hers. "Perfect." The last word was an impassioned plea as he captured her mouth with his, not pulling back until she melted into the kiss.

"Good." He took in the dazed expression on her face when he straightened, needing to stop before he said screw their friends waiting in the living room and screwed his girl-friend instead.

He dressed in a pair of sweats and a Blizzards t-shirt since his boys were playing that afternoon, took Holly's hand, and went to join the rest of their motley crew.

It looked like they called *everyone* because Sammy and Jamie were playing pool with Maddey and Becky while Kyle and Lyle rushed Holly, sandwiching her between them in a group hug.

"You okay, Sweets?" Lyle asked, holding her out at arm's length.

"Yeah, I'm okay." He liked that she looked to him as she answered.

"How do you think they found you?" Kyle wrapped an arm around her shoulders.

She shrugged. "I have no idea. It doesn't matter, they figured it out. What's done is done."

"Actually," Jordan cut in, breaking from her conversation with Justin. "I might."

She had an almost guilty expression on her face, which didn't make any sense. Linking his fingers with Holly's, he led them both to the open recliner in the room, pulling her down to settle across his lap, while they tried to untangle the events of the last twelve hours.

"Hold on," Gemma cut in handing him a bowl filled with steel-cut oats, fresh fruits and chopped nuts. "Eat this."

"Aye-aye." He gave his usual salute. "What's going on, JD?" he asked around a spoonful of oatmeal.

"I think I know how Holly's family figured out she was in Jersey."

He ran a soothing hand along Holly's thigh when she tensed. He understood why the topic caused her stress, but he'd be damned if they would actually get close enough to hurt his girl again. Not a fucking chance.

"Can you stop dragging things out? That's Beck's style, not yours. Spit it out already, because not gonna lie...you're kinda freaking me out with your face right now."

Jordan's hands flew up to her cheeks. "What's wrong with my face?"

"Oh...you are so lucky Jake has a day game today because Brick, would kick your ass for that, Vin," Skye taunted, sticking up for her bestie.

"Oh, don't start, Red," he said, unconcerned with the threat. "You know it wasn't an insult."

"Oh, yeah?" Becky was never able to resist stirring the pot. "How is one *supposed* to take a comment like that? *Please*, enlighten us."

He heard Gage snort, only to have his brother-in-law hold up his hands in surrender as if to say *you're on your own and I'm glad I'm not you right now* when he shot him a dirty look.

"I mean," he started, shooting daggers at Nick and his not helpful gesturing—"you look unsure of yourself, and you're *never* unsure of yourself, JD."

It was Jordan's turn to snort. "Yeah, right. But if that's what you want to believe, don't let me stop you." The smile she gave him told him she wasn't offended in the least by what he said and their friends were just being their usual smartass selves. "So yeah...this is what I was referring to."

He took the phone she offered, the latest meme featuring the girls at a Blizzards game on the screen. In the picture, the now eight Covenettes, plus the twins, were standing and caught in various stages of yelling at something happening on the ice. There in the middle of it all was his girlfriend, looking a little wide-eyed at what was happening around her. He couldn't blame her—those girls got vicious if anything happened to one of their guys, and Ryan had taken a nasty hit during the game.

Holly leaned into him, resting her chin on his shoulder while she looked down at the phone, her hand rising to cover her mouth as she saw herself immortalized in meme form.

"If I had known you were trying to stay out of the public eye, I would have *never* suggested you come to the game."

Holly sought out Kyle, the two sharing a silent exchange before she returned her attention to Jordan. "No. The game was the most fun I can ever remember having."

"Hey." They had gone on a few dates leading up to the hockey game, and they were hella fun, if he did say so himself.

"Present company excluded." She ran a thumb along his

jaw. "I'm done running. I didn't know a life like this existed. I'm not giving it up just because my family doesn't approve."

He was so damn proud of her.

THIRTY-THREE

Counterfeit Coven Conversations

**From the Group Message Thread of the Boys— AKA
Counterfeit Coven Conversations**

DAUNTLESS SUPERMAN (Vince): Ok. We need to come up with a plan for what to do about Holly's family. There is NOTHING I like about this situation.

THE BIG HAMMER (Jase): You know I got your back bro.

BIG DECK (Deck): Same.

CAPTAIN AMERICA (Ryan): *GIF of Captain America strapping his shield onto his back*

THE BOONDOCK SAINT (Nick): *GIF from *The Boondock Saints* of the guys sitting in a car saying "I'm strangely comfortable with it"*

. . .

THE GREEN MONSTER (Damon): *GIF of *The Boondock Saints* lighting up their cigarettes together outside*

THE SEAL DEAL (Justin): Just keep it "legal"

THE KRAKEN (Gage): Just make sure your sister won't want to kick my ass for it.

HUGE HOSE (Wyatt): *GIF of guy pointing up saying "THIS."

HUGE HOSE: But for Beth, not Rocky.

THE FEROCIOUS TEDDY BEAR (Griff): *GIF of waving grizzly bear*

THE BRICK WALL (Jake): I take it this isn't a Coven sanctioned mission?

JUST RAY (Ray): You know we give the girls shit for texting when they are together…

BIG DECK: Well not all of us are together so it's ok.

. . .

WANNA TUCK (Tucker): Why do I have to be so far away? I wanna kick some ass.

ROCKSTAR MAN (Jamie): I might have an idea.

DAUNTLESS SUPERMAN: Sammy…NOT A WORD to Madz.

THE SPIN DOCTOR (Sammy): *GIF of Genie from *Aladdin* zipping his lips into a zipper.*

DAUNTLESS SUPERMAN: Glad to have you onboard, Jame.

CAPTAIN AMERICA: I knew I liked you for a reason.

THE BIG HAMMER: Agreed… knew we let you into the group for a reason.

WANNA TUCK: Yeah… he's a ROCKSTAR.

THE SPIN DOCTOR: Or… Uh… you know… my husband.

DAUNTLESS SUPERMAN: Let's plan.

Chapter Thirty-Four

Holly cranked up the speaker volume, belting out the words to "This Christmas" with Christina Aguilera. She needed something to take her mind off life and focus on the Ninja Turtle cake she was making. At her current rate, she would be at the shop well after closing.

It had been a week since the creeptastic break-in at her place, and she hadn't been able to shake the eerie feeling of being watched. She told herself there was a better than likely chance her family had hired someone to keep tabs on her whereabouts, cataloging her comings and goings, but hadn't spotted anyone that fit the bill.

The feeling of unease only went away with Vince. He managed to do the one thing she never thought possible after coming face-to-face with her old reality—he made her feel safe.

She wasn't naive enough to think her family was done with her or that they would fade quietly into the night. She'd been avoiding most discussions about her family, wanting to stay a resident of Denialville for as long as possible. She knew she had important things, *crucial things,* to figure out if she was going to remain free from their clutches.

That was a problem for another time. For now—she had a cake to decorate.

The cake was baked, a delicious death by chocolate, filled with fresh cannoli cream with both mini milk and white chocolate chips. The baking itself didn't take long, even when mixing things from scratch. It took longer for the layers of the cake to bake than mixing up ingredients. The time-consuming part—and her money-maker—was decorating. Cutting, shaping and creating the pieces out of fondant was what took her hours, if not days, to complete.

Each layer of the cake was trimmed, the crumb layer of frosting laid down as a base for the fondant. The eight-inch round she'd prepared for the bottom layer was waiting on the island.

She brushed hair from her face, smiling at the glimpse of purple tips she allowed Lyle to convince her to get. She wondered if whoever her family sent to find her took pictures. Diana Vanderbuilt would shit a brick—metaphorically of course, because ladies didn't poop *insert eye roll here*—if she saw that not only had she chopped off the locks to just above her shoulders, but that she was being lowbrow by putting such a blasphemous color in it.

Her mother, ladies and gentlemen. She gave new meaning to *stuck-up elitist bitch*, among other terms.

Taking the container of fondant she'd sectioned out for the bottom layer, she dumped it out onto the counter. As she kneaded the fondant to warm it up and make it more pliable, her mind wandered to the wicked things Vince did to her in bed the night before. If she wasn't sleeping at his place, he was crawling into her bed, usually with a pleasurable way of letting her know he was there.

The frustration of her situation bled into her movements as she used more force than necessary to roll out the fondant to the proper thickness. She didn't like the uncertainty of what her family planned hanging over her head. Honestly, it straight up pissed her off. They'd showed their hand with the mistletoe message, now they were toying with her like a cat would a mouse before killing it. She didn't like it. Not one bit.

Each day she spent with Vince, the more certain she became she was in love with him. Though he didn't say the words, she suspected he felt the same. It was in the way his steel gray eyes turned molten as they looked at her from across a room, or the way he always found an excuse to touch her. She expected to feel smothered, but didn't.

Not once did he try to control her, or make her feel like she needed to check in with him. If he asked what she was up to or what her plans were for the day, it wasn't so he knew where she was at all times, or because she needed his approval, it was because he wanted to see her, not keep tabs on her.

There was no pomp and circumstance to it. It wasn't to put on a show, to say *look at my pretty trophy, be jealous of our perfect relationship.* She knew firsthand how deceiving looks could be. She'd lived it and had no plans of ever going back to that way of life.

Trimming the edges of the rolled out fondant to the correct size, she draped it over the rolling pin to position it on the cake.

She set to work on the tedious task of pulling, tugging, and smoothing so the fondant lay flat without any bubbles or creases. She wanted to focus on it and not what it would cost her if her family got their way.

Family, in her experience, was a four-letter word. But not the way the people here did it. Family *meant* something to them. It stood for so much more than the standard definition.

When she escaped, she drove away from millions of dollars, and yet now, as a baker in a town in the middle of New Jersey, she had so much more to lose.

She linked her hands behind her back, bringing her elbows together to stretch out after being hunched over for so long. She needed a break before starting the intricate detail work of the actual design.

"Hey, Sweets." Lyle held out a coffee to her when she made it out front.

"Hey, Ly." She gratefully accepted the mug. A quick sip revealed it to be an eggnog latte, his holiday creation and one of her favorites. Starbucks had nothing on Lyle's barista skills.

She spotted Maddey tucked away in her usual corner by the window and headed that way. It was still surreal that one of her favorite authors was quickly becoming one of her closest friends in real life.

She pulled out the Dobby-printed chair across from where her friend was furiously typing away on her laptop and sat down.

A minute later, Maddey lowered her headphones to wrap around her neck, pushed her glasses on top of her head, and blinked herself away from the scene she'd been writing.

"Hey, Hol." She closed the laptop and moved it to the side.

"Hey, Madz."

"So whatcha working on today?"

Holly pulled up the Pinterest photos for the cake's inspiration. The bottom layer of the cake was designed to look like a pepperoni pizza, while the two towers rising from the "pizza" were the sewer pipes the turtles used to get to their underground home. On the sides, she would put the birthday boy's name and the number 6.

The top was her favorite part. She was going to use fondant to create the heads of each of the Ninja Turtles and have it look like they were climbing out of the open manhole cover. It was so much fun to create.

"Oh my god." Maddey squealed in delight. "You *have* to show this to Rocky. She'll flip."

"I'll make sure to take a picture when I'm done."

"Hell no." Maddey gathered her things into her bag. "Let's show her now."

"Umm…" Her words trailed off uncertain. Though Vince stopped by to visit while she worked every day, she had yet to go by the gym while he trained. She may not know specifics about MMA yet, but she understood how serious his training and upcoming fight were. She didn't want to distract him from that goal. Another thing her family could mess with.

"What?"

"Won't we get in the way of the guys and their training?"

"Hell no. I write out of The Steele Maker all the time." She looped the strap of her bag over her head. "Hey, Lyle."

"What's up, doll?"

"Wanna go objectify some hunky men?"

"Always. The answer is always." He walked from behind the counter, paper to-go cup in one hand while he waited for them to join him at the door. When they did, he took her mug and dumped the remainder of her coffee in the to-go cup, before they all pulled on their winter coats and headed across the street.

As they stepped onto the sidewalk, the hairs on the back of Holly's neck stood on end, the same way they had whenever she was in public that week.

Maddey, never one to miss anything, noticed how she tensed. "What's wrong?"

She wanted to blow off the concern. She didn't have any concrete proof, but at the same time, she'd never been known for being dramatic.

"I'm…not sure," she hedged. "All week I've been getting this feeling like I'm being watched or something."

Maddey's eyes immediately started to scan the area, her icy blue eyes missing nothing, thanks to being raised by a former SEAL.

Was it better or worse someone else was taking her

concerns seriously? That itchy, *bugs crawling under her skin* feeling flared full force now that she wasn't hidden away in Espresso Patronum.

"Idiots." Maddey cursed under her breath, then said, "Stay here."

Neither she or Lyle listened, following a few steps behind Maddey as she approached a dark SUV parked down Main Street.

Maddey stalked to the driver's side window and knocked on the glass for it to lower. Her hands went to her hips, and she said, "You boys want to tell me what you're doing here?"

Vince dipped his shoulder for what felt like the hundredth time that day, shoving it into Deck's armpit and hooking his arm up around his neck. Arms locked tight, he jutted his hip out to swing Deck around his body, dropping him to the mats in a textbook perfect judo hip throw.

"Again," Papa Steele commanded, arms crossed over his broad chest, serious expression on his face as he waited for his directive to be followed.

This time Nick took up the position across from him as Vince alternated between him, Deck and Damon for practice.

Over and over, he tangled with his teammates, tossing them around his body and onto the padded floor. The move was so ingrained he could do it in his sleep.

He reached out a hand to Damon after another hip throw when movement by the reception desk caught their attention.

Lyle leaned back with his elbows against the desk like he didn't have a care in the world, and Maddey and Holly stood next to him.

Vince instantly brightened seeing his girl. She never came to watch him practice. Except as he looked at her, *really* looked at her, she did not look like she reciprocated his feelings. No, she looked down-right pissed. And Maddey, well, *yippie-ki-yay*, she looked ready to go full-blown *Die Hard* on his ass.

Uh-oh.

"Oh, man. *Someone's* in trouble," Deck sing-songed.

"Shit yeah," Nick agreed. "I don't think I've seen an expression that fierce since the day after Tommy attacked Jordan back in college."

"Oh, yeah, she was *not* happy to catch that team meeting, that's for sure," Damon added.

"If those girls are feeling even a tenth of what JD was that day, you are screwed." Nick clapped him on the shoulder, backing away, out of the line of fire.

They were probably right. Maybe a little charm could get him out of whatever trouble he now found himself in.

"Hey, Cupcake." He gave her the smile he knew she loved because it showed off the dimple in his left cheek.

"Oh, no." Holly crossed her arms over her chest. "Don't you *hey, Cupcake* me."

Okay, so charm isn't going to work.

Swallowing hard, he started to try again but was cut off by her slashing a hand through the air.

"What did you *do*, Vince?" Her voice cracked.

"I'm not quite sure I know what you mean, babe," he hedged.

"Don't play dumb, Vin. It doesn't suit you," Maddey cut in. "She's talking about the SUV filled with a security detail she had no idea about."

Welp. This wasn't good.

"They were there to keep you safe." He spoke directly to Holly. Sure, having a Covenette mad at him was never ideal, but he could handle Maddey. Having his girlfriend pissed at him, that wasn't acceptable.

"How long?" Holly asked.

"How long what?" He moved in her direction, his long

legs eating up the space between them until he stood directly in front of her.

"How long have you had them watching me?"

He didn't want to answer the question but had to.

"Since Monday."

Her whiskey eyes flashed like fire at his admission.

"So for almost a week, you've had people...what...tailing me? And not once did you think to bring it up to me?" The wounded tone of her voice gutted him.

"I needed you safe." Maybe he went about things the wrong way, but he wouldn't apologize for taking steps to make sure nothing happened to her. She was too fucking important to him.

"Safe?" she cried. "Safe from what? My family?"

He scrubbed a hand over his face, the cotton wraps absorbing some of the sweat beaded on his forehead. He cast a glance around the gym as he tugged on his hair, every eye locked on them. The middle of the gym was *not* the place for this conversation.

Taking Holly by the hand, he pulled her to the back. He needed privacy for the groveling he was about to do. He led her through the open door of his sister's office, shutting and locking it behind them. He wasn't risking any interruptions.

He nudged her until the back of her legs hit Rocky's desk, caging her against it with his body. His hands lifted to her face, his wraps preventing him from cradling it the way he wanted. His thumbs put pressure under her chin until she lifted her face to his, her eyes watery when they locked onto his. The sight damn near broke his heart.

"Vince, what the hell is going on?"

"I hired a few of Jamie's security guys to keep an eye on you and make sure you stayed safe."

"From my family?" Her voice was resigned as if she already knew the answer.

"Of course from your family." His fingers flexed against her face.

"Oh, Vince." Her voice softened, and her forehead fell to his chest.

He scoffed, her head snapping up at the sound.

"They *can't* have you back."

"What do you think they are going to do? Kidnap me off the street?"

"How the hell am I supposed to know?" He threw his hands up, pacing away from her. "All I know is there's a threat out there. A threat I can't see, and if I can't see it, how am I supposed to fight it?"

Anger and discontentment bubbled under his skin in a way they never had before. He was one of the jokesters of the group, a good time guy, things rolled off his back like water off a duck. If the threat was against him, he could shrug it off, but that wasn't the case here. Holly was being threatened. A fact that was completely unacceptable.

"Look." She cleared her throat as she watched him pace. "I understand why you did what you did. What I don't under-stand is why you didn't tell me about it. Do you have *any* idea how freaked out I've been this week, feeling like I had a target on my back? That someone was watching my every move?"

The way her voice broke at the end pierced his heart. He was back at her side, lifting her onto the desk, arms holding her to him as he dropped his forehead to hers.

"I'm sorry I had a hand in making you feel that way. It was never my intention. And I'm sorry I didn't tell you about hiring security, but I'm *not* sorry I did it."

He placed a finger over her lips, stopping whatever protest was about to come.

"I want you safe. No, I *need* you safe." He linked his fingers behind her neck. "You have become an essential part of my life. I need to know you're safe even if I'm not with you."

Her breath hitched.

"If anything happens to you, and I could have prevented it, I would never be able to forgive myself. So no, I won't apologize for taking the steps I deemed necessary in protecting you when I couldn't be there."

"It wasn't your decision to make."

"The fuck it wasn't."

"Don't you dare go all growly alpha man on me right now." She leveled him with a hard look. "I understand *why* you did it. If you had asked me about it, I would have agreed. But that's the thing, Vince...you didn't ask." She pulled back from him. "You *never* ask."

Well, shit. He fucked up.

"If this"—she flicked a finger between them—"you and me is going to work, you need to learn to *ask* me. When you just act without asking, you're taking away my consent."

He was like her douchebag father. He may not have put his hands on her, but she was right, it was like he was trying to control her. That was never his intention.

"I'm sorry." He pressed his forehead to hers again, took a deep breath and prepared for what he was about to say.

Because once he did, there was no taking it back.

"I love you, Holly." His head dropped as she ripped hers away to lock eyes with him, mouth slack in shock. "I don't care if it's too soon or if people think I'm crazy, but I do. I think I've loved you since that first day I caught you dancing around in the kitchen at EP." His thumbs caressed her cheeks. "I love you and I'm going to marry you one day. And I don't give a fuck how much money your family has, or how much power they *think* they have, there is *nothing* that will keep us apart."

A sob escaped. Her arms wound around his neck as her legs went around his hips. She crashed her mouth to his in an all-consuming kiss. No, kiss was too tame a word for what was happening. It was more like a blending of their souls.

Fuck. Love was turning him into some sort of weepy poet.

Whatever, it didn't matter.

Nor did the fact that she didn't say the words back.

He didn't need them.

Her kiss said it all.

Chapter Thirty-Five

Hours later, Holly put the finishing touches on the Ninja Turtle cake. She was the last person in the coffee shop since Espresso Patronum had closed a half an hour earlier. It was super rare for her to be there that late, but after everything went down with Vince earlier, she'd spent a few hours decompressing with Maddey before returning to finish the cake.

Her thoughts were a jumbled mess, tangled together like Christmas lights at the start of the season. Even singing along to Mariah Carey's "All I Want For Christmas Is You" wasn't doing anything to help process all the emotions.

First, there was the threat of her family.

Then there was the whole going behind her back and hiring a security detail. She'd confronted Kyle about it, but he and Lyle both claimed ignorance. They had no reason to lie, and Lyle looked just as shocked as she and Maddey when they made the discovery.

It wasn't that he hired security. What hurt the most was how he kept it from her, not once thinking to include her in a decision that directly affected her. For twenty-three years that was her life, she wasn't going back to it—at least not willingly.

The cherry on top of the emotional maelstrom of the day was hearing the three words she *never* expected from him. And holy Buddy you're not an elf, talk about delivery. The way he declared not only his feelings but his intentions, she was floored.

Though she felt the same—there was no doubt in her mind, she did love him—she didn't say the words back. A part of her was too pissed about being kept in the dark to allow them to pass her lips. It was also why she didn't text him about working late. She told Becky and Gemma, knowing they would pass along the information, but avoided reaching out to him directly. It was petty, but she was ticked off enough not to care.

She ran the fondant trimmer down the long rectangle of white fondant rolled out on the counter. All the other layers were done, now she worked on the finishing touches of the pizza base. A group of red speckled fondant cut out to resemble pepperoni, as well as the dime sized black donut shaped circles for olive slices waited for her to place the cheese of the pizza down. Though the cheese pieces were the easiest to cut, it took the longest because she needed so much of it.

Section by section she sprinkled her "cheese" on the pizza, letting the pieces fall like they would before it melted flat inside an oven. As she placed the last of the "olive slices" on the pie, she wasn't at all surprised to see a large shadow fill the doorway to the kitchen. It took him longer to show up than she'd thought it would.

Ignoring him, she concentrated on lifting and balancing the heavy cake to move it to the fridge until it was picked up in the morning.

"Vin." She turned to face him, wiping the remnants of sugar left from the fondant on her leggings. She ate up the sight of her sexy AF boyfriend leaning against the doorjamb, black joggers, white henley, backward Yankees hat, sheepish expression on his face. Why did she have to be so taken with him? She wanted to stay mad, she *really* did, but how the hell was she supposed to do that when he looked like *that*?

He tried to hide the wince from her not calling him Muffin, but she caught it.

"Hey, Cupcake." He didn't enter the kitchen like usual. As if waiting for permission to enter like a vampire needing to be invited inside.

"What are you doing here?" She started to wipe down her work station, needing to look away before she jumped him. She may be mad at him, but the sight of him was enough to have her wet.

"I came to apologize." His deep voice rumbled through her body, and her nipples stood up in attention.

"You already did that." She tossed the last of her tools in the sink to be washed.

"I did. But this time, I'm going to apologize properly." With her back to him, she couldn't see but heard him push from his post and head in her direction. His hands went to her hips, spinning her around and lifting her onto the freshly wiped counter. He spread her knees as he stepped between them, crowding into her space.

His silvery eyes were the deep charcoal color they turned when supremely turned on, the thick fringe of black lashes around them only adding to their intensity. For such a fun-loving guy, he was *intense* with her. It was a heady thing to experience.

He stroked a thumb across the arch of one of her brows, continuing down, following the line of her jaw, not stopping until it came to rest on her bottom lip.

"*Fuck,* I'm sorry, baby." His eyes stayed locked on her mouth. "I didn't mean to hurt you. I only hoped by not telling you it wouldn't *add* to the stress of the situation."

I know.

Her fingers played with the ends of his hair exposed underneath his hat.

"I really am sorry, baby."

"I know. And I forgive you." And she did. Deep down, a part of her knew that, though misguided, his actions came from a place of love, not control.

"Good." A mischievous gleam entered his eyes. "Now… time for me to apologize properly."

"Isn't that what you just did?"

"Sure. With my words." He reached for something behind her. "But haven't you ever heard the phrase, actions speak louder than words?"

He tunneled his fingers underneath the hem of her 'It is NEVER too early for Christmas music' t-shirt, lifting it from her body and tossing it over his shoulder. Deftly he popped the clasp on her red bra, giving it the same treatment as her shirt.

Her nipples stood out, both from the chilled air in the kitchen and the wanton look on his face as he stared down at her half-naked on the counter.

Then as if she weighed no more than a bag of flour, one arm hooked around her middle, lifting her enough to peel her leggings over her ass and down her legs, her sneakers and socks sliding off in the process. His effortless display of strength sent a fresh wave of heat so strong she barely noticed the chill of the countertop beneath her bare ass.

Once resettled, Vince grabbed the mixing bowl of leftover red frosting, holding it between them as he dipped one long finger into the buttercream.

Wordlessly, he stretched his red-coated finger out, traced a line across her collarbone and down to her right nipple, before dipping back in for more frosting and doing the same to the left.

Again he went back for more, this time following the

zigzag pattern of freckles down her belly, playing connect the dots with the beauty marks, stopping before he reached her pulsing clit.

"Whatever you do," he leaned in, millimeters away from her buttercreamed collarbone, "don't tell Gem about this. She'll kick my ass for breaking my diet, but *fuck*, if I haven't imagined licking frosting off of you from the moment I met you."

Then no more words were needed as his tongue licked the sweetness from her body, scraping his teeth across the small bump of her collarbone, the sensation mimicking itself in her clit begging for attention.

Completely unhurried, he continued down the drawn path, sucking first one then the other nipple into his mouth until they were extremely clean.

He bent, skimming the plane of her stomach, his dexterous tongue driving her into a frenzy. He told her once his hands had to be registered as lethal weapons, but his mouth should be too. The combination of the dirty words he loved to whisper and the wicked things his tongue knew how to do was lethal.

At the end of the line, his slight scruff grazed across her pubic bone. She whimpered as he pulled back, holding her thighs open as he stared at the place that wanted him the most.

"Fuck, baby. You are the most delicious cupcake I've *ever* tasted."

Another whimper escaped when he went back for another dollop of frosting, this time tracing between her lips to coat the swollen bud underneath.

"Do you know the *one* thing missing?" He stroked the outside of her lips with his thumbs, waiting for her response.

Does he seriously think I'm capable of intelligent thought right now?

By the way he continued to wait, the back and forth

motion of his fingers just outside where she needed them most, he did.

"What's that?" she asked so he would finish what he started.

"It needs something to sweeten it up some."

"The *hell* it does." She was the professional, and her frosting recipe was legit, the perfect balance of sugar without being *too* sweet.

He tsked. "It does, babe." His mouth hovered over her already weeping pussy. "It's missing *you*. Now be a good girl and come for me."

She started to roll her eyes at the *good girl* comment, but as his tongue started to trace figure eights on her clit, they rolled for an entirely different reason.

VINCE HAD BEEN out of sorts since Holly discovered what he did. When she still wasn't home *hours* after her usual time, he couldn't sit around and wait any longer. A quick drive to the Samson boys for the key to Espresso Patronum, and he went to see his girl.

Now on his knees, literally, in apology for being a moron, he lapped up every drop of sugar—and he wasn't talking about the frosting—from her delicious pussy. His Cupcake was quickly becoming his favorite dessert of all time.

He bit down on her clit, and she gushed into his mouth, her orgasm bursting. He continued to lick until the last of her tremors abated. He placed a few kisses on her thigh before rising to stand. Her lust-drunk eyes were heavy, lashes opening to look at him. A surge of male pride filled him at being the one to put that look on her face.

His dick was screaming for release, but he ignored the way it tented his joggers, now wasn't about him. Holly, however, was not about that life. Her hands came out, gripped the bottom of his shirt and tugged until he bent to help pull it over his head, his hat getting dislodged in the process.

"My turn." Her smile was sinful as she hopped off the counter, reversing their positions and pushing him against it. She hooked her thumbs in the waistband of his joggers, pushing them down until they were at his feet, his dick bouncing as it was freed from the confines of the material.

Unconcerned with her own nudity, she reached for the container of frosting, tracing her own pattern in the cuts of his six pack and the deep v framing his groin.

"I have dreamt about doing this to you since the day you blatantly stripped in my kitchen."

He loved knowing she thought about him as much as he thought about her. He'd practically given himself blisters jerking off so many times thinking of all the naughty things he wanted to do to her.

But as she lowered herself in front of him, little sounds of pleasure humming in her throat while she licked the frosting from his torso, he had to calculate the number of calories his own dessert exploration was to prevent blowing his load prematurely. His girl may claim to be one of Santa's besties, but she was pure vixen when it came to sexy times.

The container went to the floor beside her knees, her finger drawing a line down the length of his dick right at her eye-level. She sat back on her heels as her thumb circled the head, swiping across the drop of pre-cum that had leaked free and sucking it between her lips.

Fuck if that wasn't the hottest thing he had ever seen.

Then without warning, she took the entire length of him in her mouth, swallowing him down her throat until her lips brushed against the skin of his groin.

She hummed around his cock, the vibrations almost tipping him over the edge as she worked him.

Out to the tip.

Down to the base.

A drag of the tongue on the underside of his dick.

A swirl of it around the sensitive head.

He was seconds away from coming down her throat, but no way he could when he was the one who was supposed to be apologizing.

He snapped his hips back, his cock falling from her mouth with an audible pop. He hooked his hands under her arms as she blinked in confusion.

"I am *not* coming without you," he growled, reversing their positions again, this time bending her over the counter, her glorious ass on full display. He smacked it once just to watch the muscles bounce.

He stretched her arms out in front of her, his hands curving around hers to grip the opposite edge of the counter.

"Hold on tight, baby," he advised, dragging the head of his cock through her wetness and slammed himself home inside her in one thrust.

He groaned as the heat of her pussy squeezed him in a viselike grip.

He wasn't going to last long. This was going to be a quick, hard fuck at its finest.

He curved one arm around her hip to strum her clit, and the other snaked between her stomach and the counter to pluck a nipple while his hips pounded into her in an almost punishing pace.

Over and over, he drove himself into her.

"Vince," she cried.

Pull back, push inside.

"More," she pleaded. "More. Give me more."

There wasn't a chance he was stopping.

His fingers on her clit sped up until she was coming around him with a scream, her wetness soaking him to the balls. He squeezed the tit in his hand and emptied himself inside her, following her over the edge.

His body draped over hers like a blanket, utterly spent

from the most intense orgasm of his life. This woman wrecked him in every single way.

When he finally felt like his legs were strong enough to support him, he shifted to pull her into his arms, sinking down to the floor, cradling her in his lap, pressing a kiss on the crown of her head.

"Now *that's* what I call makeup sex." He spoke into the wild waves of her sex hair.

She let out a surprised giggle. "I think I like the way you apologize."

Fuck, he loved this girl.

He meant what he'd said earlier. He was going to marry her one day.

Now all he had to do was deal with her family.

Chapter Thirty-Six

With Christmas only a few days away, the orders for Holly's custom cookies had tripled. To accommodate the increased demand, she no longer handled the everyday baking for Espresso Patronum, only focusing on the cookies until the holiday season was over.

Needing a break from all the snowmen, Santas, reindeer and wreaths, she chose to spend an hour at The Steele Maker, unabashedly watching her sexy fighter boyfriend train for his fight just over a week away.

"You coming to the game with us tonight? Or are you stuck making cookies again?" Maddey asked from her own oversized beanbag chair as they watched Vince and Gage grapple on the mats in front of them.

"No game for me. I'll be slaving away late into the night, finishing the last of the special orders. But then I get three days off, so it's okay."

"You're coming to Jordan's for Christmas, right?"

Maddey's question went unanswered because Holly was distracted by watching Vince scramble out of Gage's python-like arms, slipping out, flipping them over so he was behind the heavyweight champ, legs wrapped and ankles locked around his belly, arms crushed around his head in a headlock, while bending back in a way that caused both their backs to arch.

She had no idea what any of the technical terms were but the strength a move like that required was impressive enough that even a layman like herself could appreciate it. It also helped that both guys were shirtless, every muscle on display in all their bulging glory.

"Hol?" Maddey's voice broke through her lustful thoughts.

"Hmm?" What would it feel like to have Vince wrapped around her so tightly?

"Girl," Maddey chuckled. "You got it bad. I don't blame you, but damn." Her eyes shifted to look over Holly's shoulder to the treadmill area behind her. "Ray, take it easy on my dog. I'm spending the next few days at Jordan's, he'll get plenty of exercise."

Holly turned to watch as Ray ran on a treadmill with Trident on the machine beside him. When Vince's roommate first called the dog over to the treadmill, she'd thought he was out of his mind, but Maddey explained Trident ran on a treadmill a few times a week when it was too cold for her to take him outside. She couldn't make this stuff up if she tried.

Grunting from the mats brought her attention back to where the two guys were practically rolling around trying to get the other to tap out. Why was it so hot to watch?

"*Now* you see why I write out of here sometimes?" Maddey leaned over to whisper.

"Oh, yeah." She nodded, still transfixed by the display in front of her.

"Okay, that's enough for today," Rocky said from where she observed her husband and her brother training. "It's leg day for you both, so get to work." She pointed to the free weight area at the front of the gym.

"Hey, Cupcake." Vince greeted her with a kiss, bending down to grab a towel and water bottle.

"Hey, Muffin."

He matched her smirk with one of his own, his dimple popping out because he knew she loved it. She still had yet to say the words—too scared to utter them out loud—but she loved him with her whole heart. Even the pieces tattered by her past loved him. He healed her in ways she never thought a person could.

"How much longer do I have you?" His teeth ripped open the Velcro on his red Flash hand wraps, unraveling one before repeating the action on the other.

Even when he was working, training, he made her feel that she was a part of what he was doing. He included her though she was merely a spectator.

"I've got at least a half an hour before I have to head back. And I might even be able to be convinced to extend my time-line for the right incentive."

She let out a startled yelp when he scooped her out of her seat and into his arms, pulling her flush against his sweaty body, the musk and soap filling her senses in a heady rush that made her want to lick him all over.

She should not be thinking about licking him while around other people because all it did was remind her of the frosting foray a few weeks earlier.

"Vincent." Papa Steele's hard voice cut across the gym. "You know the rules. If you want your girlfriend—a girl-friend I'll remind you that you haven't brought by for family dinner yet—to be able to hang out here, you keep all *that*" — he circled a finger at them—"out of my gym during working hours."

Properly chastised by his father, Vince lowered her to the ground and took her hand in his.

"Come on, Cupcake." He tugged her forward. "You can help me workout."

"Umm." She hesitated even as she let him lead her toward the weights and machines. "I'm not sure if you noticed this about me, but I'm not the most athletic person. And I sure as hell am not strong enough to lift anything you can."

"Oh, you think I'm strong, baby?" His tone was gleeful as he let his ego out to play.

He walked her to the leg press machine. He stood back, examining the machine until he settled on which weights to use. He loaded up each side with a large forty-five-pound plate, then turned back to face her.

"Hop on up." He patted the top of the shelf.

"Come again?"

"I'm saving that for later when I have you back in my bed." His words made her blush. "But for now, you're gonna help me lift. Now put that perfect heart-shaped ass of yours right here." He smacked his hand on the shelf again.

"You're serious?"

"Abso-fucking-lutely." His dimple was out again. "This is child's play compared to the ways Rocky added to Gage's workouts before she let him knock her up. Now come on, chop-chop."

"Aww…look, Blue. Vin is trying to play with the big boys, having Hol sit on the leg press," Gage said as they joined them in the weight area.

"Oh, how cute. Our boy is growing up," Rocky said, a familiar mischievous sparkle in her gray eyes.

"We'll talk once you graduate to doing pull-ups with your girl hanging on you. But A for effort." Gage clapped Vince on the back and shared a laugh with his wife.

"Wait." Holly held her hands up in a time-out gesture. "You've done that?" She waved a finger between Rocky and Gage.

"Oh, yeah." Rocky pulled her phone from the pocket on the side of her leggings. "Got pictures of it too." She passed her phone to Holly. Snap went the gingerbread man, it was impressive. She couldn't even lift her own body in a pull-up, let alone do it with another person wrapped around her. She looked at Gage with new respect.

"Hey now," Vince cut in. "He's a married man, Cupcake, and *you're* a taken woman."

"Like I could ever forget you claimed me, Muffin." She smiled at him as she walked up to the leg press. "But you can't blame a girl for being impressed."

His gray eyes narrowed at her. "Well, let's go then. Hop on me and let's do some pull-ups."

"First off, eww. I don't need to hear your dirty talk." Rocky mimed gagging. "And second, it's leg day. Sit your ass down and push your girlfriend up and down."

Law laid down, Vince hoisted her onto the shelf and settled himself in the seat below on his back, sneakers positioning themselves under her. He released the lever and slowly started to lower her down toward him until his knees were bent at a ninety-degree angle before pushing back up again.

He made it seem effortless as he lowered her and the weights up and down.

Down to him.

Up away from him.

Down.

Up.

Bend the knees.

Straighten the legs.

She counted off two dozen reps before he reengaged the locks and rose to stand. He told her to stay on her perch, he had two more sets to do.

She admired the way his gym shorts tightened around his thighs as he pulled his foot behind him to his equally spectacular ass in a quad stretch. Before he could reclaim his seat, a commotion by the front counter captured their attention.

Becky was out from her usual perch behind it, holding up

her hands in an attempt to stop whoever had shown up from entering the gym further.

The breath whooshed from her lungs as the man came into view and her heart stopped—literally felt like it stopped beating—as shock set in.

Blue eyes she knew well met hers across the room, the same ones she'd wished never to see again when she escaped. The Steele Maker was the last place she ever expected to see them.

Goosebumps rose on her skin, and she went clammy as she locked eyes with her *least* favorite person on the planet.

Her fiancé.

Chapter Thirty-Seven

N *o.*

No, no.

No, no, no, no, no.

This is not happening.

I'm dreaming.

This is a nightmare.

Holly froze as if the blue eyes locked on her were Medusa's, and she was turned to stone.

She knew her family had found her and were trying to scare her into returning home, but she never thought *he* would show up.

Chad Montgomery.

Heir to the Montgomery fortune.

Son of Connecticut's current Senator.

The Montgomerys had been a staple in American politics since the American Revolution. They were the Kennedys before the Kennedys were the Kennedys.

If the rumors were true—and in this case they always were—Chad would be running for office when his father stepped down in a few years to make a run for the White House.

Chad Montgomery was the picture-perfect All-American good boy. With his coiffed blond hair and blue eyes, he was preppy perfection in a polo and khakis or the bespoke three-piece suit he currently wore.

He was everything her family expected for their daughter. A Yale undergrad alum and a JD from Harvard Law, the former polo player was the quintessential future politician. Those were the things that mattered most to the Vanderbuilts, what *connections* they could make, what would help grow their empire—things like love, or the fact that Chad was eight years older than her, never even entered the equation.

How she ever managed to last three years with the guy, let alone being engaged to and living with him, she would never know.

"Oh, Holly." Disapproval rang clear in Chad's voice. "What in the world did you do to your hair?" His face scrunched in distaste.

She didn't answer. She remained on top of the leg press machine, praying she was hallucinating and this wasn't actually happening.

"It's got to be the influence of that fag friend of yours and his fairy husband."

The gym sucked in a collective breath, and a dozen fists clenched and cocked.

"Who the hell do you think you are?" Rocky stepped forward, ready to throw a punch to defend their friends.

Gage quickly wrapped an arm around her, pulling her back to his side. "Blue, baby, you're pregnant. Probably best you *don't* get in a fistfight right now."

Chad's eyes briefly flicked in Rocky's direction before returning to Holly, not bothering to respond.

"Imagine my disappointment to find you in this hovel looking like a punk rock skank."

There he was. The man she'd seen more and more over the last year. Chad Montgomery was a master at emotional abuse.

He knew exactly what words to use to whittle away at your confidence until there was nothing left. It was surprising that he would show that part of himself in front of so many witnesses. It was a testament to how pissed he was.

"Hovel?" Becky rolled her eyes at the ludicrous description of the state-of-the-art gym.

"Where the *fuck* do you get off calling my girl a skank?" Vince's voice roared throughout the space.

"*Your* girl?" Chad stepped in closer to Vince as he looked at him for the first time. "Guess skank really is an apt description seeing as she's sleeping with you while engaged to me."

WHAT. THE. ACTUAL. Fuck?

Vince wiggled a finger in his ear, sure he misheard Captain Douchepants. There was no way Holly—*his* Holly—was engaged to the Ken doll standing before him. Sure, there were details about her past he didn't know, but he knew in his gut she wasn't a cheater.

"Imagine my surprise when my father's press secretary showed me a clip from the latest UFC promo video, only to see you canoodling with this ape"—he spoke to Holly and waved a hand toward Vince—"while they interviewed another one of the knuckle-draggers."

Vince's molars snapped together as he clenched his jaw, fighting the urge to bury his fist in the twat's face.

He turned to face Holly as she scrambled down from the leg press machine and marched in their direction.

"We. Are. *Not*. Engaged anymore. I stopped being your fiancée the moment I put the ring on your nightstand and left."

The conviction in Holly's words eased the uncertainty that had crept inside him.

"Tsk, tsk, tsk…oh, Holly," Douche Ken said in a patronizing tone. "We all know you're going to return home where you belong once you're done slumming it with this barbarian. Why drag this out any longer?"

Holly wasn't going anywhere, not if he had anything to say about it.

"I'm not going anywhere with you, Chad."

Chad—*what the fuck kind of name was Chad anyway?*—rolled his eyes as if Holly was being ridiculous. "Of course you are. This"—his finger bounced between the two of them—"has been arranged for years. But if you are having fun playing the whore for this Neanderthal, I can be more than accommodating to the notion once we are home. Heaven knows you'll be spending a lot of time on your knees to make up for the inconvenience you've caused me."

Vince *knew* he shouldn't hit the guy, he could get in a lot of trouble for fighting outside the cage, but he had reached his breaking point. He would not listen to one more disgusting word from this asshole's mouth.

He stepped around his girl, hooked an arm around her to push her safely behind him, cocked his arm back and laid the fucker out with a single jab to the face. The satisfying crunch of bone sounded as he broke *Chad's* turned-up nose.

"Vince! Don't." Holly wrapped her hands around his arm as he readied to throw another punch. "He's not worth the trouble it will cause."

Maybe not, but it would sure feel good to lay this fucker out again.

As if able to read his thoughts, she stepped into his body, wrapped both arms around his neck, rising on tiptoe and placed a kiss to the underside of his jaw, the act automatically soothing the beast inside.

"I'm going to sue you for everything you're worth," Chad roared, holding a hand over his nose to stem the bleeding.

"Sue him? For what? For you tripping over a loose free weight and smashing your face against the rack? How is *your* clumsiness *Vince's* fault?" Gage asked.

Chad sputtered. "That is not what happened."

"That's what I saw," his brother-in-law was quick to say.

"Me too," his sister agreed.

A chorus of "Us too" was heard as everyone one from the gym had his back. It was what family did.

"You really should watch where you're walking in a gym," Becky advised. "I try to teach them to put the weights away when they are done, but being *knuckle-draggers*—that's what you called them, right?—well, they don't always comprehend the concept."

God, he loved Becky. She was the sister he never wanted but wouldn't trade for the world.

"Now why don't you get the fuck out of my gym before you have another accident." The threat was clear in Vince's voice.

Chad's eyes bounced between Vince and Holly before he spoke again. "Whatever...you can have her. She was only good for the money that came attached. But now that she's slumming it with you, she'll be cut off just like her little rainbow friend was."

"First off, I'd be careful what you say about Kyle. He's more of a man than you'll ever be." He turned his attention from the dickhead and looked down at his girlfriend, pushing a few pieces of purple-tipped hair from her face and behind her ear. "You, Cupcake"—he stroked a finger across her cheek then her bottom lip—"are worth so much more than money. The only thing I need from you is to love me the way I love you."

She hiccuped out a sob at his words, burying her face against his chest as her arms locked around him like a vice.

You wouldn't hear any complaints from him.

"Aww, how cute, you love the little slut." The guy was really angling for a beatdown. "Have fun living in squalor with a man who makes his living acting like a barbarian, Holly."

Vince kept his arms wrapped around her so he didn't give in to the overpowering urge to use this asshole's face like a speed bag.

"Sorry to break it to you," his tone was anything but apologetic, "but my barbaric living earns me millions. So thanks so much for your concern, but I think we'll be fine. Now someone *please* get this douchecanoe out of here before I make him my new punching bag."

He'd had enough. The guy didn't deserve one more second of his attention. He needed to forget about him and focus on the girl trembling in his arms. *She* was what mattered.

With Ozzy Osbourne's "I Don't Wanna Stop" blasting through his earbuds at earsplitting volume, Vince beat a relentless pattern against the tethered punching bag.

Jab-cross-jab-cross-jab-cross-jab-cross.

Roundhouse kick.

Jab-jab-jab-jab.

Roundhouse kick

Jab-cross-jab-cross.

Knee-knee-knee.

Over and over, he beat the bag, his frustration from the fucked-up day flowing from his body and into the bag. Snippets of the day flashed through his mind like a highlight reel.

Each insult Chad hurled Holly's way.

Every derogatory slur he spat.

The revelation that Holly had been engaged to the douche played on a loop in his brain.

Needing to be alone with Holly immediately, he took her by the hand and led her to his sister's office.

He shut and locked the door, leaning against it. His arms looped around her hips, stretching out a hand to cup her ass. He loved her ass, he couldn't help himself.

"Are you mad at me?" Holly's voice was small as she kept her face trained on their feet.

One finger curled under her chin to raise her face until he could look into her whiskey eyes. His own eyes narrowed at the uncertainty swimming in hers.

"Why on earth would I be mad at you? You didn't invite that fuckwad here. He ambushed you." His own anger over the situation simmered under the surface. What if the fucker had gone to EP looking for her instead? What would he have done if she was alone and not surrounded by a legion of friends?

Jab-hook.

Cross-hook-cross-hook.

Jab-jab-jab.

Each hit was harder than the last as he imagined all the possibilities of what *could have* happened if Holly wasn't with him at the gym that afternoon.

"Be-Because I never told you I used to be engaged." She tried to look away again.

Both hands now cupped her face as he held her gaze on his.

"I'd only be mad if you were still engaged to the prick...Pfft...I probably wouldn't even be mad then." He lifted his thumbs to caress her cheekbones. "I've told you...I knew you were meant to be mine from the moment I laid eyes on you. I doubt there's anything that could have kept me away."

She melted against him, hands clutched in the waistband of his shorts since he was shirtless.

"I meant it." Her head lifted, making eye contact again. "I broke off our engagement."

"Cupcake."

"No." She cut him off with a shake of the head. "I need to tell you this. Honestly, I should have before today. When I ran away, I left both my ring and a note saying I wouldn't be marrying him. I

was done with him and my old life from the moment I loaded my
bags in the car and drove off."

"That's good, because you're not going anywhere now. You
belong here. You belong with me, *and now that I have you, I'm*
never letting you go."

He shook himself out of the memory of his sappiness and
landed another punishing roundhouse kick to the bag,
earning back some man card points.

Shaking his head, he internally laughed. Book club was
seriously affecting his way of thinking. All those goddamn
romance novels—no matter how much he loved them—were
making him wax poetry.

Him.

A professional MMA fighter.

A fighter about to take his shot at the light heavyweight
title.

And fuck if he didn't mean every sappy word.

Chapter Thirty-Eight

Vince took Holly's hand as they walked toward the front door of the Donovans' home. Though *home* might be too simple of a word to describe the six-bedroom, gray and tan bricked mansion with large white columns and contrasting black shutters.

The estate served as a home base for their squad. With the exception of training, they spent most of the hockey off-season either lounging around the Olympic-sized swimming pool in the back or down the shore.

"You ready for this?" Vince asked before opening the door in front of them.

Holly's brows scrunched together under her knitted beanie. "You do realize I've spent a lot of time with these people over the last two months, right?"

He loved that each one of the girls had accepted her wholly, making her one of their own. But what they were about to find on the other side of the door was an entirely different brand of crazy.

"Alright, Cupcake." He gave her hand a squeeze. "Don't say I didn't warn you."

Entering without knocking, they were immediately

engulfed in a swirl of sound. Voices and laughter sounded over the Christmas music playing in the background as a round of barking started and a mob of dogs ran to greet them. Leading the charge was Navy, Jordan's six-year-old black Labrador, the newest addition to the growing Donovan clan, Stanley, a five-month-old chocolate lab puppy, following closely on his heels. Rounding out the crew were Trident, Maddey's more sedate yellow lab, and Pebbles and Bam Bam, Chance Jenson's black, white and gray spotted Great Danes.

While the dogs wiggled at their feet, weaving between their legs, he hung their coats in the double-doored coat closet in the hall. He gave Holly one more amused look and guided her down the hall until the house opened up into a large open-concept kitchen and living room.

Holly's feet came to a stop as she took in the people filling the rooms—there were almost too many of them to count. He wrapped an arm around her as he pointed out different groupings of people. The dozens of people celebrating included the Covenettes, the gym rats, the hockey players, a rockstar, and all their assorted family members. It was like a Steele family dinner on steroids.

Lyle and Jamie were in a heated Mario Kart battle with Sean and Carlee, while Kyle and Sammy watched with bemused expressions as they listened to the two grown men trash talk a pair of nine-year-olds.

"Well, *hey* there, sexy," Tucker said flirtatiously, making his way toward them. "You must be the baker I've heard so much about." He took Holly's hand in his and brushed a kiss across her knuckles.

Vince pushed his friend back by the shoulder—okay, maybe he pushed a little harder than necessary—before going in for a one-armed, back-slapping hug.

"Don't be flirting with my girl, you Abercrombie model wannabe," he threatened while Holly giggled beside him.

"Touchy, touchy, Vinny-boy."

"Don't call me that, M-Dubs," he tossed back the girls' nickname.

"Ouch." Tuck mimed being stabbed in the heart.

"M-Dubs?" Holly's eyes bounced between them.

"It stands for Man Whore," Skye answered, passing off a glass of wine to Holly. "A title he's more than earned."

"That's only because I can't convince you to sleep with me again, Bubble." Tucker dropped an arm around Skye's shoulders which she quickly brushed off.

"I've already told you, *M-Dubs*…it's never going to happen."

"You've said that before and I distinctly remember a time dur—" Tucker's sentence was cut off by Skye's hand smacking across his mouth.

"We will *not* be mentioning that. I blame the magical powers of weddings and alcohol. Lots and *lots* of alcohol."

"Oh, come on, don't be like that, Bubble."

"Do. Not. Call me *that*." Skye bit out the words. "Keep doing it, and I'll sick my bestie on you."

"Bubble?" Holly whispered to Vince while Tucker and Skye bickered.

He leaned down to speak directly in her ear, taking a moment to inhale her sugary scent. "It stands for Bubble Butt." He chuckled at her wide-eyed expression. "See why she doesn't like being called it?"

"BB3," Jordan called out. "Stop being a shit-stirrer. It's Christmas, take a break for a day."

Tucker jogged over to wrap his arms around her in a hug from behind and rested his chin on top of her head. "Aww, Blondie…why you gotta be a fun sucker?"

"Please," Jordan rolled her eyes, clearly used to Tucker's gregarious personality. "Holls, ignore my BB3, we all do."

"BB3?"

"It stands for Big Brother 3. Tuck here didn't think having two older brothers was enough when Jake and I first started dating, so he declared himself an honorary one," Jordan explained as she handed off a sippy cup to her mom for one of her girls.

"And she's not bitter at *all* over me being seven minutes older either." Jase earned himself a backhand to the chest from his twin as he came to greet them. "Wanna go a few rounds in the ring tomorrow before I have to head back to the city?"

"Hell yeah," Vince said, always willing to spar with his best friend. Tomorrow was another day off from training, but it wouldn't hurt to mess around in the ring with the enforcer.

Becky came to whisk Holly away while he spent some time catching up. He worried the drama with her ex would still be bringing her down, but the happy smile on her face told him all he needed to know.

HOLLY'S HEAD SPUN as she followed Becky out of the bustling kitchen and into the equally populated living room. She guessed she probably should have taken Vince's concern a smidge more seriously. It was a good thing Jordan owned such a large home because there were people *everywhere*.

Becky led her to a group of couches where Rocky and Gemma sat with women she assumed were their mothers, given how strongly they resembled each other. She settled herself between her two roommates and cast a glance at Vince laughing with his friends in the kitchen. It was nice to see him smile. He had been extremely tense since Chad's unwelcome visit.

"So, Holls." Rocky smiled when she caught her checking out her brother. "You haven't met the moms yet have you?"

Rocky made quick work of introductions, the three matri-archs of the Steele family—make no mistake Tracy Reese, Becky's mom, was included in this—looked at her with an almost awed expression on each of their faces.

"You grew up with our Kyle?" Vicki Steele, Vince's mom asked.

"Yes." She looked over to her closest friend, receiving a smile when he caught her staring. "We were in the same schools since pre-school. We did have a few years where we didn't get to see each other as much as we would have liked, but we've always remained close."

"It was because his family are a bunch of assholes?" She snorted at Hope, Vince's aunt's spot-on description of the Huntingtons.

"Pretty much. Mine too," she added as an afterthought.

"So we heard," Tracy said. "At least our boy taught that dick a little thing about respect." Her statement was met with nods from the group.

"Coo-key, Coo-key," one of the Donovan twins said with outstretched arms as she ran at Holly.

She scooped the toddler into her arms, checking the color of her earrings to know which twin she held. "Hey, Lu."

"Coo-key." The blonde cutie squealed, grabbing both of her cheeks in her little hands. The girls had taken to calling her Cookie thanks to the numerous times they received the treat when she was around.

"I don't have any," Lucy's face fell, so she added quickly, "but I *did* bring some. Would you like one?" Her emerald green eyes sparkled as she clapped her hands and chanted *coo-key* over and over.

Unable to say no to the excited toddler—who could say no to those green eyes? No one, that's who—she rose from the couch with the toddler on her hip and snuck into the kitchen for a cookie. She reached for one of the reindeer she had decorated the day before, passing it off to Lucy and earning a wink from Jake as he caught them, obviously unconcerned with his daughter having sweets. She made sure to grab a second cookie just in case Lacey found them out and wanted one of her own.

"You're really good with them," Mama Steele observed as she resumed her seat, and as expected, Lacey ran over trying to steal her sister's cookie. Holly deftly averted crisis by handing off the extra one.

"They make it easy." She shrugged off the praise even as Rocky warned, "Mom."

"What, honey?" Vicki feigned a look of innocence. "I was merely making an observation."

Becky snorted, and Gemma attempted to cover a laugh.

"Uh-huh. Suuuurrrre. Leave the girl alone…they've only been dating for like a month."

"Time is relative, my dear. Look at how quickly you married Gage. When you know, you know." Vicki's eyes once again went to Holly. "Did you know you are the first girl my son has ever brought around the family?"

"*Mom.*" Rocky tried again to rein her in.

"Oh, relax, dear." She waved off her daughter's concern. "There's never even been a *hint* of a chance of your brother giving me grandkids one day—at least legitimately—so hush while I get to know Holly."

She felt like she was hit by a Stupefy curse from a Harry Potter character when Vicki's words registered.

Babies?

She sent up a silent message to the IUD gods, praying her birth control continued to do its job and keep any aliens from invading her uterus for the near future. She needed to find the courage to actually say the words *I love you* to Vince before she even entertained the idea of kids.

"You okay, Cupcake?" Vince must have noticed her mini freak-out.

"She'll be fine," Gemma answered.

"Yeah…your mom is only planning out the nursery for your future children, but she'll be fine in a minute," Becky added with a devilish smirk.

One of Vince's black brows rose to his hairline. "Something you want to tell me, Cupcake?"

She shook her head so fast her hair whipped both her and Lucy in the face. "That would be a *hard* no. The only thing taking up residence in my uterus right now is my IUD."

"What's an IUD?" Sean asked the room.

Well, shit. Maybe I shouldn't have announced my method of birth control to the room?

To be fair, the *last* thing she needed was for Vince to have even the notion that she could be pregnant. He was already way more overbearing than she needed in her life, she could only imagine how insufferable he would be if he thought she was carrying his child. She had enough family stress at the moment, she didn't need to add any baby daddy/baby mama drama.

"Girl stuff, bro." Ryan handled the awkward question from his youngest brother. "Trust me, you don't want to know."

"It's Christmas." Vince dropped onto the armrest next to her. "Can we *not* turn this into a Steele family dinner."

"Oh, don't be a buzzkill, Vin," Becky complained.

"Agreed," Gemma added. "Don't go ruining our fun just because *you* always seem to become the topic of conversation."

"Yeah." Becky snorted. "Him and his procreations."

Both her roommates lost it in a fit of giggles.

Rocky was the only one to take pity on them.

"Mom." She rubbed a hand over her belly. "Is this guy not enough for you to be excited about for now?"

"Guy?" Mama Steele jumped off the couch, squealing in excitement. *"It's a boy?"*

"I'm getting two nephews this year?" Vince included the baby Jordan was having into the equation.

"When did you find out?" Gemma asked.

"How could you not tell me?" Becky screeched.

Rocky's face did its best imitation of a fish as her mouth opened and closed wordlessly. Holly had a feeling she hadn't meant to say that.

Everyone watched them as the three moms danced around in celebration.

"Blue?" Gage was at Rocky's side immediately, his large hand spanning most of his wife's bump as he rubbed it in soothing circles. "Everything okay with the baby?"

"I'm pretty sure she's fine," Holly answered when Rocky continued to stay silent. Gage's electric blue eyes turned her way as she spoke. "I *think* she's just trying to come to terms with accidentally spilling the sex of your baby. Congratulations by the way."

"Hold on." Gage raised a hand in the air and returned his attention to his wife. "You know what we're having?"

Rocky nodded.

"And…"

"We're having a boy." She smiled up at her husband who threw his arms up in the air like he'd just defended his heavyweight title.

"Fuck yeah!" Gage scooped Rocky from the couch into a bear hug, spinning her in a joyful circle. "When did you find out?"

"Last week."

"*Last week?* Why didn't you tell me?"

"Well, I was planning on telling you today. It was actually part of your present, but it kind of slipped out now."

"That would be the pregnancy brain," Jordan said, and they shared a moment over having boys. "Just wait until you have number two and it's combined with mommy brain. The struggle is *real*."

The next few minutes were spent with Rocky and Gage getting passed around from person to person wishing them congratulations.

"Can I be the first to say"—Jase wrapped an arm around

both his sister and Rocky—"I'm happy you're both having boys. Because we need a *break* from the creation of future Covenettes."

The comment set off a fresh wave of laughter. Holly noticed no one denied the truth of the statement.

Presents were opened, the delicious meal was eaten buffet style, clean-up was completed and the parents returned home, leaving behind their cast of friends plus Sean and Carlee.

Holly snuggled in Vince's lap, cursing him for being the only one in the room not nursing a food baby due to his meal plan. He was at the weight he needed to be for his fight, now he just had to maintain it until weigh-ins in six days.

"Oh, come on." Sean threw his hands up in frustration at the basketball game playing on the flat-screen above the fireplace. "You were *barely* touching, dude."

She was having too much fun tracing the outlines of Vince's abs under his shirt to pay much attention to the game, but at Sean's outburst she shifted so she could see the basketball player from the Boston team being helped off the court while he held his shin.

"Basketball players are such wimps," Carlee said. "They need to toughen up. Learn to take a hit, dude."

"Why do you think I play hockey, babe?" Sean put his arm around his best friend, and snorts and chuckles sounded around the room at the little charmer.

"Donovan, have I ever told you I love how bloodthirsty your sister is?" Chance said to his teammate.

"Careful, bro," Jake cautioned. "Those two may not even be double digits in age, but they are *ruthless*." He pointed to Sean and Carlee.

"I love it."

"You would," Gemma said with an eye-roll. "You are a *goon,* after all."

"Oh, Princess." Chance tsked under his breath. "You and I both know I'm as much of a goon as your boy Jase. Don't even try to deny my skill on the ice."

The crazy tension between her roommate and the hockey player was entertaining to experience.

The couch dipped as Tucker plopped down beside her and Vince.

"So, Hol." The arm Tucker slung over her shoulders was quickly knocked away by a scowling Vince. "Can you make cookies that look like *anything*?" he asked while munching on one of the Santas she'd made.

"Pretty much."

Tuck bit off Santa's head, swallowing before he continued. "So if I needed to order a bunch of cookies that looked like dicks, you could make that happen?"

"What?" She barely got her question out through her laughter.

"Ooooh." Lyle was intrigued. "We can *totally* branch out into the erotic side of the bakery. You gonna model for the cookies, Tuck?" He waggled an eyebrow.

"Oh, god. Don't encourage him," Skye said.

"It doesn't have to be mine. But I would be happy to show you if you'd like a private viewing of my hockey stick." Tucker was somewhat charming as he made the suggestion.

"Tuck, next time you offer to show my girlfriend your dick, I'll break it off," Vince threatened, leveling him a look that had her curling in her lips to hold in a giggle. He was so over the top, even when he had nothing to worry about. The only dick she had interest in seeing was his.

Ryan reached over and smacked Tucker upside the head. "Dude...watch it. Impressionable minds." He shifted his eyes to the two kids, and luckily both were too engrossed in the basketball game to pay attention.

"Chill, Cap," Tucker said to Ryan, then turned back to her. "Anyway…I don't mean with a picture of my"—he gestured to his crotch—"I was thinking the cookie could be in the shape of the stick and pucks and you could do 'em up all fun with your icing and whatnot."

"I mean…yeah, I guess I could. But what I don't understand is *why?*"

Tucker's face broke out in a beaming smile. "Well, Nick Murphy gave me the idea as a good prank for people. I would need *a lot* of them."

Nick Murphy? Why did that name sound so familiar?

"Oh my god," Maddey called out in disbelief. "Tuck, no. No, no, no."

"What?" He shrugged. "It's a great idea."

"No, Tuck. You *cannot* have Holly make a thousand dick cookies for you to prank or revenge plot with." Maddey's voice was sterner than she'd ever heard it.

"Wait. Hold up." Holly made a T with her hands. "Why does this sound so familiar?"

"Have you ever read Pippa Grant?" Maddey asked.

"Oh, yeah, I *love* her books. Ares is one of my favorite book boyfriends. Her books are hilarious. I always laugh out loud like a crazy person when I read them."

"Girl, same," Maddey agreed. "I want to be funny like Pippa when I grow up. But anyway…I made the mistake of including her books in our book club—because you know she has her characters do book club too—and Tuck likes to take prank inspiration from the Berger twins and Nick Murphy. Biggest mistake *ever.*"

"What?" Tucker feigned innocence. "Don't they say art imitates real life?"

Maddey groaned and threw herself back onto Ryan, burying her face in his side as if she didn't have the strength needed to deal with Tucker. "I can't even."

Holly looked around the room, more content than she

could ever recall being, especially during a holiday. Back in her old life, holidays were all about photo ops and projecting the *right* image. There was none of that here.

Kyle caught her eye, giving her a soft smile. "It's great, isn't it?" he asked.

She answered with a smile, snuggling deeper into Vince, his strong arms automatically wrapping around her. Inhaling the fresh scent of his soap, at peace and safe in her boyfriend's arms.

This.

This was the life she'd dreamed of while lonely inside her gilded castle. She wanted nothing more than for it to be hers for the rest of her life.

Too bad life had other plans.

Chapter Thirty-Nine

With Christmas over, Holly was back to baking the standard fare of scones and muffins for Espresso Patronum. They say a watched pot never boils, well, the same could be said for muffins baking. She was counting down the minutes until they were done, planning to head across the street to The Steele Maker as soon as she pulled them from the oven.

She was washing the last of the mixing bowls when Lyle entered, a peculiar look on his face.

"What's wrong?" she asked immediately. Lyle looked like he was going to be sick.

"Umm…" His words trailed off as he looked away.

"Ly?" She shut off the water, moving to stand across from her friend. "You're kinda scaring me right now."

"Well, Sweets." Again he didn't finish his thought until she prodded him in his inked-up arm. "Your dad is here."

She blinked.

And blinked again.

There was *no* way she heard him right.

Her father was here?

No way.

"Say that again."

"Your dad"—Lyle pointed to her—"is out there." He pointed toward the front of the coffee house.

"My father, Randall Vanderbuilt, is here?" Shock laced her words.

"Yup."

"Are you sure?"

"Stuck up old guy. Salt and pepper hair, wears million dollar suits, and looks down his nose at everyone?"

Yeah, that was a pretty accurate description of her father.

"Did he say *why* he was here?"

Lyle crinkled his nose as if the memory was unpleasant. "He said, and I quote, 'Go fetch my daughter.'"

Yeah, that sounded like something he would say. He treated anyone who didn't have as much money or power—which was most people—as if they were merely his servants. Was it really any surprise she wanted away from her family?

She *so* didn't want to talk to her father. There weren't enough words in the English language to describe how much she didn't want to go out there. But knew if she didn't he would only come barreling into the kitchen as if he owned the place.

She tightened the bow of her bandana headband, steeling herself for what she was about to face.

He spotted her the moment she rounded the front counter. She hadn't seen him in months, but he was still the same stick-up-the-ass, haughty man looking down at the "peasants" around him as she remembered. The whiskey eyes she inherited were as hard as amber as they watched her approach.

"God, Holly." His voice dripped with disappointment. "When Chad told us what you looked like I was hoping he was exaggerating. But look at you"—he waved a hand up and down her body—"you look… You look so…*pedestrian*."

Randall Vanderbuilt may have billions, but no amount of money in the world could buy the man class.

"It's nice to see you too, Father." She wasn't able to keep the sarcasm out of her voice.

"We need to talk. Come with me." He turned on his heel, walking away without waiting for an answer. Why would he? It never occurred to Randall Vanderbuilt that people wouldn't follow his directives.

More than anything, she wanted to ignore the command, to reaffirm her new-found independence and stay where she was, far away from *anything* remotely connected to her past. Unfortunately, she knew ignoring it wouldn't make it go away. It had the potential to make things worse.

With a heavy sigh, she grabbed her winter coat from the rack by the door and stepped outside into the blistering cold December air.

"Let's talk in the limo." Her father gestured to the black stretch limo parked at the curb.

She shook her head, rejecting the idea *immediately*. She wouldn't put it past him to have his driver whisk them back to Connecticut the second the doors were closed.

"Charles." Her father barked at his driver as if reading her mind.

"Yes, sir?"

"I need a moment with my *daughter*." He spat the word like a curse. "Wait for me in the coffee shop until I am done." He didn't ask or use words like *please*. No, he commanded— manners were a foreign concept to the man.

"Now, shall we?" He held out a hand toward the limo the moment his driver disappeared inside Espresso Patronum.

She glanced across the street at The Steele Maker, not wanting to get in the vehicle, but knowing it was probably best not to be seen on the street having this conversation. If Vince happened to look out and see her, it was almost *guaranteed* he'd come outside.

Opening the door to the limo—because god forbid Randall Vanderbuilt opened it for himself—she slid across the leather seat inside the custom interior, her senses assaulted by the rich scent of the cologne her father preferred and the scotch he drank. Her stomach churned.

She moved to the long bench seat along the left side of the car, needing to face him head-on for whatever diatribe he wanted to spew. He didn't waste any time.

"It is time for you return home."

It took everything in her not to roll her eyes.

"I am home, Father." She kept eye contact as she spoke, not showing an ounce of weakness. "This"—she pointed down—"is my home."

"Don't be ridiculous," he snapped. "You've had your tantrum. Now it is time for you to grow up and come back to Connecticut. You have a duty to fulfill. A role you need to serve."

Now she did roll her eyes.

"The only *duty* I have is to be true to myself. I'm worth more than a bargaining chip in a business agreement. I'm done being used as one."

"Oh, grow up, Holly." He paused to pour himself a tumbler of thirty-five-year-old scotch. "You will return home. Pack your bags, and move back in with your fiancé before the week is out."

At the mention of Chad, there was no stopping the laugh from escaping.

"Yeah…no." She shook her head for emphasis. "You have a better chance of Mother leaving the house without any makeup on than me going back to Chad. I don't love him… and now that I know what *real* love is, I don't think I ever did."

"Real love," he scoffed. "Please god, tell me you aren't referring to that Neanderthal?"

"You and Chad claim I'm pedestrian." She massaged the

tension she felt building under her brow. "Yet the two of you are so unoriginal in your insults. What makes him a Neanderthal? Because he's an athlete? He makes his living fighting? His money isn't as old as yours?" She was careful to not include herself when referring to her father's money. "It doesn't matter where his money comes from, it's just as green as yours."

Her father's cold eyes went molten at the challenge. He believed wholeheartedly that his money meant more, not because he had more, but because he could trace their family's fortune back to before America was a country. The Vanderbuilts were a pharmaceutical empire now, but they were some of the oldest of the old when comparing old to new money.

"You listen to me." He leaned forward, invading her personal space, and she retreated immediately. It didn't matter how strong of a front she tried to put up, years of abuse had conditioned her.

"I am done with you acting like a petulant child. You will be in Connecticut in less than forty-eight hours, or I will *ruin* your little boyfriend."

Her blood ran cold at the threat. She'd been handling her family's threats and manipulations for twenty-three years, but Vince was off-limits.

"You have no power over Vince. And lord knows your fists are no match for his."

"There are ways to break a person without laying a hand on them. It's too bad he doesn't have any pets." He stroked his chin in thought.

Her blood turned to ice, and she swallowed down bile.

He was a monster, and she was done being scared.

"Vince isn't a business you can take over. You have *nothing* he could possibly want. You *can't* buy him off."

"No, you're right, I can't buy him off."

The easy acceptance made her skin crawl.

"But I can ruin him. I can destroy his career like that." He snapped his fingers.

"How?" The question came out as a choked sob.

"The timing is very fortuitous. The drug test for his upcoming fight will show evidence of doping."

He wouldn't.

"No fight. No purse. No funds for his little women's shelter he wants to fund. What a shame."

How did he know about Vince's plans?

"Don't look so surprised, Holly. I know *everything* about him."

"It won't work. He'll get it cleared. It may delay things, but that's it."

"Yes, you are correct." He buffed his nails on his suit jacket, eerily calm.

"But after the original tests keep him from fighting this fight, other documents will indicate that his family's precious gym has been paying off officials to falsify records to show *all* their fighters have been clean, when in reality, they have been dirty for *years*."

She gasped.

He wasn't just planning on going after Vince, but his entire family and their livelihood. The worst part? He had the means to do it.

He knew he won.

"Clock starts now. Forty-eight hours." He tapped his watch and reclined back in his seat like a king on the throne expecting his peasants to obey.

With a heavy heart, she exited the limo, already dreading what she knew she needed to do.

Chapter Forty

Holly was already thirty-plus hours into her forty-eight deadline. Lyle swore not to mention their surprise visitor, not even to Kyle. Thank god Maddey hadn't been writing out of EP.

Until she figured out what to do, spending as much time as possible with Vince was the priority.

It was after hours when she keyed in the code to the gym to see him. The absence of the sound of weights clanking or fists hitting punching bags was eerie.

She hesitated at the white door of the locker room, not sure what she would find on the other side of it. Sure, it *should* be empty with the gym closed, but what girl wanted to accidentally come across a strange man with his trouser snake catching some air.

She navigated her way through the rows of lockers and padded benches to where the cedar door of the sauna was tucked away in the corner.

Again she hesitated before pushing the door open, unsure what she would say when she faced Vince.

Pulling on her big girl panties, she stepped inside the steam-filled room.

. . .

VINCE SETTLED INTO his usual spot on the middle bench inside the sauna. It was his last session inside the steam room before he had to leave for Manhattan. With all his promotional obligations for the fight, it was easier to spend the last days leading up to it there. His weight had been holding steady at two hundred and three pounds—two pounds under the requirement—now he was in maintenance mode.

The usual music wasn't playing, so the only sound in the room was the hiss of steam as the water burned off the hot coals. His mind was preoccupied with Holly's peculiar behavior the last couple of days.

The door to the sauna pushed open, and as if conjured by his thoughts, his gorgeous girlfriend stepped inside. It had been less than an hour since he left her baking at Espresso Patronum, but still he couldn't get enough of her.

"Hey, Cupcake." He shifted on the bench, his dick stirring to life at the way her purple 'I don't always bake, oh wait… yes I do' v-neck dipped low enough to show off a generous amount of cleavage.

"Hey, Muffin." She smiled at him, but the wattage wasn't as high as normal.

He watched her kneel on the bench below him, her hands going to his knees as she shifted between them. His towel parted as he made room for her, the terry cloth barely remaining overlapped as he went from half-mast to fully erect when he caught a whiff of her sugary scent. He craved her more than the sweet treats he had been denying himself during camp.

But she was the treat he didn't deny himself. *Ever.*

Like something straight out of his fantasies, her hands skimmed along his thighs, burrowing underneath the towel and pushing it until the knot holding it together on his hip finally lost the battle and gave way.

A bead of sweat that had nothing to do with the heat of the sauna and everything to do with the hungry way she stared at his cock cut a path between his pecs and down to where that cock leaked pre-cum onto his belly.

"Babe?" he questioned, not all that sure what he was asking.

She didn't say a word.

Her hands continued up his legs until they hooked around his hips, using them as an anchor, she pulled herself until she was in the narrowest part of his spread legs.

Her left hand continued north, over the bumps of his abs, up to his pecs, her fingers fanning out over the muscle so it sat inside her palm while the right one wrapped around the base of his dick.

He hissed through his teeth as she squeezed him. Slowly stroked him from base to tip and back down again.

Eyes on him, she lowered her head and her tongue licked the sensitive head, before swallowing him down her throat until she kissed his manscaped pubic hair.

"*Mmm,*" she moaned, the vibrations from the sound only serving to heighten the pleasure around his dick.

Without preamble, she bobbed her head up and down.

Up.

Down.

The squeeze of her throat as she swallowed around him.

The tease of release as she pulled back until only the very tip remained inside her mouth, her tongue licking across the small slit weeping constant pre-cum.

The bandana headband slipped loose when he tangled his fingers in her hair, holding on as she worked him to the brink.

Not wanting to finish in her mouth, he gave a gentle tug on her locks until she released him with a pop.

"Straddle me," he growled.

She scrambled to do as he asked, rising from the bench and settling herself in his lap.

The position put him at eye level with her breasts, and he *needed* them in his mouth, his tongue stroking across the hard bud of her nipple as he suckled and teased the pillowy flesh.

He had her shirt and bra off and tossed to the side before she took her next breath, her hips rocking into him.

"*Vince,*" his name was a broken plea as he bit down on her nipple.

Another rock of her hips pushed on his dick trapped between his belly and the cotton of her leggings.

He needed inside her.

He needed inside her *now*.

He cupped her ass, following the seam of her pants until he found the perfect spot, tugging until the sound of ripping fabric filled the room as he tore the pants from her body.

Her head fell forward as a shocked gasp left her mouth at his caveman actions.

"Sorry, baby." He adjusted so her center lined up with his erection. "I'll give you some sweats." He trailed a path of kisses across her collarbone. "I can't wait. *Ride* me."

Lust-drunk eyes met his before looking down. She took him in her hand, shifting until he was braced at her entrance, then lowered herself inch by inch until he was buried to the hilt inside her.

Heaven.

Sweet baby Jesus, he had died and gone to heaven.

HOLLY LOST THE ability to breathe as she lowered herself onto Vince. The all-consuming fullness made it impossible to process anything else except for how *right* it was to be with him like this. Him and *only* him.

She was so keyed up she was already on the verge of coming.

Hell, when he literally ripped her pants from her body, she swore she had a mini orgasm.

She needed a moment to adjust to the way his over-whelming size stretched her body.

"Fuck, you're so tight," he groaned into her neck. The whispered curses only intensified as she rocked in his lap.

She circled her hips then used the muscles of her thighs to lift and lower back down.

His large hands cupped her ass, squeezing to help guide her body up and down his length.

Faster and faster she rode him, breasts bouncing in his face from the force.

There was almost no gray to be seen when she locked eyes with him again, keeping eye contact as she swiveled her hips like a stripper giving the lap dance of her life.

If this was going to be the last time she could have him like this, it was going to be the best sex of either of their lives.

One hand rose to cradle the back of her head as he pulled her down for a kiss with so much passion she was surprised they didn't burn the room down around them.

She poured everything she had into the kiss.

She had no idea how she was supposed to give this up.

This was so much more than sex.

It was more than their bodies coming together, it was a joining of their souls.

There wasn't a part of her that didn't love him.

Her heart.

Her mind.

Her body.

Her soul.

Every part of her claimed each of his.

Leaving him was going to do irreparable damage, but what choice did she have? She loved him too much to stay.

Faster.

Faster.

She slammed her body down on his cock one last time, exploding around him, her orgasm knocking the breath from her body. Sweat from more than the sauna coated her skin as she melted against him while his own orgasm ripped from his body.

He continued to pump inside her, the thrusts easing as they came down from the high of release.

She didn't climb from his lap, soaking in every last second she could, branding herself with the memory of what it felt like to be in his arms.

"I love you, Cupcake."

She choked back a sob as he whispered the words into her hair.

I love you too. So fucking much, Muffin.

She couldn't bring herself to utter the words out loud though.

She couldn't quantify how much she was going to miss him.

Chapter Forty-One

Vince shifted awake, automatically reaching for Holly since she wasn't cuddled against him. Except as he stretched out all he found were sheets—cold sheets.

He pushed himself up onto an elbow and looked at the empty spot on her side of the bed. As a baker, it was pretty common for her to be up and out before him, but she hadn't woken him up to kiss him goodbye before she left. What was up with that?

Left to right, he dropped an ear to each shoulder, neck cracking with the movement, his sleepy mind trying to remember if she said she was going in to work that morning.

He was leaving for Manhattan in a couple of hours and needed to get his butt in gear and out of bed.

He caught a flash of hot pink, the bright color at odds with his spider web sheets. Reaching out, he lifted the object, realizing it was a sticky note attached to a phone—Holly's phone.

Brow creased, he took in the familiar cartoon drawing of a cupcake on the back of the case, before flipping it back over to read the note written out in her bubbly writing. "Watch me," was all it said.

He slid his thumb across the screen to unlock it, hitting play on the video already queued up. His lips twitched as her beautiful face filled the screen, but he frowned at the sadness on it and the red rimming her eyes as if she'd been crying. His pulse thumped like a speed bag as scenarios for why she would be upset sped through his mind.

"Hey, Muffin." She tried to smile but it missed its mark.

"I don't even know where to start."

Then don't. His mind screamed as he scanned the area behind her, trying to determine where she filmed the video. From the limited amount he could see, he guessed she used the stairwell of their apartment building based on the plain white wall behind her and the slight echo of her voice.

Her shoulders rose as she pulled in a deep breath.

"I need you to watch this entire message before you react. Please, Vince, don't hit stop until the end."

Another deep inhale.

"By the time you watch this I'll already be back in Connecticut."

The fuck?! How had her family gotten to her? He was going to kill Chad.

"Now I need you to take a breath and calm down. I wasn't kidnapped, this isn't a ransom note or anything. Can I say I wanted to leave?" She shook her head. "No, I can't say that. But I was the one who made the decision to leave."

He watched as a tear fell from her eye, cutting a path down her cheek. Nothing she said made sense. If she didn't want to leave, then why did she?

"I need you to promise you will not come after me. You have to go to the city for your fight. Please, please, focus on winning the title you've worked your whole life toward and don't come looking for me."

Was she crazy? How the hell did she think the title was more important than her? Had he not done enough to *prove* how much she meant to him?

"I mean it, Vin. Go. To. Your. Fight. Do. Your. Job. I—"

Her words cut off as a sob broke free.

"I love you too damn much to have you throw away your life's work."

His heart turned over inside his chest. She loved him. It was the first time she said the words out loud. Why the hell did it have to be as she was saying goodbye?

"I'm sorry I was too scared to tell you before, but I've loved you for so long. And even though I have to give you up, which"—she looked up as if struggling to get the words out—"is harder than I imagined, I'm grateful I was able to experience what real love was, even if it was for such a short time."

It didn't have to be a short time. They didn't have to be over. He would get her back and prove it to her. She was crazy if she thought he was just going to give her up without a fight.

"I love you so much and I'm pretty sure I'll never stop, but I need you to let me go."

The tears were now pouring down her face in a steady stream.

"Go to your fight. Win your fight. Use the money to fund the shelter. Forget about me. Live your life and be happy."

How the fuck did she think he could be happy without her?

When he got her back, he was tying her to his bed and he wasn't letting her out of it until *any* thought of him being able to "live" without her was permanently erased from her mind.

"I love you, Vince. You will forever be my Stud Muffin. Now go kick some ass and become the Light Heavyweight Champion of the UFC."

The video ended, Holly's tear-stained face frozen on the screen.

He was out of his bed in a flash. There wasn't a chance in hell that he *wasn't* going after her. She was the *only* thing that mattered.

Not training.

Not the million promotional engagements Jordan and Skye had lined up.

Not the fight.

Not the belt.

Not even funding the women's shelter.

Nothing.

Nothing mattered except bringing Holly home.

Home with him, in New Jersey, not in some mansion in Connecticut with douchewaffle Chad.

He was about to piss off *so* many people but he'd deal with it *after* he got his girl back.

He was grabbing his keys from the rack by the door when it pushed open, and his sister stepped in. From the expression on her face, he had a feeling she already knew what he had planned.

"No." Rocky's tone was commanding and left no room for argument. Steel gray eyes met his as she stared him down—hard. He might be the professional fighter in the family, but his sister was the true badass.

"I'm going." He tried to go around her, but she side-stepped, using her body to block his exit.

"No, you're not." She crossed her arms, resting her forearms on the growing swell of her belly. "Didn't you listen to what she said to you?"

"I don't *care*, Rock." He ran a hand through his hair, pulling on the strands in frustration. "I *love* her."

Her eyes softened as she looked at him. "I know you do, Vin. But she *wants* you to go to the city and do your job."

"So what? You're saying forget about her. Ignore how my heart is breaking and go out and fight like it's not? Like the thought of her even spending *one second* around that real-life Ken doll isn't tearing at my insides?"

"Actually, comparing Chad Montgomery to Ken is an insult to the doll, not the man. Ken super loves Barbie and is an A-plus boyfriend."

He growled in the back of his throat. "Not the point, Rock."

"I know." She ran a reassuring hand down his arm. "I'm sorry."

"Forgiven." The last thing he wanted to do was fight with his sister. It wasn't her he was mad at, it was the situation.

"Listen." She pushed him toward the stools at the island in the kitchen. "This is what you're gonna do."

He held up a hand to cut her off. "Wait. How do you even know what happened? Did she tell you she was going to leave me?"

"*God,* no, Vin." She made a face, clearly offended he even made the accusation.

Now it was his turn to apologize.

"I had an email from Holly this morning. It was a video message telling me what she was doing and *begging* me to make sure you went to your fight and not after her."

"How did she email you when I have her phone?" he asked, trying to piece together the timeline.

"She must have scheduled it, because I got it right before I came over."

Ray and Deck made their way out of their rooms, not saying a word as if reading the tension in the room.

"You really want me to go to the city like everything is fine? Like Holly didn't leave me?"

"The fuck?" the guys said in unison behind him but they ignored them.

"What I'm saying is…" Rocky leveled him with a look "… first, you go and win your fight. Then, you go and fight for your girl. Because"—she held up a finger when he tried to speak—"if you *don't,* Holly is only going to be pissed when she sees you."

He was quiet as he considered her words.

"Don't forfeit one fight when you can win them both."

Chapter Forty-Two

Vince was a mess, an utter disaster. He was in a holding pattern and he fucking hated it.

He was a man of action who wasn't allowed to act.

It sucked big hairy balls.

Holly was gone.

She loved him, but she was gone.

He had a job to do, but she was gone.

His head needed to be in the game to win his fight, but she was gone.

If he didn't win the fight, he wouldn't be able to fund the women's shelter. A shelter he had worked for years to be in the position to help build.

But still—she was gone.

He was in the city, and she was gone.

The real kick in the balls was that he knew she went back to people who had hurt her before.

Nightmares plagued him, the possibilities of what could happen to her without him there to protect her gutting him.

He had learned to ask instead of command, giving them each options when it came to the things that would affect their relationship. Then she went ahead and cut him out of the equation entirely.

He was pissed.

Holly was gone, and for the time being, he couldn't do *anything* about it.

It needed to be tomorrow—Fight Night—because he *really* needed to hit something.

FORTY-THREE

Coven Conversations

From the Group Message Thread of The Coven

MOTHER OF DRAGONS: Meet in the lobby of the hotel in 1 hour.

MAKES BOYS CRY: Where we going?

ALPHABET SOUP: What's up? This sounds serious.

PROTEIN PRINCESS: How can a text sound serious?

QUEEN OF SMUT: I think it's more the fact we're being summoned.

YOU KNOW YOU WANNA: What's going on?

• • •

THE OG PITA: Isn't it too early to meet up for the fight?

MOTHER OF DRAGONS: I know what happened with Holly.

MOTHER OF DRAGONS: And more importantly, I know where she is.

YOU KNOW YOU WANNA: Man you guys say I know how to leave you in suspense. But look at Jordan stepping up her game.

ALPHABET SOUP: Should we loop in Vince?

YOU KNOW YOU WANNA: Seriously…

YOU KNOW YOU WANNA: Boy has been like a chick in a rom-com when they go through the usual breakup scene.

YOU KNOW YOU WANNA: Pathetic.

MOTHER OF DRAGONS: NO!!!!

MOTHER OF DRAGONS: DON'T say anything to Vince yet.

MOTHER OF DRAGONS: This shit has already fucked with his head enough. He needs to concentrate on the fight. There's still the possibility my plan won't work. I'm not going to let this cost him everything he's worked for.

PROTEIN PRINCESS: Shit. This must be serious if we broke Jor enough to have her texting like Beck *crying laughing emoji*

QUEEN OF SMUT: *GIF of Whitney Houston pointing to herself then up saying "This"*

QUEEN OF SMUT: *GIF of Mike Tyson clapping hands and laughing*

THE OG PITA: GOD…we are THE WORST. We can't even stay on topic when it's serious.

YOU KNOW YOU WANNA: *GIF of dog from *Up* turning his head saying "Squirrel"*

ALPHABET SOUP: *praise hands emoji* *praise hands emoji*

MOTHER OF DRAGONS: Can we be serious now?

MAKES BOYS CRY: Rock, Beck, will you be able to dip out without the guys getting suspicious?

ALPHABET SOUP: Yes?

. . .

QUEEN OF SMUT: I'm in the restaurant downstairs. I'll just come get you like any other time we would do something Covenish. They won't think anything of it.

YOU KNOW YOU WANNA: *GIF of Seth Meyers pointing saying "That's a freakin' great idea"*

QUEEN OF SMUT: *GIF of guy gesturing to his temple as if to say he's smart*

ALPHABET SOUP: Gem you good to meet us?

PROTEIN PRINCESS: Yup. I finished at Dickhead's a little while ago. I'm already on the train headed to the city. Be there in about 30.

THE OG PITA: Dude...you and Chance just need to fuck each other and get it over with.

PROTEIN PRINCESS: *puking emoji*

MAKES BOYS CRY: Umm hmm...doth protest too much me thinks

YOU KNOW YOU WANNA: Besides...

. . .

YOU KNOW YOU WANNA: Aint nothing wrong with a little hate fucking.

QUEEN OF SMUT: Ooooo I FLOVE a good enemies-to-lovers story.

THE OG PITA: *GIF of girl saying "Girl, Same"*

MOTHER OF DRAGONS: OMG…Me too…But truth be told I would have thought that would have been Skye and BB3… except they aren't "enemy" enough…but you and Chance…100%.

ALPHABET SOUP: I'd read it.

THE OG PITA: Kindle crack right there.

MAKES BOYS CRY: Yeah…me and Tuck again…not gonna happen

MOTHER OF DRAGONS: Famous last words.

PROTEIN PRINCESS: O

. . .

PROTEIN PRINCESS: M

PROTEIN PRINCESS: G

PROTEIN PRINCESS: I can't even.

PROTEIN PRINCESS: Hurry up and meet in the hotel lobby. We need to get Holly back, because clearly I need new friends.

Chapter Forty-Four

Four days.

Holly had been back in her parents' house for four days.

She was *not* going to make it to day five.

Her soul felt poisoned, every second she spent in her prison disguised as a mansion only added to the feeling like ingredients added to a recipe.

The silver lining—the fake silver, the kind that turns your skin green when you wear it—was at least she was at her parents' house and not Chad's. Her father tried to pressure, or force depending on your definition of the word, her to return to her old home, but she vehemently refused.

It was the day of Vince's big fight. Her heart was both overjoyed at the thought of him accomplishing his dream but broken at missing out on getting to experience it with him.

Leaving him had felt like she'd ripped her heart out of her chest and left it behind next to her phone. Walking away had been the mermaid in the non-Disney version of the tale, where each step felt like walking on razor blades.

She had left her phone behind, knowing if she kept it she would have been too tempted to give in to the attempts she knew Vince would make to reach her. But that didn't mean she wasn't keeping tabs on him.

Quite the opposite.

The moment she'd stepped inside the mansion, she commandeered one of the numerous iPads her parents had, using it to keep tabs on what Vince had been up to. Luckily for her, he was easy to track. Between the UFC and social media, thanks a lot in part to Jordan and Skye handling his accounts, she was able to take her internet stalking game to expert levels.

She was hiding out in the library, a room so grand it would make even Belle from *Beauty and the Beast* green with envy, as she scoured social media to find any crumb of information on Vince and how he was handling the lead up to his fight.

Some of the guys had posted here and there, but the girls were suspiciously inactive.

She'd watched the broadcast of yesterday's weigh-ins, but it wasn't the sight of him standing on stage in a glorified pair of boxer briefs that caught her attention—okay, who was she kidding, seeing him practically naked would *never* get old. But the haunted, almost dead look in his eyes had tears falling from her own. Gone was the playful alpha she fell for, in his place was a shell of her Stud Muffin.

The worst part?

She had done that. It was *her* fault. To protect him, she had to break him. It sucked. It sucked big hairy donkey balls.

"Miss Holly," the accented voice of Mrs. Rodriquez, the long-time housekeeper and only person she held any affection for in this mausoleum, startled her. "I'm sorry, Miss Holly."

"No, it's fine." She waved off her concern. "Did you need me?"

"Sí. You are needed in your father's study." There was a

hint of a smile on her face, which was strange given the directive delivered.

Ugh. That was the *last* place she wanted to be. The only reason she pushed out of the large wingback chair she was curled up in and headed for her least favorite room in the almost ten-thousand-square-foot mansion was because it would only be worse if she didn't.

"Chin up, chiquita." Mrs. Rodriquez had used the endearment most of her life. "It's good."

She respected the older woman too much to roll her eyes, but she highly doubted it. Her biggest hope was that she wasn't being summoned to be ambushed by Chad again. The Vanderbuilt/Montgomery tag team was getting old.

Stepping over the threshold, she let out an audible groan spotting, not one, but both Montgomery men in the room. Posed to flee, she caught sight of the other occupants in the room—all seven of them.

The Coven had arrived.

Standing at the front of the group was Jordan, and she looked pissed. Like full-on ready to live up to her Mother of Dragons text handle and breathe fire all over the room.

"What are you guys doing here?" she asked the girls, ignoring the men in the room completely. She had said everything she needed to say to them—repeatedly.

"Bringing you home," Gemma answered.

"*Duh,*" Becky added, causing her to laugh for first time since Christmas.

"Plus you're already one of us, and I don't feel like going through the process of breaking in another potential sister-in-law," Rocky said lightly, as though the words weren't as heavily weighted as her maiden name. Holly would *love* to have her as a sister-in-law.

"Holly will not be going anywhere." Her father's voice boomed in the room.

"I'm pretty sure *Holly* is a grown woman and can make

decisions for herself, but thanks for the input." Skye's voice dripped with sarcasm.

"Holly is staying here to fulfill the obligations set forth by this family."

"Dude, we're in the twenty-first century. Why don't you join us?"

A snort escaped Holly at Maddey calling Randall Vander-built *dude*.

"Holly knows her place. And it is not with the gym rat." Chad made the mistake of adding his two cents.

"Listen here, you wannabe Ken doll." Beth stepped into Chad's personal space. "Vincent Steele is *so* much more than a gym rat. Why don't you educate yourself so you're not such an ignorant ass the next time you open your mouth."

"And Holly"—Holly added, spurned on by the show of force from her friends, her true family, her Coven—"can speak for herself, thank you very much." She detested when people referred to themselves in the third person, but she gave herself a pass seeing as the males in the room wanted to speak about her as if she weren't standing there.

"If you must." Her father looked down his nose at her as he spoke. "Can you please get it over with so we can be rid of this nuisance and get back to discussing the benefit you will be accompanying Chad to this evening. You and I both know what will happen if you don't."

She'd had enough.

From the moment she stepped back into her childhood prison, she had been laying the groundwork for returning home—her real home in New Jersey.

She wasn't the same meek girl who grew up there. She was no longer afraid of what her father could do to her. Sure, he could physically hurt her, but she was no longer afraid.

The Coven may have arrived to fight for her, and though she loved them for it, she didn't need them to fight her battles. She could fight them herself—Vince had taught her that.

Shoulders back, chin up, she declared, "I'm leaving."

"No, you're not," her father scoffed.

"Yes. I am."

"Holly, stop being ridiculous and go get cleaned up for tonight. I can't be seen with you looking like"—Chad looked her up and down—"*that*."

"There's nothing wrong with the way I look, so fuck off, Chad."

"Aww, it's so cute when you can blatantly tell a man is trying to overcompensate for something," Jordan said.

"It's not much to write home about," Holly agreed. "And on that note…" She turned for the door, and her father stalked in her direction.

His hand was raised to slap her across the face as he had done more times than she could count throughout her life. This time things would play out differently.

Instincts honed from hours spent learning from Vince, she blocked the hit, circling her hand around his wrist and twisted, while her other hand shot out and landed a solid jab to his nose.

There was a crunch, followed by a gush of blood.

Did I just break his nose?

"Damn, Rock," Becky laughed. "She *really* was meant to be related to you."

"For reals," Gemma said. "At least if the way you two go around breaking douchebags' noses is any indication."

Her Covenettes surrounded her with hugs, and this time they turned for the door as a group.

"You step one foot outside that door and you know what I'll do, Holly." Her father's voice was muffled with his hands cupped around his nose.

"You can try." She stopped in the doorway to face him.

"But if you do, I'll release this to the media." She pulled a flash drive from her pocket.

Randall Vanderbuilt's eyes narrowed.

"You didn't *really* think I came back here without a plan, did you? Come on, *Dad*, that's so pedestrian."

There were snickers behind her.

"I spent the last four days gathering all sorts of shady information on the three of you." She pointed to all three men in front of her. "You even breathe wrong in the direction of my family—my *real* family—I will *ruin* you." She tossed his same words back at him.

Surrounded by her people, she gathered the one bag she brought with her and settled into the leather seat of Jordan's luxury vehicle, knowing there was one stop she needed to make before she went and got her man.

Chapter Forty-Five

"**D**ude." Jase put his hand on Vince's shoulder to stop his pacing. "Seriously, Creed, you need to chill. You're going to be too tired to fight if you continue to wear a path in the carpet."

Vince rolled his eyes. First, that was a ridiculous nickname solely based on his sister's name. And second, the floor was tile. But Jase Donnelly loved to embellish, it was practically in his DNA. Vince blamed the amount of time his friend spent with Maddey—her flowery words were clearly rubbing off on the puck head.

"He's right, Vin."

He shot Deck a look that screamed *not helping, bro* and continued pacing.

"Don't look at me like that," Deck countered with an *I'm not the enemy here* look.

One.

Two.

Three.

Four.

Five.

A squeak of sneakers against tile as he turned.

Five steps back the other direction.

He kept pacing, ignoring his friends. Didn't they get it? Without Holly, this all meant nothing. Not that he could utter those words out loud, at least not to anyone but his sister.

His currently should-be-there-but-wasn't sister.

Lifting his head for another pass of the room didn't reveal anything he didn't already know—no Rocky. His dad and uncle were huddled in a corner, most likely bitching about how off he'd been for the last four days—four days since his heart up and walked, ran, bused, or however the fuck she chose to get back to Connecticut—without Holly. He was a mess. He knew it. He would admit it.

"Will you *stop* your fucking pacing for like one minute, asshole?" Jase grabbed his arm, pulling him to a stop and not letting go.

The look he sent his friend would have most men pissing themselves, but no, he had to go and become best friends with a guy who was one of the toughest enforcers in the National Hockey League. He growled in frustration.

"Look," Jase said, finally relinquishing his hold on him. "I'm not saying the situation doesn't suck major Yoshi balls, because it does. But what I *am* saying is…did you ever stop brooding long enough to note who *else* is missing right now?"

"*Brooding?*" Sarcasm dripped from the word. "You need to lay off the romance novels, bro."

"Fuck you, asshole, you read the same amount as me, so don't even start." Jase looked almost bored at his attempt to insult him. "Now stop being a dick and open. Your. Eyes." He waved an arm around the room. "Who isn't here? Rocky maybe? You know, your *sister.* Also known as the person who wraps your hands for *every* fight."

"Fuck. You." One long stride had them toe-to-toe, his fingers doing their best impression of jazz hands to rid himself of the irritation coursing through his body while he reminded himself *not* to punch him. "*Now* who's the one being a dick?" Vince arched a brow. "I may not be as superstitious as some of the wonky *Major League*-type shit you guys get into—"

"Bro." Jase chuckled, cutting him off. "Do not use a *baseball* movie as your reference point." He facepalmed.

He gave in to the urge to roll his eyes. "Anyway…like I was saying…I have *one* tradition." He held a finger up for emphasis. "And that is to have Rock wrap my hands before every fight. So can you *please* refrain from pointing out how she is *not* here right now?"

"But that's my point." Jase's hands slapped his thighs.

It was a toss-up who was more annoyed with the other.

"You know," Deck cut in while buffing his nails on his shirt like he didn't have a care in the world. "I'm a little disappointed you haven't picked up what Jase is throwing down. You *both* were the ones to name The Coven. Don't you think it's a little weird that *none* of them are here right now?"

Was that true?

Another inspection of the room and sure enough, there wasn't a female in sight. All the guys from the gym were there: Nick and Damon yucking it up in the corner, Griff most likely texting his girlfriend, Simone, while talking to Ray, and Gage was sitting on the same treatment table he would use when his hands were wrapped under the watchful eyes of the officials soon.

"Where's your wife?" he snapped at his brother-in-law. The dude looked way too calm for his pregnant wife to not be at his side.

"Your *sister*"—he cocked a brow sarcastically, not at all intimidated by Vince's harsh tone—"told me they had 'Coven business' to take care of, but she promised to be back in time to wrap your hands. So can you *please* untwist the panties that are currently bunched in your vagina and take a chill pill, man?"

He flipped him off, but couldn't work up a good mad over

the comment. He'd said pretty much the same thing to Gage when he was mooning over Rocky.

"Thank you!" Jase threw his hands in the air, holding them up and looking to the ceiling as if praying for patience. "*This* is what I've been trying to get you to realize for fifteen minutes. JD and Skye have never missed an important event for any of us. If they aren't here now, well…" He let his words trail off for them to fill in the blanks.

Vince dug his knuckles into his brow ridge. The maelstrom of emotions churning inside left him feeling unmoored, like a buoy at sea in the middle of a hurricane. He could *never* admit it out loud, but he was counting down the seconds until his fight, but not so he had his shot at the title. No, the sooner the fight got started, the sooner it would be over and he could go after Holly.

Holly.

Holly.

Holly.

Her name was a staccato pulse in his brain with every beat of his heart.

Fucking hell, falling in love was the toughest fight he'd ever faced. Though his heart felt like it had already gone four rounds inside the cage, it was smacking gloves, ready for the final five minutes left to win. His record was unblemished, not one defeat on it. His Cupcake *would not* be the first.

He'd do what his sister told him. He'd win the fight, then go and win the girl.

Maddey had better prepare herself to take notes, because this was going to be the sweetest victory of all.

The tinkling sounds of feminine laughter trickled in, and heads snapped toward the open door as the girls stepped through. His eyes raked over the faces of the most important women in his life, aside from his mother, looking for the one vital to his existence. His heart sank when he didn't see the flash of purple hair.

Chapter Forty-Six

Holly worried the edge of the bandage wrapped around her wrist as she followed the girls through the tunnels of Madison Square Garden. No matter how many times they tried to reassure her Vince would be happy to see her, she couldn't rid herself of the anxiety the thought of facing him again brought on.

There was *so* much she'd done wrong in how she handled things.

For starters, she left.

She told him she loved him and left. She didn't even want to think about the fact that the first time she told him she loved him was in a video message while she dumped him. There was not one thing she'd done right in that entire scenario.

"Relax." Rocky linked their arms. "He's going to be beyond happy to see you."

"He's got to be pissed."

"Not at you," Rocky said with confidence. "Actually…if he is pissed, it's going to be at me."

She snorted. "Why would he be pissed at you? You're not

the one who told him you loved him and then broke up with him in the same breath…over voicemail."

Rocky placed a hand over the swell of her belly as she laughed. "Whatever. He should be happy someone as awesome as you even wants to put up with his punk ass. But I'm the one to wrap his hands before a fight, and"—she pulled her phone from her pocket and checked the time—"I'm cutting it *a little* close to when that needs to happen for him *not* to be freaking out. I'm sure he'll forgive me when he realizes I'm late because I brought him *you*."

Rocky's words washed over her, a soothing balm on each of her frayed edges.

As each of the girls disappeared inside the room—the room where Vince was—she unlooped her arm from Rocky's for her to go on. She needed a moment to compose herself.

The man she loved was in there.

The same man she loved and dumped.

She left to protect him. Now she just needed to explain and beg for forgiveness.

She could do this.

She hoped.

With a fortifying breath, she straightened the hem of her shirt and went to get her man.

Chapter Forty-Seven

Like a vision, there she was.

Not giving one fuck about their audience, Vince strode across the room, wrapped an arm around Holly's body, lifted her into his arms, pinned her to the wall, and crushed his mouth to hers.

Mine.

Vanilla and sugar filled his lungs and danced across his tastebuds as he devoured her mouth. In four days, he'd missed her taste more than the treats he denied himself during the three months spent in training camp.

Everything in the room faded into the background, the hyperfocus he fought with taking over as he reacquainted himself with the flavor, the smell, the feel of his girlfriend.

Four days.

Four long, torturous days he was without her. Never again.

She was his, and he was hers. And as soon as he could ask without worrying he'd scare her off, he was asking her to marry him. He needed her tied to him in *every* way.

"Vincent."

The use of his full name spoken in his father's gruff voice

was the only thing capable of penetrating. Not willing to part from Holly for a second, he maintained their position against the wall and turned his head to lock eyes with Papa Steele.

"It's time to get your hands wrapped." He nodded toward the official from the UFC and his opponent's chief second standing inside the room.

Arms crossed under her ass, he shifted them from the wall and carried Holly with him to the treatment table, setting her down in the spot Gage vacated, needing her close now that he had gotten her back.

Automatically he held his hand out to his sister, keeping his focus on Holly, having done the hand wrap dance so many times it was muscle memory. "Nice of you to show up," he said to his sister, eyes still on Holly.

The thin, soft gauze of the base wrap circled his hand and wrapped around his wrist.

"Yeah, well, I knew you needed to have your Cupcake"—clearly she meant his nickname for Holly and not the actual treat—"before the fight, so I went and got it."

He loved his sister something fierce.

His fingers spread as she threaded the gauze between them, then he clenched them into a fist to keep it from getting too tight and affecting his circulation.

"Good lookin' out, sis," he relented, unable to hold on to his anger now that his other half was back with him.

The gauze layer was signed off by the official, and Rocky set to work with ten feet of surgical tape on top. She completed one hand fully before moving onto the next.

Once both hands were signed with black Sharpie, he was able to slip on his black fingerless gloves, then the UFC official and O'Doyle's chief second left the room. After they were gone, he hooked an arm around Holly's middle and pulled her over to straddle his lap where he sat on the table. Her gasp of shock filled his ears, causing his lips to tip up.

His grin turned into a full-fledged smile when he saw how

wide her whiskey-colored eyes were. Male pride filled him at the swelling in her berry-hued lips, no doubt thanks to him claiming them. He yearned for more.

His heart skipped a beat, and he barked out a laugh as he read the writing on her v-neck t-shirt. Written in the blue, yellow, and red color scheme of Superman were the words, 'I'm just a Cupcake looking for her Stud Muffin.' The wrapper on the cupcake had little Superman emblems on them, and the muffins had Steele printed over and over.

"You know I fucking love this, right?" He ran a finger around the muffin printed near her belly button. "*Almost* as much as I love you."

"I love you too, Muffin." Her mouth quirked the way it always did when she used the nickname. "I'm sorry I didn't say it soo—"

He cut off her apology with a kiss.

The last thing he wanted was for the first time he got to hear those three magical words spoken in person to be tainted with an apology. Just hearing them uttered in her soft voice had his heart swelling three sizes like the Grinch.

Her hands came up and fisted in his Superman-inspired shirt. His own hands trailed down the silky skin of her arms, over the bump of her elbow before coming to rest over her slender wrists. The crinkle of bandages wrapped at the base of each hand had him pulling back.

Cradling her wrists, he lifted them for inspection, his heart straight up stopping at the sight of the harsh white bandages wrapped and taped all the way around her wrists—both wrists. The implications had bile churning in his gut, and he had to choke it back.

What the fuck had his girl gone through while she was gone?

. . .

HOLLY TREMBLED IN Vince's arms, the look of devastation on his face as he looked at her wrists rocked her to her core.

Does he know what I did? Is he mad?

She swallowed thickly, barely managing it around the elf-sized lump in her throat.

"*Holly.*"

She wasn't sure if it was the use of her actual name or the almost broken way he said it that sent a shiver of pain skirting down her spine. He sounded *nothing* like the cocky fighter she had grown to love.

"Vin? What's wrong?" The words whipped out of her.

"It—what—how?" He spoke in a staccato, his eyes not once leaving the bandages.

"Vin?" She tried again, attempting to lift her hands to cup his face, but his hold was too firm. "Do they really upset you that much?" She choked back a sob, unsure what she was supposed to do if he answered yes.

"*Upset?*" His voice rose as his agitation escalated, and thunderclouds swirled in his gray eyes when they snapped to hers. "Upset? You're damn fucking right I'm upset. Wait… No." He shook his head. "Upset is too tame of a word for what I'm feeling right now, Holly."

Shit. Way to go, Hol. It's not like it's permanent or anything.

"I can't believe you can even ask me that right now." His thumbs ghosted over the inside of her wrists.

"I didn't think you'd be so bothered by it."

He reared back in shock. The thunderclouds rolled as they locked back on her.

"*Bothered?*" The look he gave her was so savage it was no wonder he never lost a fight. Having that look turned on her when she knew he loved her, she could only *imagine* what his opponents felt like having it trained their way. "Well, aren't we the queen of the understatement right now." His knuckles went white as they tugged at the longer hair on top of his head.

"I mean—" she tried again, only to be cut off.

"If this is what they fucking did to you, *why* would you go back to them?"

Wait? What?

"What are you talking about?"

He continued on like she hadn't spoken.

"*Fuck,* Holly." Another tug on his hair. "It was bad enough having you leave, knowing you wanted me to wait to come after you. But what the fuck?" His gaze was probing. "How the fuck do you think I would have felt when I *finally* was able to come get you and you were wearing bruises from *them*?"

Her brain scrambled to put the puzzle pieces together.

"Vin."

He ignored her to stare at her hands.

"Vin."

Now he wasn't even looking at her.

"VINCENT!"

His eyes finally snapped to hers.

She yanked until he relented his hold on her wrists. She went to work loosening the tape securing the bandages, her movements jerky as she unraveled the adhesive.

"No one hurt me. That's not what these are from." She peeled back both bandages. "Look."

He stubbornly refused to look down at her wrists. A growl of frustration escaped her throat at his obstinance.

She shoved her wrists in his face, so close he wouldn't be able to focus on what she was trying to show him, but hoping it was enough to get him to pay attention.

"I'm. Not. Injured. I'm inked."

Her friends giggled in the background, not even trying to pretend they weren't listening to every word. Good. She might need them to knock some sense into her boyfriend if he was determined to act like an idiot.

"W-What?"

There he is. Nice of you to pay attention.

"They didn't hurt me. They never got the chance. *You* made sure of that." The conviction rang out with each word she spoke. He might literally be the fighter in their relationship, but she was no shrinking violet. It may have taken her twenty-three years to stand up for herself, but now that she had, she was never stopping. Even though she did leave, it was always her plan to make it back to him.

His calloused thumb stroked along the outline of the small black witch's hat she had tattooed on her right wrist like the other Covenettes.

"You know what this means, right?" Awe-filled eyes bounced between the tattoo and her face. "It's official. You're stuck with us for life now. Tattoos are permanent, you know?"

Yeah, she had been well aware of that fact as the needles went to work marking her forever. She had to bite her tongue to keep from quoting Rachel Green when she and Phoebe got tattoos and said they were licked on by kittens.

"Are you saying you don't like it?"

"Are you *crazy?*" His head shook frantically. "I fucking love it."

"Good."

Now for the part that *might* make her seem crazy.

"Well...I hope you still feel that way when you see the *other* one I had done."

She brought his attention to her left wrist, the skin still pink around where she had *Muffin's* inked in black script across it. She'd taken the personalization a step further and had the possessive "s" shaped into a mini Superman emblem.

It was his turn for his eyes to go wide like a cartoon character.

"Marry me."

Okay, so *he* wanted to be the insane one in the relationship obviously.

"Are you out of your mind?"

"Maybe." He shrugged. "Doesn't matter. Marry me."

"Oh my god. This is totally going in one of my books." Maddey's attempt at whispering failed.

"Not now, Madz," Vince called out before returning his steely gaze to her. "I'm serious, Cupcake. Marry me."

"And I'm serious, *Muffin*. No, I will not marry you. It's *way* too soon."

"But it wasn't too soon to get my name tattooed on you?" One of his black brows lifted with the admittedly perfect counter-argument. *Damn him.*

"Fine." She relented with an attempt to scowl. "Think of it as a promise ring of sorts."

"Promise ring." Jase snorted.

"How high school virgin of them," Deck added and the room lost it in big, leg-slapping guffaws.

"You need *romance*, man," Gage choked out through his laughter.

"Says the guy who proposed inside the cage after a fight," Vince grumbled.

"Hey." She turned to find Gage grinning like a schoolgirl as he stood with his arms wrapped around Rocky. "She said yes, so *clearly* I have more game than you."

Vince's gloves creaked as he flipped off his brother-in-law, and she couldn't stop her own laugh from breaking free.

"You find this amusing, do you?" Her nipples puckered and her clit throbbed at the dark promise she heard lurking in his words.

"A little." She held her fingers about an inch apart.

"Well, you know what this means now?"

She shook her head, not at all sure how far he would take things in front of an audience.

He lifted her wrist a pressed a kiss to the tattoo of his name. "I have to figure out where to get my cupcake." He waved a hand over his body.

"Ehhh." She made a sound like a buzzer. "First thing you have to do is go out there and kick some ass to win the belt. *Then*, if you can manage that, you'll have earned your cupcake."

"It's in the bag, baby."

Chapter Forty-Eight

Not long after Vince's impromptu proposal—and hold on a sec because *what the fuck was that?*—Holly followed the bulk of the squad out to their cage-side seats for the fight, while Rocky, Gage, Jase, Deck and Ray stayed behind with Vince. Rocky would be one of his cornermen—the people who actually went inside the cage between fights—while the rest would be his support outside the octagon while he fought.

"You nervous?" Becky asked, giving her hand a squeeze as they sat down beside Sean and Carlee.

She nodded as her eyes went to the fight currently happening. She would never admit it to Vince but she was. Violence was never her thing—no surprise, given her history.

"Don't be," Gemma said from her other side. "Now that you're here, there's not a chance he's losing this fight."

Though the words made her feel squishy inside, a knot of anxiety still formed knowing she was about to watch her boyfriend get beat up.

"Don't worry, Holly." Sean came to stand in front of her as the fight ended and everyone settled in to wait for the start of

Vince's. "O'Doyle is good, and he may get a few lucky hits on Vince, but if our boy manages to get him on the mat, there's no way he stands a chance."

"How do you know all this?"

"It's what I do." He shrugged. "I drink and I know things."

"You're nine. Why do you know *Game of Thrones?*"

"Because I'm awesome."

With the confidence of someone three times his age, he turned on his heel, Superman cape flapping in the wind as he returned to his seat and dropped an arm around Carlee.

"We are so screwed when he actually goes through puberty." Ryan leaned forward in his seat behind them, nodding in Sean's direction. She agreed wholeheartedly.

"He's not wrong though," Griff chimed in. "Vince won state multiple times in high school thanks to his wrestling skills. If he can get O'Doyle off his feet, he's done for."

"Oooh, oooh." Maddey waved her hands in the air before scrambling for her phone. "I have just the thing that will make you feel better." She scrolled through something on the screen, then climbed onto Ryan's lap to get closer as she handed off the phone.

Holly squinted at the image. Maddey stood between two guys dressed in wrestling singlets, one in black and one in maroon. As her fingers swiped to zoom in, she let out a snort when she realized the guys in wrestling gear were younger versions of Vince and Griff.

"Rocky and I had cardboard cutouts made of them in all their high school glory for April Fools' Day one year," Maddey answered the unvoiced question.

"Oh my god. This is *ah-may-zing.*" Her eyes didn't leave the screen. "Is it wrong I kind of want one?"

"No way. I'll make it happen."

"Vince isn't going to like it." Becky's smile said she was fully on board with the idea.

"Especially since it's not one of him in his little fighting shorts," Gemma agreed.

"Eh." Holly waved it off. "I don't need that, I have it in real life. But this"—she pointed to the phone—"is everything."

Even back in high school, Vince was hot. She was sure he had all the girls chasing him. As the girls played keep-away with the phone to prevent Griff's attempts at hiding the image, she knew Maddey accomplished exactly what she set out to do—distracting her from her worry.

The hairs on her arm stood on end as electricity crackled through the audience at the Garden. The lights dimmed, the Jumbotron in the arena sparking to life with the pre-filmed footage the UFC used to promote the fight. Her eyes, along with the twenty thousand other pairs in the arena, lifted skyward to watch.

When the clip ended, the speakers boomed a remixed rendition of the classic Superman theme song. Vince and The Steele Maker team made their way down the security-blocked pathway to the cage.

Sean and Carlee stood on their padded folding chairs, flapping their own red Superman capes as countless others did the same around the arena. Vince wasn't the champion, but it was obvious fans loved him.

After Vince's entrance and what she was told was an inspection by a UFC official, he stepped inside the octagon, prowling around it like a lion inside a cage.

The arena lighting dimmed a second time, the rings separating the different levels of seating flooding with the green, white and orange lights of Ireland's flag as "Shipping up to Boston" by the Dropkick Murphy's played, announcing Kevin O'Doyle's entrance. The crowd cheered for their champ.

O'Doyle went through the same pre-fight formalities as Vince before also stepping inside the cage. The two fighters paced the space on their respective sides, Vince grinning around his mouth guard.

"I swear." Nick chuckled. "Vin is the only person I know who could pull off looking like a kid in a candy store before a fight."

"True," Damon agreed. "Everyone else goes for *intimidation* with a hard ass scowl, but not our boy."

"Are you kidding me?" Jake shifted to see the fighters behind them. "Why do you think him and Jase are BFFs? He's the same damn way out on the ice. Unless the Storm are playing the Bruisers and he's up against Bishop, he smiles the *entire* time he drops the gloves and goes for it."

"For real." Skye shook her head. "Do you know how many memes trend because of it?"

"It's scary how much they think alike. There are times I question which one of us is Jase's twin," Jordan added.

Holly let the mindless banter of her friends distract her from what she was about to witness.

"Ladies and gentlemen."

The main ring announcer's voice boomed through the arena.

"This is the main event of the evening."

He ran down the list of judges, introduced the referee, and ended with the sponsor of the fight.

"Aaaaaaand now. This is the moment you have been waiting for. Live from the sold-out Madison Square Garden in New York City, we have a fight to decide who will take home the UFC Light Heavyweight Championship belt."

The crowd of thousands let out a deafening cheer.

"Introducing first, fighting out of the Blue Corner, coming in with an undefeated record of seventeen-and-oh. Standing at six foot four inches, coming in at two hundred and three pounds, fighting out of The Steele Maker in New Jersey, the challenger, Vince 'The Man of Steel' Steele."

Capes waved in the air as the roar from the fans greeted the announcement.

"Now fighting out of the Red Corner, also with an impressive undefeated record, standing at six foot three inches, coming in at two hundred and five pounds, fighting out of Dublin, Ireland, I present to you your current, reigning, undisputed UFC Light Heavyweight Champion of the World, Kevin 'The Knockout' O'Doyle."

Jase, Deck and Ray hung over the top of the cage, fists pounding on the black links that made the walls. The guys dropped to join Rocky, Gage, Vic and Mick outside the cage.

The referee called for the time to touch gloves, and both fighters stepped forward. Eyes wide, heart in her throat, Holly prepared herself for battle.

THE SPARK VINCE had been missing during the four days Holly was gone now surged through him like he was Thor first getting his lightning powers. Fighting was in his blood—literally, coming from a line of Judo and boxing champions—it bubbled through his veins as he waited at the mouth of the entrance to the Garden. The belt was so close he could practically taste the leather and gold on his tongue.

With Holly watching, there wasn't a chance the night would end without him crowned the newest Light Heavyweight Champ.

He didn't posture to the crowd as he walked to the octagon, but he did exchange a few fist bumps along the way to those stretching their arms out, his smile in full bloom. Most fighters went for the tough guy scowl—one of the best in the biz was Ronda Rousey when she fought—he, however, preferred the mindfuck of a happy grin.

He kicked off his sneakers, grabbed his black and gray Superman t-shirt from behind the neck and tossed it to the ground before stripping out of his joggers, leaving only the white fight shorts of the challenger.

He stepped up for inspection, allowing the UFC's cutman to apply a layer of Vaseline to his face, making the skin elastic and slippery to minimize the amount of tearing caused by hits.

Walking inside the cage, he circled it while waiting for O'Doyle to make his entrance. Unlike when Gage had defended his title the year before against Curtis "The Cutter" Cutler, there was no bad blood between him and the Irishman he was about to fight. He had met the guy a few times through the years and respected the hell out of him. However, that didn't mean he wasn't going to enjoy taking the belt from the current champ.

Scanning the audience, he searched for his girl and found her amongst their rowdy group of friends. She probably couldn't tell he was looking at her, but the sight of her was enough to fuel him for what was to come.

He'd been so caught up in the fact that she was *back,* he never got the chance to question why she left. The time for that would come later.

He stayed loose, shaking out his arms, hopping from foot to foot.

He tapped gloves with O'Doyle and dropped back into his fighting stance, bouncing on the balls of his feet, keeping his limbs fluid to react at a moment's notice.

The months of training.

The hours of watching footage of O'Doyle's previous fights.

The numerous strategy planning sessions.

It all played through his mind at warp speed as he waited for O'Doyle to make his first move.

Thanks to his Uncle Mick, his boxing skills were ranked amongst some of the best, but O'Doyle didn't earn the moniker of "The Knockout" by not being one of them as well. The guy had one of the deadliest right hooks in the world.

He struck out with two jabs in rapid succession, then dropped back onto his right heel as O'Doyle faked left then tried to come at him with a right, his own weight barely shifting enough to avoid contact.

Another circle of the cage.

He blocked a jab.

Took a cross to the ribs.

O'Doyle tried to back him against the fence with a flurry of punches. At the last second, Vince was able to duck under, reversing their positions so O'Doyle's back was to the covered links.

Jab-jab-cross.

He grabbed O'Doyle by the shoulders to deliver two quick knees to the gut before his opponent managed to break the hold and shoved him back.

Again they circled.

Back and forth punches were traded, some blocked, some connecting.

As his sister called out the time left in the round, O'Doyle's lethal right hand connected with his temple, and Vince had to shake off the cartoon birds flying around his head. He didn't go down but was dazed. Thanks to Rocky, he knew he only needed to last a few more seconds before he'd get a minute break he could use to get his bearings.

He managed to land a powerful right hook of his own before the *ding-ding* of the bell sounded, announcing the end of the round.

Acting as his cornermen, his sister and father entered the cage as he dropped onto the stool set out for him. Rocky immediately placed a gallon-sized bag of ice over his throbbing temple.

"You're a great boxer, Vin, but you're not going to beat this guy boxing." His dad jumped right into fight strategy, the minute timeframe not leaving time to waste on pleasantries. "Take him down to the mat. Make him fight you on *your* turf."

He nodded.

"Seriously, bro." Rocky pushed harder on the ice held to his face. "Why do you think I spent so much time watching you grapple with Gage? As hot as I think it is to see my husband in action, it loses a *little bit* of the appeal with my *brother* in the mix."

Leave it to his sister to give him shit in the middle of the biggest fight of his career.

"Love you too, Rock."

She puckered her lips at him.

"Go for a single leg takedown to his right leg. With his right cross being his best weapon, it leaves that leg slightly more vulnerable than the other," Papa Steele said.

"Careful of leaving yourself open to being hit while he's on his back though," Rocky added. She was their secret weapon—the amount of information she retained on other fighters was unparalleled.

"Your sister's right. Get behind him if you can."

"Rear naked choke it up in here." Rocky did a little jog of excitement.

"You're a nut, you know that?" There was no stopping his grin at her ridiculousness.

"I know." She shrugged. "You love me anyway." She held out a fist to bump twice and exited the octagon for the second round.

O'Doyle came at him with a storm of punches as soon as the round started, obviously changing up his strategy as well. He blocked as many as he could and ducked those he couldn't, waiting for his opening to go for a takedown.

He fell back a step.

Waiting.

Watching.

There.

O'Doyle shifted, leaving his leg open as his dad predicted. Vince dove down, wrapped both arms around O'Doyle's calf underneath the knee, lifted it toward his chest, dropping his shoulder, then released his right arm to hook behind O'Doyle's left knee, taking them both to the mat.

Gripping the mat with his toes, he scrambled around, wedging himself behind O'Doyle when he lifted his body to strike. He took a few punishing hits to the ribs before he was able to seat himself behind the champ, but finally got in position for one of his favorite submission moves—second only to the arm bar Rocky was also partial to—the rear naked choke.

His legs went around O'Doyle's hips before hooking over his legs so his feet could anchor themselves under the champ's knees to give him control over his lower body. At the same time, his right hand sliced underneath his jaw, keeping his arm as tight to his neck as possible, as his left hand came up to join in a classic seatbelt hold over O'Doyle's chest.

Every muscle in his body bulged and flexed as he tightened his hold, continuing to slide his right arm around until he had his opponent's throat in the crook of his elbow, eliminating any space he could use to gain a hold for an escape.

O'Doyle bucked his massive body against his, trying to break free, the two of them rocking back across the mat.

Thanks to sweat and blood, O'Doyle was a slippery motherfucker, but he held firm, determined to come out the victor.

His left arm continued to snake its way up O'Doyle's sweaty chest, curving behind his neck and wrapping onto his right bicep.

He squeezed.

And squeezed some more, not allowing any oxygen to fill O'Doyle's lungs.

More thrashing from the champ. Every last-ditch effort

thrown that could possibly break him from Vince's python hold.

In his black latex gloves, the referee hovered over them, watching for either the moment O'Doyle tapped out or passed out. Whichever came first.

Then, right as Vince was sure the champ would pass out, he felt the *tap-tap* on his forearm and instantly eased the pressure on O'Doyle's windpipe.

He flopped back onto the mat, taking a second to lay there and allow the fact he was now the new Light Heavyweight World Champion of the UFC to sink in.

He won.

Seconds later, he popped to his feet. The ref raised Vince's arm and the declaration came and made it official. Jase wrapped the belt around his waist, it's heavy weight barely registering.

He and O'Doyle shared a handshake and a one-armed hug as journalists circled them for interviews and sound bites of their reactions.

He moved to the entrance of the cage, leaning a shoulder against the padding looking out at his girl. She beamed at him from across the space.

He pushed off to go to her but she was already running to him, leaping into his arms.

"You won." Kisses rained all over his face.

"Did you doubt me, Cupcake?"

"No." Forehead kiss. "Still." Nose kiss. "Wow." Finally the lips.

Holly's lips on his was better than the belt around his waist.

"I love you so much, Cupcake."

"I love you too, Stud Muffin."

He'd done it.

He'd accomplished the goal he dreamed of practically his entire life.

He'd get to sponsor the women's shelter.

But what he didn't expect?

None of it meant as much as the girl in his arms.

He'd taken *a lot* of hits in his life, but Holly was the one he never saw coming.

Stunned, knocked out, down for the count—for life.

Epilogue

Hours later, after the interviews, clearance by medical staff, and all the other hoopla that apparently came with the aftermath of a UFC fight, Holly and Vince retired to his hotel suite along with the rest of their friends. It didn't bother them one bit that it was after two o'clock in the morning, none of them seemed ready to call it a night.

"Hey, Gem," Vince called out while pulling Holly down on the couch with him. "Were you able to get the stuff I asked for delivered?"

"You questioning my power, cuz?" Gemma retorted as she disappeared into the suite's kitchen.

Vince's body bounced under Holly as he chuckled—at least until it broke off into a groan of pain. Why wasn't he sleeping? He may have won the fight, but even a novice like her could tell he took a beating on his journey to champion.

Her fingers skimmed beneath the hem of his shirt to trace along the bumps of his abdominals, the muscles twitching under her touch.

"Perfect." This time when Vince groaned, it sounded like a different kind of pain. He lowered his mouth to her ear, inhaling deeply. "Mmm. You have *no* idea how much I missed your scent, Cupcake."

A shiver chased down her spine as his teeth scraped the shell of her ear. Her body cried out for all the dirty things he *wasn't* saying. Her heart wasn't the only thing that had missed him over the last four days.

"What I don't get," Gemma said as she held out a container of store-bought icing to Vince, "is why do you want this crap when you date a baker who can make this stuff from scratch. I can tell you from experience that Holly's is better."

"Yeah, it is." He took the red-topped container from Gemma. "But I know *just* what to put this on to make it taste better."

"Muffin!" She squealed when her world went topsy-turvy as he stood up and tossed her over his shoulder like Santa's sack of toys. "What are you doing?"

"I'm about to gorge myself on you for dessert, while simultaneously teaching you to *never* leave me again."

She yelped when he smacked her ass, then he gave the abused cheek a squeeze as he walked backward to face their friends.

"I love you guys, and thanks for being there for me tonight, but I'll have to see you all in the morning."

"We still need to work out the details for the shelter," Skye said.

"Tomorrow is fine, as I will be otherwise occupied for the rest of the evening."

Whistles and catcalls followed them down the hallway, the sound not diminishing until Vince kicked the door shut with his heel and locked it for good measure.

When he set her next to the king-sized bed, her breath stalled in her lungs at the graphite hue his eyes took on as he stared down at her. Even with the swelling and discoloration around his left temple, he was still the hottest thing she had ever laid eyes on.

"Strip."

The single word was a command, not a suggestion.

She pulled off the custom t-shirt, tossing it carelessly to the ground while he did the same with his. Her breath caught for an entirely different reason as his magnificent torso was revealed. The muscle definition was so defined he didn't seem real, but the usual Photoshop perfection of it was ruined by the mottled pattern of violets and blues blooming along his ribs from where he endured the worst of the beating.

The way he stared, like he could see through her body to where her hands stilled on her bra clasp behind her back, was intoxicating. He watched her with a new intensity she didn't recognize.

"Why do you still have clothes on?" That gravelly tone broke her from her stupor, and her red lace bra went the way of her shirt.

His fingers hooked in the band of his pants but paused, as if waiting for her to remove her own before doing the same.

The button of her jeans slipped free.

The hiss of her zipper echoed in the room.

Her thumbs mirrored his on her sides.

A shimmy of the hips, the denim and lace panties peeled down her legs, and she kicked them to the side.

She waited, expecting Vince to give her another command, his alpha side already prominently on display, but none came.

He toed his own pants away, then without a word, scooped both her and her panties into his arms, not releasing either until she was sprawled out in the middle of the mattress, the soft cotton of the duvet silky on her back.

Before she could blink, her arms were pulled overhead and tied to the intricate wrought-iron headboard, restrained by her own underwear.

She tugged on the lace.

"I wouldn't do that if I were you. You don't want it to move and put pressure on your pretty new ink, now do you?"

His hands reached out to cup each breast, thumbing her nipples and making her squirm.

"Now." He reached for the container of frosting.

The creak of plastic from the top

The hiss as the foil seal was broken.

Each sound amplified as her heart pounded, laid out at his mercy.

His finger swirled inside the pint-sized container before coming away covered in dark chocolate. He hummed as he drew a pattern on her body similar to that night back in the kitchen of Espresso Patronum.

"That's good enough to start," he said as he inspected his work.

To start?

She lifted her head to see more of her torso covered in the frosting than not.

"To start?" Lust had her voice cracking.

"Yes, Cupcake." His head bent until his mouth hovered over the dollop circled on the jut of her hip bone. "I'm going to lick, suck and bite you until you're out of your mind. I don't care if I have to use the entire tub, it's not like I have to worry about the calories anymore."

His tongue laved a path to her navel, her stomach concaving from the strained breath she took.

"The only thing I want you to be able to think about is me. I'm not stopping until any thoughts you could ever *possibly* have of leaving me are driven from your mind completely."

A swirl along her ribs.

"I understand *why* you did what you did, but *never* again, Holly." His eyes were molten silver as he lifted them to look at her, chocolate rimming his mouth like a goatee. "You. Are. Mine. And. I. Am. Yours. We fight together, not apart. It's the only way to have it."

She swallowed thickly. "Have what?"

"Sweet victory, baby. Together, the end result will *always* be a sweet victory."

First his words slayed her, then his mouth.

THE SIGHT OF Holly's lithe body bound by her own panties and spread out had his dick bobbing, nodding its own approval. His blood roared with the same adrenaline rush he experienced before his fight.

When she explained after the fight why she left, she had asked for forgiveness. But there was nothing to forgive. She loved him and was only doing what she thought was best for him.

It was the time to prove to her the only way to conquer the things against them was to stand together.

True to his word, he didn't stop his oral assault on her body until he consumed more than half the frosting from the container and she had three orgasms.

With his dick threatening to break off if he didn't slip it inside her in the next few seconds, he hooked his hands under her trembling thighs and positioned himself at her entrance and slid home.

He sucked in a breath as her slick heat grabbed him like a pulsing vice thanks to the last orgasm he pulled from her.

"Vi—" She hiccuped a sob. "*Vin*...untie me," she begged. "I—I *need*...I need to touch you."

Who was he to deny her? He wanted her hands on him just as much. He stretched to where the delicate lace was knotted on the iron. Finding the weak point in the material, he tore through it, freeing her to roam.

One hand clutched his hair as the other scored his back with her nails.

His hips pulled back and snapped forward, driving them both into the memory foam.

Pump.

Pump.

Pump.

With each thrust of his hips, the pressure inside him increased.

"I'm spending the next *week* buried inside you." He groaned into the curve of her neck.

"*Mmff*," was her response.

"You."

In.

"Were."

Out.

"Made."

In.

"For."

Out.

"Me."

He swiveled his hips to graze her clit, and she went off like a rocket, soaking his balls as he emptied himself inside her.

As the high from the most intense orgasm of his life started to fade, he maintained their connection and rolled them to the side to keep from crushing her.

Her eyes were glazed, skin flushed pink, hair a riot of waves. She was a post-sex masterpiece. He felt more pride from putting that well-fucked expression on her face than he did holding the championship belt overhead.

Feathering kisses on her face, he grazed her forehead, each closed eyelid, her cheeks, the tip of her nose and finally her sweet lips.

"I love you, Cupcake."

"I love you too, Stud Muffin."

She may not have taken his proposal earlier seriously, but he'd meant every word. He was going to marry her one day. This beautiful, strong, independent girl had taught him that accomplishing his career goals was amazing, but the best victory, the sweetest victory of all, was winning her heart.

Did Vince ever get Holly to accept his proposal? *Turn the page to find out.*

Can't get enough of the BTU Alumni Squad? *They will are back in Puck Performance.*

Are you one of those cool kids that write reviews? *Sweet Victory can be found on Amazon, Goodreads, and BookBub.*

Bonus Epilogue

onus Epilogue 1

Vince had lost count of how many times he had proposed to Holly over nearly a year only to have her shoot him down. Every. Damn. Time.

He was done playing games. Come hell or high water, he was going to have his rock on her finger before the end of the year. Time to bust out the big guns.

Once again, he swallowed his pride and sought out the advice of The Coven.

Back in college, he and Jase thought they were *so* clever when they nicknamed their favorite group of girls. No one made more Coven references than the two of them, and they certainly didn't expect it to come around and bite them in the ass all these years later.

Because now, not only were their sisters members, but so were the women they loved. *Super screwed.*

Also, since Holly was a full-blown member of the crazy

girl squad, it was difficult to get them all in one place *without* her around.

As he let himself into the Donovan house, he double-checked his phone, making sure he had enough time before Holly finished at Espresso Patronum and showed up.

He was on a mission and would not fail.

As always, he was first greeted by Navy and Stanley, the two dogs weaving between his legs while Jordan reminded them to stay quiet as she walked past with a passed out baby Logan on her shoulder.

The remaining seven girls were spread out around the living room, laughing at god knew what. He'd learned early on it was better not to know what was discussed when they got together.

"Hey, bro," Rocky called out when she spotted him.

"Hey, sis." He dropped a kiss to the top of her head as well as his nephew, Ronnie's. And yes, his *Harry Potter*-loving sister and husband named him after one of the main characters.

"Is Jase with you too?" Melody, the newest Covenette, asked.

"No." He shook his head as he flopped onto the couch next to Rocky. "He's with the guys. I'll be meeting up with them soon but I needed to talk to you all before Holly got here."

"How have you not figured this out yet, cuz?" Gemma asked with a knowing smirk.

"Figured what out?" Beth asked.

Seven sets of expectant eyes watched him as they waited for his answer. No one spoke. They knew damn well what he was talking about, but they were going to make him say it. Enjoying the torture a little too much. *Karma's a bitch. How much shit have you given them through the years?*

Gah. Even his subconscious was on their side.

"Fine." He slapped his thighs. "How do I get Holly to finally say *yes* when I ask her to marry me?"

"Vin." Becky leveled him with a *you're an idiot* look. "You really do have me questioning if you took too many hits to the head."

"For reals. Can you check that out, Rock?" Skye asked.

"His brain is fine." The mischievous look in his sister's eyes told him he wasn't off the hook with her either. "He just suffers from a condition know as being a man."

"Thanks, Rock. I'm really feeling the love." He reached out and took his nephew from her, needing support from the only other male in the room, even if he was six months old.

"Vin, don't you know by now if you ask a stupid question you're gonna get a sarcastic answer from us," Jordan said, joining them and placing a baby monitor next to her.

"And besides," Beth cut in, "you're the one who keeps coming to us for advice. You'd think you'd be used to it."

Holly. Remember you're doing this for Holly.

He grumbled to himself and rubbed at the tension building behind his brow.

"Vin." Maddey spoke his name softly, waiting until he lifted his eyes to hers before continuing. "Do you want to know why Holly hasn't said yes to any of your proposals?"

He gave her a *why else would I be here* look.

"Come on, Vin." Maddey tapped a finger to his forehead. "Use that romance junkie brain of yours."

She sighed at his blank expression.

"Romance, Vince. You're missing the romance. The grand gesture." She put her hands up like she was putting the words on display. "You have to woo her in a way that she can't say no when you *ask* her."

"Remind her why you guys are best friends," Jordan added as the dogs started barking, announcing a new arrival.

A moment later, the subject of conversation arrived, cutting off any further discussion.

Holly placed a platter of cookies on the coffee table and collectively greeted the room.

Vince pulled her against him, kissing her long enough that the girls started to catcall, then he left them to their girl time.

He may have spent his time at the Donovan house getting picked on, but it paid off—he knew what he needed to do.

Bonus Epilogue 2

Holly directed Deck and Ray where to place their boxes of Christmas decorations, while Vince and Gage wrestled with getting the tree set up in the corner.

"You know, I used to think you guys went all out for the holidays before," Nick said, carrying in his own container of ornaments, "but *this* is like Christmas on steroids."

"It's awesome, isn't it?" She clapped her hands in front of her.

"I don't know why you're surprised, bro," Damon said, clasping Nick on the shoulder.

"For real," Ryan agreed. "Look at how much she went out for Halloween." He held up the skeleton lantern he was about to pack for emphasis.

"You guys are such babies. It's awesome and festive. So stop complaining and get to work," Becky commanded.

As Sammy cranked up the Christmas mix he'd put together for their tree trimming party, Holly looked around at all the people who had made up her new family. There were *way* too many people stuffed into the space, but they wouldn't have it any other way.

An arm fell around her shoulders, and she let herself be pulled against Kyle's side. "It's like a movie, isn't it?"

She tipped her head back to meet her oldest friend's eyes,

a smile she was sure was almost cartoonish spreading across her face.

"No." She shook her head, looking at the room. "It's better."

Who would have thought two kids from elitist, blue-blood families would escape and find their true place with the same group of friends.

The past year had been like something out of a storybook, and a lot of it had to do with the hunky man pulling her from her best friend's arms and into his.

"Hi, Muffin."

"Cupcake." She flushed as she recalled him drawling her nickname the same way in bed that morning.

Vince bent and captured her lips with his, tangled his hands in her hair, angling her head back, kissing her long and deep like they weren't standing in the middle of a room filled with people. But that was her Vince, her alpha man, her Muffin. He did what he wanted without apology.

Snaking her hands between their bodies, she clutched at his shirt, making sure to give as good as she got.

Tongues stroked.

Teeth nipped.

And when Vince sucked her bottom lip into his mouth, she was ready to say screw decorating and drag him into the closest room available.

He moved back, the dimple in his left cheek revealing he knew exactly where her thoughts had gone. *Knowing bastard.*

"Later, baby," he promised.

She whimpered as he pulled away.

His stubble scratched along the shell of her ear, sending tingles down her spine, as he bent to speak so only she could hear. "I promise once this is over and everyone's gone, I will do things to you that will put us permanently on Santa's Naughty List."

Oh my Frosty.

Another whimper escaped, and he chuckled.

"You excited?" he asked, tucking her against his side.

"So excited."

In her old life, things like Christmas trees and other holiday decor were handled by professional designers, but not anymore. This would be the first year *she* got to decorate a tree, *and* she got to do two, the guys giving her free rein over theirs next door as well.

"*Ewww.* Eww, eww, eww," Jordan cried, running in from the guys' apartment across the hall. "So gross."

"What's wrong, babe?" Jake asked, going to his wife.

"Relax, JD," Jase said, also making his way from next door.

"*Don't* tell me to relax, Jason Richard." She jabbed an aggressive finger at her twin.

"Oh, shit, she *must* be pissed if she's middle-naming you, bro." Ryan clutched his stomach as he bent over laughing.

"Haven't you heard of knocking?" Jase asked Jordan.

"Haven't you heard of *locking* a door?" Jordan countered.

"Must have forgotten in the heat of the moment." Jase shrugged his shoulders as Melody buried her face against his chest in embarrassment. All the eyes in the room were ping-ponging between the two twins.

"Nothing worse than walking in on your sibling getting jiggy with it," Justin said sympathetically.

"Oh, *don't* even go there, Just. It's not my fault you came over uninvited and entered my house without knocking," Maddey said from her perch on her husband's lap.

"Aren't you glad you're an only child?" Vince asked Holly, reaching out to bump knuckles with Jase as Jordan advised the room he should change his sheets.

It may be true that she didn't have any blood siblings, but this insane group of people was the family of her heart.

❀

Hours later, Vince still hadn't managed to get his nerves under control. He racked his brain for the perfect way to ask Holly to marry him before he figured out what he'd been doing wrong—he'd never *asked*.

He was an idiot.

It was like trying to get her to date him all over again. He'd gotten better at asking for things instead of demanding, but it looked like old habits died hard.

What he came up with might not be all that *grand*, but he thought it would be perfect for Holly.

She was putting the finishing touches on the Christmas tree in the girls' apartment—it was now or never.

Moving into position, he retrieved the box he'd hidden earlier. "You missed an ornament, Cupcake." He held out the unassuming white box.

"Oh, whoops." She took the box from him, joy radiating from her.

There was nothing cuter than his girlfriend in the holiday spirit.

Box in hand, she returned her attention to the tree.

With her back now to him, he dropped to one knee, holding his breath while he waited.

A gasp, followed by an "Oh my god," filled the now silent room as she whipped around to face him.

Those whiskey eyes he loved to drown in widened when she saw him down on one knee.

"Vin?" There was a wobble in her voice as she said his name.

"Cupcake." He had to pause to clear the emotion from his as well. "I've lost count of the number of times I've asked you this."

A chorus of laughter filled the room as their friends didn't even attempt the hide their amusement.

"But I realized I never really *asked* you."

He reached out, cupping his hands around her hips and tugging her closer.

"So…Holly, baby, Cupcake. I only have one thing on my Christmas list this year, and that's to have you *finally* say yes. What do you say? Will you make all my wishes come true? Will you marry me?"

"Oh, Muffin." Her head fell forward, the purple tips of her hair obscuring his view of her beautiful face.

His heart sank as he prepared himself for another rejection.

Without warning, she launched at him, knocking him back, both of them tumbling to the floor along with the ring box.

"Is this your new way of telling me no? Because I gotta say, it's a little better than the others, but still not what I want."

He rolled them, propping himself on his elbow to see her. With his free hand, he brushed the hair from her face, trailing a finger down her jaw and across her bottom lip.

"No."

He was really starting to hate that two-letter word.

"I *will* get you to say yes to me one day."

Her hair fanned out as she shook her head side-to-side. "No, my answer isn't no."

"Come again?"

"Vince." She playfully smacked his chest. "*Now* is not the time for dirty talk."

He gave her a wolfish grin, knowing he had spoken those exact words to her that morning.

"It's *always* time for dirty talk."

Another smack.

"Not when I'm trying to accept your proposal, it isn't."

His heart leaped from his chest at the words, soaring with Santa and his reindeer as they registered.

"About fucking time, Cupcake."

"The same can be said about you, Muffin. Took you long enough to *actually* ask."

His mouth was on hers in an instant, not even the raucous round of applause from their friends enough to break them apart.

"See, babe." Jake's voice was the first thing to finally register. "We aren't the only ones to get lost in the moment and forget about the ring."

"Oh my god." Holly pushed him back and sat up abruptly. "The ring." She frantically patted the ground, looking for the box.

He spotted it down by her leg, scooped it up and lifted the custom engagement ring from the foam it rested in. The round ruby winked at him, the emeralds inside the twisted band the perfect complement for his Christmas-inspired piece.

"You sure?" He paused before slipping the ring down her finger. "This is permanent, you know?"

"So's this." She flipped her hand over to reveal the *Muffin's* tattoo she had inked on her skin almost a year ago. The girl may have made him work for her to say yes to his proposal, but she had always been his.

Hell, she'd been his from the moment he locked eyes on her.

"I love you, Cupcake."

"I love you too, Muffin."

Playlist

*

One Direction: "I Want"
Jon Bon Jovi: "Please Come Home For Christmas"
Bruce Springsteen: "Santa Claus Is Coming To Town"
*** NSYNC:** "Merry Christmas, Happy Holidays"
Pentatonix: "Hallelujah"
Kelly Clarkson: "Wrapped in Red"
Muse: "Uprising"
Brandy: "I Wanna Be Down"
Ariana Grande: "Santa Tell Me"
Queen: "Don't Stop Me Now"
AC/DC: "T.N.T."
Bruno Mars: "That's What I Like"
Christina Aguilera: "Merry Christmas, Baby"
Rascall Flatts: "I'll Be Home For Christmas"
Glee Cast: "Jingle Bells"
Ed Sheeran: "Make It Rain"
5 Seconds of Summer: "Youngblood"
Christina Aguilera: "This Christmas"
Mariah Carey: "All I Want For Christmas Is You"

Ozzy Osbourne: "I Don't Wanna Stop"
Calum Scott: "You Are The Reason"
Dropkick Murphys: "I'm Shipping Up To Boston"

Randomness For My Readers

Whoop! Welcome to the craziness that makes up my mind.

I hope you enjoyed Vince and Holly's story and hanging out with the BTU Alumni Squad again.

If everyone was new to you, you can see where the group began in *Power Play* (Jake and Jordan's story) and see exactly how Vince helped Gage grow a set and get Rocky in Tap Out.

So now for a little bullet style fun facts:

* I am a Christmas lover like our girl Holly here but I *do* love me some Halloween too.

* A lot of Holly's Playlist are some of my favorite Christmas songs. And let me tell you, listening to Christmas music in the summer while writing this book was interesting.

* Holly's baking skills and cookies she's famous for actually are inspired by one of my best friends and let me tell you, she's a dangerous friend to have. Check out her amazing creations here.

* The GIFs The Coven use in their group chats are ones used all the time in my own group chats and we never stay on topic either.

* My main squad is huge like the BTU crew and most of us have been friends since high school or sooner.

* *Friends* is obviously one of my favorite TV shows and the game episode is also one of mine and The Hubs' favorite episode.

* Growing up Tweety was one of my all time faves so he had to get a nod here.

* Vince is my comic loving Homeboy.

* I'm a major and proud Potterhead and wish Espresso Patronum was real. It was born from a t-shirt I saw and I took inspiration for the stool from Señor Frogs.

* If you want to see the Ninja Turtle cake Holly bake's I have it on the *Sweet Victory* Pinterest board.

* For those of you who are in my reader group you know how much of a fangirl I am for Pippa Grant so of course I had to give a nod to some of my favorite books. But in case it wasn't obvious Ares is mine.

* I still have to get my Coven tattoo but it will happen before the end of the year.

If my rambling hasn't turned you off and you are like "This chick is my kind of crazy," feel free to reach out!

Lots of Love,

Alley

For A Good Time Call

Did you have fun meeting The Coven? Do you want to stay up-to-date on releases, be the first to see cover reveals, excerpts from upcoming books, deleted scenes, sales, freebies, and all sorts of insider information you can't get anywhere else?

If you're like "Duh! Come on Alley." Make sure you sign up for my newsletter here.

Ask yourself this:
    * Are you a Romance Junkie?
    * Do you like book boyfriends and book besties? (yes this is a thing)
    * Is your GIF game strong?
    * Want to get inside the crazy world of Alley Ciz?
    If any of your answers are yes, maybe you should join my Facebook reader group, Romance Junkie's Coven
    Join The Coven

Stalk Alley
    Join The Coven
    Get the Newsletter

Like Alley on Facebook
Follow Alley on Instagram
Hang with Alley on Goodreads
Follow Alley on Amazon
Follow Alley on BookBub
Subscribe on YouTube for Book Trailers
Follow Alley's inspiration boards on Pinterest
All the Swag
All Things Alley

Acknowledgments

This is where I get to say thank you, hopefully I don't miss anyone. If I do I'm sorry and I still love you, just you know, mommy brain.

I'll start with the Hubs—who even though he gave me crap **again** that *this* book also isn't dedicated to him he's still the real MVP—he has to deal with my lack of sleep, putting off laundry *because… laundry* and helping to hold the fort down with our three crazy mini royals. You truly are my best friend. Also, I'm sure he would want me to make sure I say thanks for all the hero inspiration, but it is true (even if he has no ink *winking emoji*)

To my Beta Bitches, my OG Coven: Gemma, Jenny, Megan, Caitie, Sarah, Nova, Andi, and Dana. Our real life Coven Conversations give me life.

To Stef, Rebecca, and Britney for and making sure Vince's true Alpha shined through.

To Jenny (again) my PA, without her I wouldn't be organized enough for any of my releases to happen. Thank you for being the other half of my brain and video chatting all hours, damn our timezones.

For Jess my editor for pushing me to make my characters

stronger. Some of my favorite scenes in *Sweet Victory* were born because of you.

To Gemma (again) for going from my proofreader to fangirl and being so invested in my characters stories to threaten my life *lovingly of course*

To Dawn for giving *Sweet Victory* it's final spit shine.

To my real life squad for giving me the memories and constant source of inspiration needed to throw a fictional twist on.

To Ley for baking up all the delicious goodies that helped inspire Holly. You know I'm always here when you need a taste tester.

To my street team for being the best pimps ever. Seriously, you guys rock my socks.

To my ARC team for giving my books some early love and getting the word out there.

To every blogger and bookstagrammer that takes a chance and reads my words and writes about them.

Thank you to all the authors in the indie community for your continued support. I am so happy to be a part of this amazing group of people.

To my fellow Covenettes for making my reader group one of my happy places. Whenever you guys post things that you know belong there I squeal a little.

And, of course, to you my fabulous reader, for picking up my book and giving me a chance. Without you I wouldn't be able to live my dream of bringing to life the stories the voices in my head tell me.

Lots of Love,

Alley

Also by Alley Ciz

BTU Alumni Series

Power Play (Jake and Jordan)

Tap Out (Gage and Rocky)

Sweet Victory (Vince and Holly)

Puck Performance (Jase and Melody)

Writing Dirty (Maddey and Dex)

BTU6- Coming 2021

#UofJ Series

Looking To Score

Game Changer**BTU Alumni Series**

Power Play (Jake and Jordan)

Musical Mayhem (Sammy and Jamie) BTU Novella

Tap Out (Gage and Rocky)

Sweet Victory (Vince and Holly)

Puck Performance (Jase and Melody)

Writing Dirty (Maddey and Dex)

Scoring Beauty- BTU6 Preorder, Releasing September 2021

#UofJ Series

Cut Above The Rest (Prequel)- Freebie

Looking To Score

Game Changer

Playing For Keeps

Off The Bench- #UofJ4 Preorder, Releasing December 2021

The Royalty Crew (A #UofJ Spin-Off)

Savage Queen- Preorder, Releasing April 2021

Ruthless Noble- Preorder, Releasing June 2021

Playing For Keeps

Untitled #UofJ4- Add to TBR Releasing end of 2021

Savage Queen: A Royalty Crew U of J Spin-Off Novel- Preorder, Releasing April 2021

About the Author

Alley Ciz is an internationally bestselling indie author of sassy heroines and the alpha men that fall on their knees for them. She is a romance junkie whose love for books turned into her telling the stories of the crazies who live in her head…even if they don't know how to stay in their lane.

This Potterhead can typically be found in the wild wearing a funny T-shirt, connected to an IV drip of coffee, stuffing her face with pizza and tacos, chasing behind her 3 minis, all while her 95lb yellow lab—the best behaved child—watches on in amusement.

Made in the USA
Middletown, DE
31 July 2021